THE CRIMSON SCARF

and Other Stories

Elliot Stanton

Michael Terence
Publishing

First published in paperback by
Michael Terence Publishing in 2020
www.mtp.agency

Copyright © 2020 Elliot Stanton

Elliot Stanton has asserted the right to be identified as
the author of this work in accordance with the
Copyright, Designs and Patents Act 1988

ISBN 9781913653064

No part of this publication may be reproduced, stored
in a retrieval system, or transmitted, in any form or
by any means, electronic, mechanical, photocopying,
recording or otherwise, without the prior
permission of the publisher

Cover images
Copyright © Samuel Sequeira, Ostill, Rawpixel

Cover design
Copyright © 2020 Michael Terence Publishing

With gratitude to all the people who have given me support and inspiration to write this book. Thanks in particular to Ellie M., Fiona A., James H., Carole H., Irene G., Sue T., Sarah S., Lorraine R. and all my fellow authors from my local writer's group, Writers In The Wood.

Contents

The Crimson Scarf

On a chilly early January night, Jack Redding and his best friend Eric Steadman were sat at a small table by the crackling open fire in their local hostelry, The Cornelian. Strings of coloured lights flashed, keeping metronomic time on the Christmas tree; gold and green decorations still adorned the wooden beams that cocooned the little old public house.

Looking around the interior, with a critical eye, Eric spoke, "You know, there's something a little sad about seeing decorations up after Christmas. When I was young, it wasn't unusual for my parents to remove any trace of them the day after Boxing Day."

"That's considered unlucky," said Jack. "We always took decorations down on the 12th day, and I dare say, that's when the landlord would remove his and box up that old tree for another 11 months."

"Well, it was certainly unlucky for my parents as they got a divorce when I was 14," said Eric. "Having said that, I'm in no doubt they would have killed each other by the time I was out of secondary school, so maybe it was lucky after all." Jack gave him a chastening glance as he sipped from his glass of claret.

"You know, I think he really should think about having a real one in future. It adds so much," said Jack, pointing at the artificial tree.

"Yeah, it adds piles of pine needles and the headache of getting rid of the blasted thing when Christmas is done and dusted," countered Eric.

"You're full of Christmas spirit, aren't you?" questioned Jack.

"I was, but it's January now, and there are ads for Summer holidays on television. Christmas has been and gone. It'll raise its head at the end of August when the Pound shops begin to stock their shelves with discount Christmas puds again," continued a cynical Eric. "Anyway, I suppose you'll be off in a moment. It's nearly half-past ten. Haven't you got another paragraph of your Opus Magnum to write? I hope it'll be more successful than your previous four attempts."

"Oh, don't start with all that again. Besides, it was three. I've had just three works rejected before. Anyway, it's part of my routine; thank you very much. I try to get a bit of work done before going to bed on a Sunday night. I'm sure it'll all be worth it in the end. Anyway it's *Magnum Opus*," Jack said, trying to justify his reason for always leaving the pub early.

"I hope you've strayed away from your previous 'hackneyed attempts at story writing.' Wasn't that one of the comments a publisher made?" said Eric cruelly.

"Just because it wasn't to their taste, it doesn't mean that someone else won't like it," replied Jack.

"Look, I don't want to be rude, but…" said Eric.

"Well, you're doing a pretty good job of that," retorted Jack.

"I *don't* want to be rude, but if you use the same old formula, you'll probably get the same old response," explained Eric.

"I'm sticking to my guns. I know what I'm doing,"

replied Jack bombastically.

Not wanting to cause an argument with his friend, Eric changed tack. "So, have you figured out 'whodunnit' yet?"

"I might have. You'll have to wait and see." Jack checked his watch, finished what was left of his wine and stood up to put his coat on.

"Well, I look forward to reading it," said Eric, who remained seated with a good half a pint of stout left in his pint glass in front of him.

"It'll be worth it. Writing a mystery novel is a protracted and sometimes arduous vocation Eric, old boy. You have to get things just right. You can't make it too apparent to the reader as he'll see right through your plot, and contrarily, you can't make things so contrived that nothing makes sense. That is why I'm taking my time."

"Ah well, I'm sure you know what you're doing, even if the publishers and agents don't. I guess I'll see you here next Sunday night?" Eric asked before taking a few generous gulps of his beer.

"I guess you will. Have a good week." Jack nodded back, unwilling to take his pal's bait. He walked over to the door, just pausing to lift his coat collar. Conditions were bitter and unforgiving outside, and the prospect of icy sleet dripping down his neck was most unappealing.

Half an hour later, Jack was sat up in bed, hands poised in anticipation over the keyboard of his laptop –

Eliza began to quicken her pace. Even though she couldn't see or hear anyone behind her, she could feel it. It was tangible. Her breathing hastened, and her heart was pumping harder and harder. A fit young woman, she ordinarily wouldn't be breathing heavily or break a sweat with a gentle jog, let alone a brisk walk, but this situation was in no way an ordinary one. It wasn't the first time in recent weeks that she believed that someone had been following her home, and these uncomfortable sensations were making her paranoid and extremely anxious.

She reached her front door, painted bright postbox red in contrast to the pastel shades of most of the other properties in her road, and frantically fished out her keys from her coat pocket. In total panic, all she could think about was getting into her house and bolting the door behind her. She dare not spare a moment to see who was following her. Finally, she found the key, located the keyhole and after a couple of attempts, made it safely inside. Slamming the door behind her, she bolted and locked herself in. Leaning back on the door, she took a deep breath and threw her keys into the terracotta bowl on the shelf beside the front door. The moment of calm was rudely interrupted by a creak at the top of the stairs. She stood rigid; heart thumping like a traction engine. An imposing shadow appeared on the landing. After all the efforts to get inside, now she needed to get out. She grabbed the keys and tried desperately to unlock and unbolt the front door. Whoever was at the top of her stairs started to decline them and with each clumping step drew closer and closer. Squealing incoherently with fear and unable to compose herself sufficiently to unlock the front door, Eliza could feel the hot breath of her intruder on the back of her neck. The figure pulled her around.

"Edwin Stafford," she breathlessly yelled. "But you're…"

"Dead? No, not quite my dear. I've just been… resting. But now I'm back to claim what is mine. I'm here for my hjosdklfjifehhhiowfhiue."

"Ruby!! You don't half pick your moments, you silly girl," Jack yelled at his portly Persian cat after she leapt up on to his computer keyboard, scaring his owner and inadvertently typing a stream of gobbledygook to the most dramatic scene of Jack's story. "You never come to me when I call, but all of a sudden appear like magic when I least expect it." Like his lead character, Jack was left breathless by this incident, and as quick as she appeared, Ruby was gone. "I've lost my train of thought now," Jack mumbled to himself. Unable to continue, he saved his work and closed the lid of his laptop. He placed the device on his bedside table and switched the lamp off. He made himself comfortable under his duvet and within minutes was slumbering gently.

The following morning was miserable and blustery, much as the night before and Jack sat calmly, immaculately dressed at the breakfast bar in his kitchen/diner and ate his usual Monday morning breakfast of porridge. It never wavered. Monday is porridge day. Tuesday and Thursday was toast and strawberry jam (or raspberry if he was feeling daring). Wednesday was yoghurt with fruit and Friday was fried egg on toast. He was very much a creature of habit and his life was ordered and considered, if not a little empty.

He looked at his watch. It was 7:25. The walk to Burnt Oak tube station took 10 minutes, and that would give him time to get on board the 7:40 train and pick his usual end seat, facing away from the platform. However, Ruby had other ideas. Once again, she surprised her owner and jumped on to the table, knocking over a mug of coffee. Before Jack could do anything about the rapidly approaching black liquid, it began cascading off the table surface and on to his clean, pressed trousers.

"Oh, I don't believe this," the volume of his voice

frightened the cat who typically disappeared from the scene. "I'm going to have to change. I'll be late for the train now, you silly cat."

Jack ran into the bedroom to change into new trousers, with the thought of catching the later train and possibly forfeiting his favourite seat perturbing him somewhat. A few minutes later, he exited the bedroom and grabbed his scarf, raincoat and briefcase. He rechecked the time; it was 7:33, and the later train was now an inevitability because he would have to now make a detour to the dry cleaners en route to the station. With briefcase in one hand and coffee-stained trousers over his arm, Jack left the flat in a fluster.

The man in the dry cleaners next to the station, who knew Jack, tried in vain to make pleasant conversation but Jack wasn't in any mood for small talk.

"They'll be ready on Wednesday afternoon," shouted the shopkeeper as jack bolted out.

"I'll pop in Thursday evening," returned Jack, barely in earshot of the dry cleaner.

Jack was in full power walk mode as he entered the station. He forwent his usual Metro newspaper, and he made his way through the barrier and down the steps to the platform. Luckily for him, a Southbound Northern Line train was pulling in to the station. Jack looked intently for an empty end of row seat as the carriages trundled past him. He spotted one just as the tube train arrived at a halt. There was no competition from any other passengers and with a massive sigh of relief, Jack slumped into his seat. The train began moving, and he undid the top two buttons of his raincoat and loosened his scarf a little. Without a newspaper, he opened his briefcase and pulled out a novel he had been reading, mainly for inspiration and ideas.

Murder in the Monastery was not a particularly well-written novel, but it satisfied the needs of this budding author. Relieved, he settled down to read.

A couple of stops into the journey and entirely lost in his literature; he didn't feel someone sit down into the seat next to him. An older and somewhat scruffy and gaunt-looking man immediately made his presence known to Jack. He felt something pushed between his left arm and torso. Somewhat surprised, Jack broke off from his reading and looked down to see a stuffed envelope under his elbow. He looked up at the man who was dressed in very unseasonable clothes; with a Panama hat and light flannels he was very much 'Our man in Havana.'

"The devil's in the detail, old boy," the old man said, staring at Jack's scarf. He found that statement amusing because he started to laugh almost menacingly. "They said you'd be here sitting in that seat. I like organisation and good time-keeping." Jack removed the scarf and placed it on the seat to his left. In the process, he almost dropped the envelope to the floor.

"I'm sorry?" said Jack in a bewildered state.

"Shhh. We don't want to be seen in conversation by anyone." The old man looked around the carriage, but no one appeared too interested in what he was doing. "You need to deliver this. A gentleman will be waiting outside the main entrance at Camden Town Station. When you reach the top of the escalator, exit the station to the left, and as soon as you are out, you'll see a tall man, a city gent, on the right-hand side. He'll be wearing a blue pin-stripe suit with a red carnation. Give him the package, and that's your job done. You understand?"

"I beg your pardon?" asked a shocked Jack.

"Shhh," the old man interrupted him once more. He put his boney fingers to his lips. Put that away out of sight." Jack stared at the envelope for a moment before slipping it inside his coat pocket.

The train stopped, and the old man stood up, doffed his hat to Jack and alighted. The doors closed, and the tube continued its journey. Jack sat pondering the last couple of minutes. Undoubtedly, the stranger had mistaken him for someone else, but how did he seem to know he'd be on the train at that time? This thought intrigued and excited him. His interest in the unusual and mysterious was in stark contrast to his ordered and almost OCD lifestyle. He convinced himself to carry out his task and deliver the envelope to the gentleman outside Camden Town Station.

Before he knew it, the train pulled in at his station, and Jack stepped on to the platform. He felt like a character from a crime novel, and this excited him. At the top of the escalator, he turned left as and exited the station as instructed. Thankfully, the rain had stopped, but there was no man in a blue pin-stripe suit to be seen. Was this all a hoax and what was in the envelope? Was it full of cash, or maybe a map? Just then, he felt a looming presence beside him. He looked up to see a tall, moustached, stern-looking gentleman with a red carnation presented in his jacket buttonhole. He just looked at Jack, who was a good five inches shorter than him without saying a word. Jack handed over the envelope, and with only the slightest nod, the man accepted it and walked up the road and out of sight.

Jack checked his watch. It was 8:15, and even though he took a later train, he was still early for work, as he was every day. Rooted to the spot, he stood for a moment in silent contemplation. Surely something was going to happen or was that it? His dabble into espionage was over. Still, it was a strange set of events, and he couldn't get his head around who 'they' thought he was. Then another question came to him – either they knew he worked in Camden or it was another coincidence? And if they did know where he worked, what else do they know? Perhaps they knew where he lived, where he socialised and with whom. They could have been watching him for ages, just like the man who followed Eliza in his book. Thoughts swirled around his head as he paced with purpose down the road and over the canal bridge to Salmon and Partners, where he had several clients' accounts to service in the day ahead. He walked into the building, up a flight of stairs and into the empty open-plan office. After taking off and hanging up his raincoat, the next port of call was the coffee machine in the kitchenette at the end of the room. Once his coffee had been poured, Jack sat down at his desk and sipped at it, pensively staring into the middle distance trying to make sense of the events of the morning.

A couple of minutes later, in walked Scarlett, a tall and striking young lady who had just recently joined the firm. Jack didn't even notice her walk in and sit down at the desk opposite.

"You look deep in thought."

"Oh, sorry. I was miles away. Scarlett, has anything ever happened to you all of a sudden and out of the blue that makes you question your very existence?" he asked.

"Wow, where did that come from? And the first thing on a Monday morning too?" she replied jokily. "If I can find a pair of tights in the morning or make toast without burning it, it's a triumph. What's brought this on?"

Jack pondered the possibility of regaling the morning's string of events to Scarlett but thought better of it. "Oh, it's nothing. When you get to my age, you begin to wonder in what direction your life is going."

Somewhat relieved, Scarlett switched her computer on and arranged her files for the day's accounting duties.

The day continued like any other at Salmon and Partners and at dead on 5 pm, Jack stretched, stood up, collected his coat from the coat rack and put it on.

"Where is my scarf?" he muttered to himself. Jack looked all around and checked the pockets, but he couldn't locate it.

"What's up, Jack?" asked Scarlett who was close by, buttoning up her knee-length coat.

"Oh, nothing. I can't find my scarf, that's all," replied Jack as he searched his coat pockets for the third time.

"It'll turn up when you least expect it. These things always do," said Scarlett. "Anyway, I'm off to home. I'll see you in the morning.

"Yeah. See you," Jack said, still looking around as if suddenly the scarf would appear.

Knowing that the fourth rifle through his pockets would be as fruitless as the previous three, he marched out of the office and out of the building.

A few yards into his homeward journey Jack was detoured to the other side of the road by the appearance of a police cordon on his side of the bridge. Nothing suggested why it was taped off, but he crossed the street and walked up to the station.

A packed train was inevitable as it was on every weekday return journey. The morning luxury of picking out your favourite seat and reading a newspaper was juxtaposed by the early evening's desperate eagerness to manage a position next to a door or even a pole to hang on to.

As soon as Jack got home, he hung up his coat and immediately set about feeding the cat who had told him in no uncertain meows that she was starving. He then got out of his work clothes and changed into jeans and a comfortable old 'house' sweater. It was an explosion of lines and colour and looked like something even too abstract for Salvador Dali. It was an item of clothing that would never see the light of day or even night outside his flat.

Within 40 minutes, Jack sat comfortably on his sofa in front of the news picking away at a rather unappetising microwaved cannelloni. To his shock, the broadcast featured a story which explained the police cordon of the bridge in Camden. A body of a man was found in the canal directly beneath the bridge. A police inspector appeared on the screen asking for any witnesses to come forward. They weren't ruling out an accident, but neither were they suggesting it was foul play. In the background, he could see the building where he worked. It looked a lot grander on television than in real life.

The rest of the evening was spent channel hopping and still trying to figure out what his part was in the morning's strange events.

In contrast to his earlier concerns, by the evening, Jack's approach had become far more pragmatic but also more fanciful. He may have found himself becoming the middle man in a cold war covert operation. Perhaps he could be the mysterious Mr X who passed on secrets to an international arms cartel. Then again, it could have just been a case of mistaken identity. In any event, these thoughts excited him. This alternative life was far more interesting than his experience as an accountant living alone in a one-bedroom flat on the outskirts of North London beholden to a self-centred Persian cat.

Tuesday morning was jam on toast day. Unlike the previous morning, there was no spilt coffee, no trouser-changing panic and more notably, no mysterious stranger on the train. The cordon was still in force on the bridge, and as usual, Jack was first into work. He sat at his desk with his mug of coffee, every now and again opening the desk drawers in the hope that his lost scarf would miraculously appear in one of them. It didn't. Scarlett arrived, and the talk centred around the news of the previous evening.

"Suicide or murder?" asked Scarlett brazenly.

"It could have just been an accident," replied Jack, willing to give balance to the scenario.

"Nah. Why would it be featured on the news if it was an accident?" Scarlett continued in a sensationalist manner.

"The police don't know. The Inspector in charge of the case said so."

"Exactly. A 'case.' You don't get an 'accident' case, but you do get a 'murder' case. I reckon the police know it was foul play — mark my words. Ooh, I love a good murder mystery. And this one's right on our doorstep. It's just so exciting, don't you think?"

"I'm sure we'll find out over the next day or so," said

Jack, attempting to downplay the situation, deliberately leaving the question unanswered. In honesty, he was just as intrigued by the whole scenario, but wanted to sound like a considered adult against his colleague's almost childlike fascination in the hope that it was a gruesome murder.

The day continued as pretty much any day would, with number crunching, lunch munching and back hunching until 5 p.m. and then it was time to go home. With the police tape removed from the thoroughfare, Jack was able to walk on his favoured side of the bridge. The same old cramped journey back, the usual desperate meows of the whining cat and the inevitable microwaved supermarket meal for one completed Jack's traditional early evening schedule. Once again, the news featured the story of the 'Camden Corpse' as Scarlett earlier dubbed the discovered body. He still didn't have a name, and the story was pretty much the same as the day before. Detective Inspector Ellie Sturridge, the same policewoman from the previous day's news, appealed for anyone who might have any information on any suspicious activity in the area to come forward.

"That's just about everybody in Camden, eh Ruby?" quipped Jack, but Ruby was nowhere to be seen. "Huh, typical! Well, if there's nobody to even listen to me talk to myself, I'm going to have a long bath and an early night."

Wednesday morning featured a healthy fruit-based breakfast which Jack carefully consumed, taking great care not to drop a rogue blueberry down his beautifully ironed shirt. The miserable skies and constant rain of the early part of the week had now been replaced with clear blue skies and even a smattering of watery sunshine. The mild meteorological conditions outside balanced with an overall feeling of beatitude within. Jack found himself humming a ditty as he arranged his tie in the hallway mirror with Ruby purring and rubbing her body against her owner's legs, which is something she very rarely did.

Jack managed to secure his favoured seat on the tube and began reading his morning newspaper from back to front as he wanted to catch up on the previous night's football reports. Before he knew it, the train pulled in to Camden Town station, and within a minute, Jack began sauntering down the road in what was now startling sunlight. Once at work, he hung up his coat, made some coffee and sat at his desk in peace.

The silence broke within five minutes as the whirling dervish, Scarlett spun into work.

"I didn't recognise him, did you? Mind you, why would I? London's a big old place," said Scarlett excitedly.

"I'm sorry?" asked Jack, not knowing what the devil she was trying to say.

"The body in the lock. The Camden Corpse. Didn't you read about him in your paper?" asked Scarlett, pointing at Jack's folded up Metro. Jack reached for his copy and laid it out on his desk.

"Page 5," added Scarlett. Jack opened the paper to page five, and the photo that greeted him turned his blood cold. It was the old man from the train.

"Oh my God," whispered Jack, unable to speak at his normal volume.

"Don't tell me you know him?"

Jack paused for a moment. "No… no. I don't know him. He bears a passing resemblance to someone I once knew. Anyway, I've got a lot to get through today." Scarlett just stood staring at her rattled colleague before walking off to the kitchenette. As soon as she was gone, Jack re-opened the newspaper and just stared at the photo in the faint hope that he'd got it wrong and he wasn't the stranger on the train. However, there was no doubt about it; it was the same person.

The rest of the day was a bit of a blur for Jack, and he found immense difficulty to retain concentration on his work. As soon as 5 o'clock came, on went the coat and he left the building as quick as a flash. On the way to the station, he paused at the apex of the bridge and leant over, staring at the murky cold water below, trying to make sense of matters. If the first mystery of the man on the train wasn't enough, then the fact that his body had been dragged out of the water within a couple of hours of their 'chance meeting' confused matters even further.

He reached his home at the same time, fed the cat and changed out of his work clothes before sitting down in front of the evening news in trepidation more than just interest.

There was the same reporter again, and with her, the Police Inspector, who Jack told a sleeping Ruby was 'getting more television airtime than Ant & Dec.' He immediately chastised himself for his brief moment of flippancy. The photo of the deceased filled the screen. He was looking straight at Jack and far from being the usual sort of sombre mug shot that is standard in such cases; the look on his face suggested a smug satisfaction – almost as if he was mocking Jack from beyond the grave, or at least the morgue. However, the most curious and concerning statement from Inspector Ellie Sturridge was her confirmation that no identification or objects were found on the stranger's person aside from – a red scarf – a crimson red scarf that was found rolled up in his jacket pocket. Jack's missing scarf? Jack couldn't understand what was happening to him. He knew the scarf had to be his, but how did it end up in possession of the old man? "Surely it would link him to the crime", he imagined. Either someone was playing a horrible game, or he was being set up as the stooge to a homicide. Cold shivers and hot flushes took turns on Jack's physicality. "What's going on, Ruby?" The cat was lying on her side, barely bothering to raise an eye to her owner. Her belly was full, and that's all that mattered to her.

Jack didn't feel much like eating, so after a bath, he once again took himself to bed, although if he believed his demeanour his nerves would benefit from a good night's sleep, he was sorely mistaken.

A protracted and restless night ensued filled with the spectral image of the old man. Jack had seriously considered calling in ill to work and taking the day off sick. This was something that he had never once done in his whole working life. He managed to convince himself that he was unwell as lack of sleep and anxiety had taken their toll on his mind and body as he barely nibbled at his jam on toast. Ruby sat by his feet, looking up in anticipation. She didn't care much for her owner's state of mind – all she was after was a bit of crust to take back to her favourite spot beside the radiator. Without even a purr or a friendly rub of her tail against his legs, she duly received her snack. Seeing as even his pet cat wasn't bothered with his presence, working would be the best thing for him. At least he could keep his mind occupied with figures and not the ghostly apparitions that had begun to haunt him.

At the station, Jack picked up a copy of The Metro and

as he boarded the Tube. He opened it up to read that the case was now being referred to as 'The Crimson Scarf Murder', at least by the media, although they were at pains to admit that the authorities hadn't yet announced it was a murder investigation.

By 8:15, as usual, Jack was seated at his office desk in muted reverence, looking out of the window.

"Did you find your scarf?" asked Scarlett, causing Jack to almost jump out of his seat.

"Where did you spring from?" replied Jack with a start.

"I've been here for five minutes. You've been in a world of your own for the last couple of days. So did you find it?" Scarlett repeated.

"Find what?"

"Your scarf?"

"Why… why do you ask?" questioned Jack sounding annoyed.

"Because you were looking for it at the beginning of the week and secondly, I was just making polite conversation," Scarlett replied meekly.

"Oh, I'm sorry. You know I don't care much for smalltalk. And no, I haven't found it yet," said Jack emphasising the last word.

"Okay, I'll let you get on with your 'staring out of the window' then," Scarlett walked off, leaving Jack to do just that.

Jack kept himself very much to himself all day, unwilling to communicate with anyone unless it was absolutely necessary. He had started to convince himself that it would only be a matter of time before the police turned up to request his presence down at the station for questioning. Every time the double doors of the office opened, he sprang up like a meerkat and his heart skipped a beat. Fortunately, his fear didn't come to fruition, and once again, Jack couldn't wait to leave the office and go home. On exiting the tube station at Burnt Oak, he made the slight detour to collect his trousers from the dry cleaners. No words were exchanged between himself and the owner, just a mutual head nod and a contrived smile.

As usual, Ruby sat in front of the door, waiting for Jack to get in and feed her. Breaking with protocol, he took off his coat, chucked it over the back of the sofa and switched on the television. Ruby was not impressed, loudly meowing impatiently. The news came on, and the first story featured was 'The Crimson Scarf Murder.' Today's revelation was the old man now revealed to be Ernest Swakeley, aged 84, a former lecturer at the London School of Economics. The reporter announced that he had no living family and had curiously been missing for years – a mystery in itself.

"If only I'd left that damned scarf at home on Monday," Jack complained to Ruby who sat at his feet apathetic to the verbal regret. "Not that you care. All you think about is your stomach. You'll have to wait for your food tonight though." Ruby just stared back at him. The police still weren't calling his death as a murder and weren't linking the scarf with the incident, although the media liked the idea that it was.

"At least they haven't come for me yet, I suppose," Jack said to Ruby who expressed herself with a loud meow. "Alright, I suppose you've been waiting long enough. Crap in a bag alright for you tonight?" Jack made his way over to the kitchen as the news moved on to stories of floods in the West Country.

"Keep yourself calm. Keep yourself calm," Jack repeated to himself as he released the cat's food from the pouch to the plate.

The knowledge that the police still weren't calling the case a murder inquiry gave Jack the solace he was craving. He couldn't remember the last time he ate adequately, and although not at all hungry he managed to prepare a tuna and sweetcorn pasta and then sat in front of the television and ploughed his way through the supper.

Stomach full from the first decent meal he'd had in days, Jack unaccustomedly drifted into a deep sleep on the sofa. He awoke to find himself on his morning train in his favourite seat, reading a crime novel. He looked up from his book and noticed that curiously, there wasn't another soul in the carriage. Unperturbed, Jack returned to his reading. A few moments later, still riveted by his book, he felt someone sit themselves down next to him.

"It must be a good read. You look completely entranced by it," the figure spoke.

"Swakeley!" Jack exclaimed, almost jumping out of his skin.

"Call me Ernest, please. I do hate formality in the morning," the old man replied eerily.

"But you're dead!" Jack screeched in disbelief.

"Dead? No, not yet, old boy. I've just been… resting. Anyway, I'm glad you now know my name. It's so much easier to have a conversation when you know who you are talking to, don't you think?"

Jack sat, unable to say a word. He noticed the old man was wearing the same clothes as he was on his first meeting, but they were soaking wet, creating a puddle of water on the floor of the carriage.

"It's a funny old business, murder, wouldn't you say? Sometimes there's no apparent motive. Well, nothing you can hang your hat on. It'll all unravel itself in the end though. Oh, have you found the killer yet?" Swakeley asked in an intimidatingly cheery voice, nodding at the book in Jack's hands. "No, you're only halfway through it, I notice. Then again, perhaps you know already, at least I hope you do; after all, you wrote the damn thing, eh Jack?"

Jack closed the book and slowly turned it around to the front cover – `*Nowhere to Run by Jack Redding.*'

"The title's a little passé, but I'm sure you know your own mind. Then again, maybe I know it better than you do." Swakeley laughed with perverse delight. Jack, sat in rigid fear, turned slowly back to the old man. Abruptly, he stopped laughing and turned to Jack, moving ever so haltingly closer to him. "In fact… I do!"

The entire carriage fell into darkness, and with a jolt, Jack's body went into spasm, and he violently awoke from his slumber, but with eyes still firmly closed. His heart was racing, and for a moment, he dare not move or even open his eyes. Eventually, he did and was relieved to find himself still sitting on the sofa with Ruby beside him licking up the remnants of his tuna supper off the plate which rested to his side. A few minutes later and with composure reinstated, Jack managed to get to his feet, take his plate and cutlery to the dishwasher and return to the sofa.

"Ruby, I think life would be far less complex if I were a cat, like you." Ruby looked up at Jack, sniffed and ran off as usual. "Suit yourself," Jack conceded as he was left alone again. The dream remained on his mind for the rest of the evening. The lucidity of it initially shook Jack up, but the eventual realisation that it wasn't real, reassured him that most of his concerns were just of his own making. His story teller's mind both nourished and punished him in equal measures.

Like so many evenings of the previous few days, Thursday evening followed in the same uneasy and uncomfortable manner. Jack did whatever he could to deflect his mind away from recent events and in particular, the horrible nightmare of the early evening. The effort was proving more difficult than he imagined. After flicking through the myriad of satellite channels, taking good care not to land on a news station, Jack even started a jigsaw puzzle his mother bought him some Christmases back. However, his mind just wasn't on the pastime. What he usually did when trying to relax was to write, but murder mystery was hardly the genre to occupy his mind at this time.

By 11 p.m., it was past Jack's usual bedtime, but the prospect of falling asleep and having another nightmare loomed largely. However, he could not put off the inevitable and with Ruby generously keeping his company; he finally managed to nod off just past midnight.

Friday morning meant fried egg on toast for breakfast, which Jack duly prepared, but only managed to eat less than half. Fortunately, the night before didn't bring any night terrors and as he stared at his harrowed reflection in his mug of black coffee, he speculated at what the newspapers and television broadcasts would add to 'The Crimson Scarf Murder.'

"I know, I'll give Eric a bell this evening. I'm sure his flippancy and dry wit will help lighten my mood," Jack told Ruby who was being unusually attentive of late. Perhaps she sensed her owner's angst. Once again, Jack avoided the morning television news. He piled his plates and mug alongside the frying pan in the sink, bypassing the dishwasher and prepared to leave for work.

"Thank heaven's it's Friday, Ruby," said Jack as he put down a small plate of food for the feline before leaving the flat.

Having arrived at the station, Jack considered not picking up his usual copy of The Metro, but he relented and once on the train, started to leaf his way through it. A sense of relief washed over him as the only reference to Swakeley's death was a column on page 11. He thought that perhaps the papers had grown tired of the lack of sensationalism, or they believed that a boy band on the verge of splitting up and a catfight on the catwalk at a Milan fashion show more newsworthy. Either way, it was not a bad thing. A few minutes into the journey, Jack felt someone sit down next to him, which made him leap out of his seat shocking the portly middle-aged woman who had planted herself down beside him. He smiled apologetically at her and went back to reading his newspaper.

He arrived at the office at his usual time, and to his amazement, Scarlett was already at her desk.

"Good morning Scarlett. You're early."

"Yes, well I wanted to get everything I had to do by the weekend, and I do not plan on staying in this building for one minute longer than I need to on a Friday night. I have other things to do," she replied, hoping for Jack to question where she might be going, but she was disappointed as he was too disinterested to enquire. So, she tried another method to get some conversation out of her colleague.

"I see they think it might be murder after all."

"What? I thought there wasn't any evidence?" a startled Jack replied.

"Didn't you see the news this morning?" Scarlett continued.

"No, I read my paper, but didn't see anything about it," Jack responded, clearly rattled. "What did they say?"

"It was that lady policeman who can't get enough of the TV cameras. She said that the pathology report found that the old man suffered a blow to the back of his head. It's so exciting that it happened on our doorstep," reported Scarlett joyously.

"So she's saying it's a murder investigation now?" asked Jack nervously, feeling angered at Scarlett's flippancy.

"Well, not quite," she backtracked.

"What are you on about, girl? Is it murder or not?" Jack spluttered angrily.

"She didn't say for sure. It could have happened when he fell, apparently," Scarlett conceded.

"You can't go around making such assumptions. Someone's liberty could be at stake."

"Okay, there's no need to be so trite. After all, it's not like they're after you, is it?"

Jack sat bolt upright. "Why would you say that? Why

would they be after me?" Jack asked.

"No reason, I'm just saying, that's all," Scarlett protested.

"Well, don't," Jack told her in no specific terms. He sat staring at his computer screen, waiting for the girl to mention his scarf again. She was the only person who knew he lost it and surely it wouldn't take very long for her enquiring mind to put two and two together and get five. Fortunately, she received a phone call from a client, and that took her mind off all things murder. Throughout the day, the workload was enormous, and the conversation remained scant. Jack was finding it challenging to stay placid under the pressure he was putting on himself.

The return journey home was busier as usual as people were in a hurry to get home for the weekend. He picked up an Evening Standard magazine that someone had discarded and flicked through it with interest. Before he knew it, he had arrived at his stop.

Once home, with Ruby fed, Jack dialled Eric's number, and he answered after one ring.

"Blimey, you must have been expecting my call?" asked Jack in a rare moment of amusement.

"No, I'm on the toilet. I was checking my emails, and your ugly mug appeared on my screen. What's up?" Eric replied in a tone that may offend some people, but not Jack. He was only one of the few people who didn't take offence at Eric's aggressive sense of humour.

"Oh, nice," said Jack. "Listen, I want to ask you something."

"The answer is no, and even if I wasn't married, I'm

afraid you're not my type. You're far too unstable and ugly," Eric jokily intercepted.

"I'm serious, Eric. Some bizarre things have happened to me this week, and I'd like your opinion, as a friend," Jack continued. He had Eric's attention and began to tell him all about the mysterious incident from Monday and the subsequent events.

"You've got yourself into a right old state, haven't you?" said Eric after he'd digested everything Jack related to him. "Now, I can't explain the whole train thing. I can only suggest that he must have assumed you were someone else. The scarf is just a coincidence. You might have just left yours on the tube. As for it linking you to his demise, then I can assure you that if they had any inkling you were involved, then rest assured they would have come after you by now. Unless you wrote your name on the scarf and they found it in his coat, I'd say you were in the clear. As for your dreams; you've wound yourself up so much, your brain is playing tricks on you. Try and relax. You have nothing to worry about. Do you understand?"

"Yes, and thank you. You make sense," conceded Jack.

"Of course I do. I'm a well-rounded, considered and thoughtful individual," replied Eric.

"Well, you're certainly well-rounded," countered Jack colourfully.

"Ooh, cutting. You really should turn your attention to comedy with that sort of rapier wit, young man."

"I'll try it out on my parents tomorrow. I'm going down to the coast to visit them," said Jack.

"You should have decent weather for it. Give them my best, won't you? I trust you'll be back for our regular

Sunday night out?" enquired Eric.

"Of course. I wouldn't miss it, old boy. See you at The Cornelian then."

They said their goodbyes and Jack finished the call in a much cheerier mood. A day away from all his worries, whether real or self-manufactured would be just the tonic he needed.

Late Saturday night and in a relaxed and confident state, Jack arrived back home. The events of the previous week were far from Jack's thoughts. Even Ruby was pleased to see him. A whole day away from home with no newspaper or television news broadcasts to bother him brightened Jack's mood. Even a brief, inadvertent listen to the radio news featured nothing to do with the mystery. Eric's advice had done the trick.

Jack rose from his slumber midway through Sunday morning, and if it wasn't for Ruby's hungry meowing, he could well have remained in bed into the afternoon. The weather continued with the sunny theme. The outlook, although not warm, was bright and crisp. A winter's day was just as appealing to a hot summer's day to Jack. With Ruby fed, Jack slumped down on his sofa in front of the television, where politics, home improvements and cooking shows were the order of the day. Once again, news programmes were deliberately avoided. Spending the day as a couch-potato, Jack only rose to feed himself and visit the bathroom. Doing as little as possible was the way he liked to spend many of his spare afternoon hours when he wasn't attempting (but not always succeeding) in writing. It was a day completely wasted, but it was precisely what was needed to recharge his batteries.

The bright sunny afternoon had substituted itself for a windy and blustery evening as Jack prepared himself for the short walk to the pub. After a day of her owner invading her domain, Ruby had returned to type and made herself scarce. The five-minute saunter turned into a marathon trek through the icy tundra only receiving rest bite when Jack threw open the double doors to the cosy public house – and sanctuary. To his left, Eric sat at the table by the fire, nursing his regular pint of stout.

"Good evening. Is it cold enough for you out there?" Eric asked. Jack removed his raincoat and shook it down, releasing hundreds of drops of water onto the parquet flooring.

"You could say that. It's as bad as last week," Jack replied.

"Is it? I can't say that I remember," said Eric, taking more of an interest in supping his drink, than discussing the thorny subject of the weather.

The evening continued with Eric downing pints of stout and Jack sipping away at his red wine.

"Watch out; it's nearly the witching hour. Hadn't you get to your waiting coach, Cinders?" Eric piped up as the time approached 10:30.

"Nice use of a mixed metaphor, but yes, you're right," Jack replied. He stood and put on his now dry coat. "Thanks for not mentioning – you know what."

"What?" Eric responded.

"The old man on the train," Jack reminded him.

"I don't know what you're on about, mate," said Eric with a quizzed expression on his face.

"Good," Jack smiled and walked over to the door and

lifted his coat collar.

"I guess I'll see you here again next Sunday night?" called out Eric, still sat at the table.

"I guess you will. Have a good week," replied Jack. With a hand on the door handle, Jack stopped in his tracks. A strong feeling of déjà vu rippled through him. He shook his head as to reboot himself and went to exit the building into the cold night, just pausing at the door to lift his coat collar.

A short time later, Jack was home and warm again. Sat up in bed with the laptop on his lap; he settled down to continue his story –

"Claim what's yours? What are you on about?" questioned a spooked Eliza.

"Eliza, Eliza, Eliza. Don't play the innocent victim. Would you mind if we moved into your living room? There's something awfully common about conducting one's affairs in a draughty hallway," Stafford eerily whispered. Without an invitation, he walked into Eliza's living room and sat down in the armchair. He waited for her to follow his lead. Eventually, she did the old man's bidding and entered the room. She placed herself at the end of her sofa as far away from him as she could.

"Now, we could go round in circles with you denying everything, or you could just confess, return what is mine, and I'll happily be on my way," said Stafford, his eyes not for one moment averting from Eliza.

"Give what back?" mumbled Eliza. Stafford sighed and at least averted his gaze.

"I feared you'd be like this. The sad thing is, you will end up giving back what is mine, but by playing games, you're just putting

*yourself at risk of danger, and neither of us wants that, do we?"
Eliza stared blankly at the old man who had re-affixed his icy glare.*

*"When you worked as a cleaner for my dear late wife and me,
you took certain objects from our house — certain rare and valuable
objects. The thing is, I need them. Living life as a dead man has its
problems and my life insurance, and indeed my poor late wife's life
insurance won't last me forever. I'm getting old, Eliza and I'd dearly
like to spend my last few years in comfort and security. You
understand that, don't you? I'm sure you want to be comfortable and
secure too?" Eliza just nodded her head meekly.*

*"Now, I've had a little look around the place while you were at
work as I'm sure you can imagine, but alas, I can't find any of my
belongings you 'liberated' from my estate. You're a clever girl, and I
should have guessed that you wouldn't leave such prized objects on
show, but I am asking you again to fetch them for me because I will
find them with your help or not. So, once again, I'd like my
possessions back… please." Eliza just sat, frozen to the edge of the
sofa.*

*"I won't ask a third time, young lady," said Stafford, his voice
changing from menacing to enraged. He stood up, took a pair of
black gloves out of his trouser pocket and crept towards Eliza. "My
poor late wife once defied me and then… she died. And what would I
have to lose if I killed you? How could they possibly suspect a dead
man?"*

*Stafford stood a couple of feet in front of a quaking Eliza and
just then…*

"Ah, caught you!" Jack shouted, lifting his laptop just
as Ruby jumped up onto his lap. "Once bitten, twice shy,
young lady. I suppose that's enough for today anyway." He
saved his work, closed the lid of the computer and
replaced it on his bedside table on top of the Evening

Standard magazine that he had still not finished perusing. He switched off the lamp, and within minutes, he was far away in the land of Nod.

Another Monday morning and another blowy and wet view greeted Jack from the windows of his flat as he sat, fully dressed at his breakfast bar with a hot bowl of porridge and steaming cup of coffee in front of him. He switched on the television news, and to his surprise, there was not one mention of 'The Crimson Scarf Murder.' He tried all the channels, and not one station was covering the story at all.

"That's strange," he said to Ruby, who was happily consuming her breakfast from a plate just a few feet away. Perhaps it's all been resolved. Maybe the whole thing was just a coincidence and an accident after all?" Ruby looked up at Jack, and in readiness for another pounce, Jack moved his coffee mug away from the right side of the table to the left. Up jumped Ruby and she made herself comfortable inches away from Jack's porridge. "I'm wising up to you and your tactics now," laughed Jack before taking another spoonful, but forgetting where he'd just placed his mug. His elbow knocked it over and what was left spilt on the table and dripped down on to his trousers.

"I don't believe this. Not again," Jack shouted, startling Ruby, who ran off into the bedroom. For the second Monday running, with time against him, he had to change trousers minutes before leaving for work. Once changed, Jack put on his raincoat, grabbed his briefcase and coffee-stained trousers and left the flat in a rush. Again, he had to divert his walk to the station via the dry cleaners.

"They'll be ready Wednesday afternoon," said the shop

owner as Jack left the premises.

"I'll be in on Thursday evening," replied Jack, just as the door shut behind him.

Just making it on to the train and without stopping for his morning newspaper, Jack was happy to plant himself in his vacant favourite seat. As the doors shut and the train continued its journey, he pulled out his novel from his briefcase. A moment later, he felt a body sit down next to him. Something was slipped in the space between his arm and his torso. Jack froze to the spot. The person leant in and spoke into his ear.

"Isn't red such a wonderfully vibrant colour?" the old man softly, but menacingly said.

It was Swakeley. Jack could feel the blood drain from his face. He felt utterly disorientated and paralysed with fear. The envelope fell on to the seat. He daren't look over.

The man continued, "The Cornelian, your favourite glass of claret, your cat, Ruby, Scarlett at work, your strawberry jam twice a week and don't forget the red front door and terracotta bowl from your tired, uninspired and unimaginative story. Then, of course, there's that lovely crimson scarf you're wearing. As I told you before, old boy, the devil's in the detail." Quivering, Jack slowly opened up his raincoat and around his neck once again was his crimson scarf. He then noticed there wasn't another soul on board apart from him and the old man. All of a sudden, the carriage fell into darkness.

"You've heard of art imitating life, but sometimes, just sometimes, life can imitate art," Swakeley offered. "Are we authors of our destiny or merely characters in a book clumsily written by a wannabe, but never will be author, Jack?"

"Quiet. Just leave me alone," Jack begged.

"Am I real? Are *you* real? Are we both figments of someone else's imagination? Is there any way to be sure? These are the questions we need to ask ourselves."

"I'm real. You're just a ghost or something. You have to be. Just go away and leave me alone," implored Jack, still refusing to look at the apparition.

Then a moment of clarity. "The clues were there. They were always there. ES… ES… ES," Jack repeated to himself, still staring ahead into the darkness. Like John Nash's beautiful mind; names appeared in front of him. "Eric Steadman, Ellie Sturridge, Edward Salmon, the ES Magazine… and then Eliza Scott and Edwin Stafford from my novel." The sound of evil laughter filled the carriage as it sped along in the dark.

"That's it. You're beginning to get it now, Jack. You're so obvious. A fool could see it. It's painful to see," said Swakeley calmly.

As soon as the names appeared, then they vanished, and Jack could see the distorted reflection of the old man in the window opposite, still wearing the light flannels and Panama hat. He spoke again, but this time the voice was deep and unearthly. With a petrifying resonance, "Oh, and don't forget, Ernest Swakeley. I'll be with you forever, old boy."

The old man started to laugh, and that laugh reverberated throughout the carriage and in Jack's mind, getting louder and louder reaching a deafening crescendo leaving Jack sitting in the blackness, shaking like a patient in a Victorian lunatic asylum. He shut his eyes and covered his ears, trying to block out the demonic senses. Then, it suddenly stopped, and he could make out the familiar commotion of the morning tube. He gingerly opened one eye and then another. The other passengers in the jam-packed carriage were staring at him. The transport was stationary – it was Camden Town. Jack drew a sigh of relief and still quite shaken, made his way through the crowd and off the train. He stood, planted on the platform as the train started pulling away, trying to compose himself. The platform emptied, and he was alone. As the guttural shriek of the train disappearing down the tunnel and the wind from its drag died away, a voice came over the public address system, "And remember old boy; the devil is in the detail… always."

A Pledge to Murder

The year is 1897, and Queen Victoria has just celebrated her Diamond Jubilee. In an empty old pawnbrokers shop in Wapping, the proprietor, Edward Scrimshaw stood at the counter talking to his new assistant, Thomas. It was coming up to five in the afternoon, and the two men were preparing to close for the day.

"It is quite a feat for Her Majesty to celebrate such a milestone, young Thomas, do you not think?"

"It is indeed, sir, but for a woman of such position and wealth, she can afford to ward off her ultimate demise. The old lady barely looks pleased to be still alive. You have you seen the new photographs of her in the Illustrated London News? The Prince of Wales will be in a bath chair before he is King."

"Hush, boy," Scrimshaw hissed. "You can't say such things. You had better be careful not to let any folk hear you talk in those tones. It could be construed as treason."

Just then, a lady entered the shop with her husband's suit.

"Ah, Mrs Winterbottom, what a wonderful surprise. Looking as elegant as ever, might I say? It is an honour to see you again," Scrimshaw fawned.

"Mr Scrimshaw, I last came into this establishment not four days since. It is always an honour to see me according to your tongue. If I were so honoured, I would have been made a Dame by this time. Now, I would like to leave my husband's suit here for the usual loan if you don't mind." Mrs Winterbottom never did stand for any false flattery, and Scrimshaw knew this. However, it was his way, and many of his customers appreciated his approach.

"Of course. Thomas, will you arrange the pledge for Mrs Winterbottom?" asked Scrimshaw.

"The usual three shillings, madam?" The customer nodded, and the assistant wrote out the ticket.

"I shall leave the bottom part with the suit, sir," said Thomas.

"Yes. I will write the tags out neatly at the close of business as usual," Scrimshaw replied, making sure the customer heard his assurance. "Really, Mrs Winterbottom, if I've told him once, I've told him a thousand times. Oh, and the state of this boy's handwriting. You would swear he never spent a day of his life in the schoolhouse," the shopkeeper added.

Mrs Winterbottom was not amused and after taking her receipt and the money, left the premises with a curt, "Good day, gentlemen."

Due to Thomas' poor handwriting, it was now standard practice for Scrimshaw to go through all of the day's pledges and attach a neat hand-written tag before stowing them away for safe-keeping after the shop had closed.

Once the customer had left the premises, Scrimshaw chastised his young employee. "You mustn't show any signs of unprofessionalism in front of the customer. After all, they are leaving their precious items with us, and they must have complete confidence in us. I know you haven't been with me for long, but that is no excuse, boy."

"Yes, sir. I understand, sir," Thomas replied timidly before walking to the front of the shop to turn the open sign around and lock the front door.

"Now, sweep the floors and empty the ashtrays while I tag the pledges and count the takings. If you're quick and I'm satisfied with your work, I may let you leave early," said Scrimshaw.

"Thank you, sir," Thomas replied and speedily got on with his task.

It had been a quiet day. Therefore, it didn't take long for the old man to finish tagging up the day's pawned items. The pledges of precious metals went into the safe in the office, which was one of the two rooms behind the counter. It was in reality, a room no larger than a pantry. The larger, less valuable pawns, consisting mainly of household items and articles of clothing, both every day and Sunday best were hung up carefully in a separate room called 'the big room.' However, in truth, it wasn't much bigger than the office.

"Thomas, you can be off now if you've finished your duties," shouted Scrimshaw from the back of the big room. "But woe betide you if they are not satisfactory."

"Thank you, sir," said Thomas, before putting the broom away. He grabbed his jacket and cap and unlocked the door.

"Be sure not to be late in the morning. 8:30 sharp," Scrimshaw shouted as he exited the room. It was too late, Thomas had already made speed his departure. Scrimshaw walked onto the shop floor to lock the door again.

The following morning at 8:20, Mr Scrimshaw sat in

his office, drinking his morning cup of tea. His peace was rudely interrupted by an incessant banging on the shop door.

"I'm coming," he shouted as he made his way to find out what all the commotion was about. It was Thomas, and he was holding a newspaper. Scrimshaw opened the door to let the lad inside.

"I know I told you not to be late, but there is no need to be so dramatic and damned noisy… and early."

"Have you seen the newspaper, Mr Scrimshaw?" asked Thomas breathlessly as he thrust it into his face.

"I believe I am, right now," replied Scrimshaw, before pushing it downward.

"He's returned," said Thomas cryptically.

"Who's returned?" asked Scrimshaw.

"Jack. Jack has returned. Look. He's murdering again."

There in black and white on the front page of The Times were two columns dedicated to the murder of a local woman. Scrimshaw took his spectacles from his breast pocket, placed them on his nose and took a look at the news story. "Gruesome discovery, blah blah… unknown assailant… blah blah… frenzied knife attack… blah blah… body lied undiscovered for days or even weeks… Police are looking for a local man in connection with the crime."

Unimpressed, Scrimshaw folded up the paper and thrust it into Thomas' chest. "While I sympathise for the plight of the young woman, I see no reason for you to believe this terrible incident to be attributed to our old foe, Jack The Ripper. He hasn't prowled our streets for a good six years, and I would think that he's long gone, either to pastures new or the pits of Hades. The newspapers love to create a culture of fear. It increases circulation. Now, I suggest you stop spreading this idle gossip and attend to your work."

"But sir, we are not a mile from Whitechapel, and Jack was never captured," insisted Thomas, rolling up the newspaper and putting it into his trouser pocket.

"Then, I hardly think he'd return after such a long leave of absence and start wreaking havoc on a neighbouring borough. I'm sure; whoever this dastardly devil is, the police force will do their best to apprehend and have him brought to justice. Now, I believe the outside privy needs some attention. Off you go." The old man shooed his assistant away to perform the most unpleasant of his daily duties. Scrimshaw turned the sign on the door around to 'Open' and made his way to his spot behind the counter.

The morning business was brisk, and it was a relief to close the shop for luncheon at midday for an hour. Thomas left the premises while Scrimshaw sat, feet up in his office, reading the newspaper that Thomas had bought that morning. He reread the article, but this time with greater care.

"I suppose it just might be him," he muttered to himself. There wasn't any definitive evidence to suggest it was and the article didn't make any references to The Whitechapel Murders. Still, if Thomas believed it could be him, then surely others would too.

Halfway through the afternoon and into the shop, marched Colonel Thackeray. A veteran of the Crimea, he was someone with breeding and wealth, but would occasionally fall on hard times due to his penchant for gambling – a pastime in which he was not at all successful. Another fault of his was he was an incurable gossip.

"I take it you've seen the newspaper, Scrimshaw. He's back. I knew he couldn't stay away forever, the beastly brute." Colonel Thackeray slapped the newspaper on to the counter.

"Ah, Colonel. As I was saying to young Thomas this morning, I hardly think this is the work of Jack the Ripper."

"No, then why are the police offering a reward of one hundred pounds for the capture and conviction of the murderer?" said the Colonel vociferously.

"One hundred pounds?" exclaimed Thomas wildly from the other side of the shop before running over to see the newspaper for himself. "I saw no mention of that in my paper."

"This must be a later edition, boy," exclaimed the Colonel.

"The police suspect the murderer is foreign too, now," said Thomas, reading further.

"They usually do," interjected Scrimshaw. "They like to whip up a bit of xenophobia. After all, such terrible deeds could not possibly have been perpetrated by one of us, could they?" he sarcastically continued. Colonel Thackeray gave him a stern stare and growled something; his huge greying walrus-like moustache twitching frantically.

"We'll have to remain extra vigilant and take extra care of our lady folk," instructed the Colonel, taking away his newspaper and folding it up neatly.

"I wouldn't worry, sir. All of his previous victims were

prostitutes," Thomas carelessly proposed. The Colonel's eyes popped out, and his nostrils flared, incensed by the suggestion.

Scrimshaw intervened, "I'm sure we can all go about our business in the usual way, Colonel. As long as we have men of courage and honour, such as your good self, we will all be able to sleep soundly in our beds at night." The carefully worded statement dampened the ire of the military man who bid Scrimshaw a good day and scowled at Thomas before making his way out of the premises without conducting any business.

"He didn't even pledge anything," said Thomas.

"Probably just as well he didn't, young man. You have to think before you speak. I thought he was going to slap you across the face for your tactless comment."

"Oh, I didn't mean to suggest that his wife was a…" Thomas spluttered.

"I should hope not," interrupted Scrimshaw.

"One hundred pounds, though, sir? That's a lot of money. They must be very keen to catch him," Thomas reasoned.

"Yes, you're right. It is indeed a great deal of money for an 'ordinary' murder, questioned Scrimshaw, making light of the terrible crime. Anyway, we'll have no more talk of this today."

"But what if a customer mentions it, sir?"

"Well, if a customer wishes to refer to it, then we will entertain the subject, but otherwise, that's an end to it. Do I make myself understood?"

"Yes, sir," Thomas muttered, before going into the big room to sort out the overdue pledges.

Naturally, there was little else customers were talking about than the murder and the generous reward money. The main point of discussion was the belief that the murderer was foreign. A similar assumption had been made years earlier, but due to no arrest, no one was sure if Jack the Ripper was from the continent or even further afield. However, the distrust and wariness of foreigners in the East End of London remained as prevalent as it was at the start of the decade.

The day ended as most days did; with Thomas cleaning the shop while Scrimshaw attached his neat hand-written tags to the day's pledges. The old man left the premises a little more ill at ease than he had done the previous day. All day, everyone had been talking about the local murder, and it was not going to disappear any time soon if past events were anything to go by.

The next day, a bright Saturday morning mirrored the previous day. Scrimshaw unlocked the shop door to the ever-excitable Thomas who again thrust the day's newspaper into his face.

"I must be paying you too much. Two newspapers purchased in two days."

"Look, sir. Look at the drawing," said a breathless Thomas. The story now warranted almost a five-column inches and was now headed by the bold headline — 'Ripper returns? Accurate drawing of suspect released.' "Do you recognise the fellow?"

"No, I don't... Hold on, yes. Yes, I do. He's one of our patrons. Yes, I'm sure he is!" shouted an excited Scrimshaw. He snatched the paper off Thomas, locked the door, strode up to the counter and laid the newspaper out.

"It says, 'Police received anonymous information from an eye witness'. This character entered and left the home of the victim in broad daylight. Good grief. 'The woman, named Mary Singleton, was 22 and unmarried; the only daughter of Tory politician Sir Richard Singleton. The family of Miss Singleton have put up a £100 reward for the capture and conviction of her attacker. It is believed that the woman had been stabbed several times with a serrated kitchen knife. Police are still searching for the murder weapon.' Well, this is a development. I must say, the image looks very familiar to me."

"I know who it is. Magnus Ericsson – he's Swedish. I told you he'd be a foreigner," Thomas announced triumphantly.

"Yes, I remember him. Hardly speaks a word of English. We have his name and his address. I'm sure we have items of his in at the moment. Fetch me my ledger," instructed Scrimshaw. Thomas did what he was told and brought out the thick, handwritten ledger for his employer to peruse.

"Now, let me see," said Scrimshaw as he began thumbing through the massive book. "Ah, he does indeed have items with us. An accordion and… wait a minute, a set of kitchen knives in a box. Thomas, go and get the knives."

A minute later, Thomas bought back the box of knives. He carefully placed it on the counter. Thomas took the tag off the box. "It was pledged a week after the murder," said Thomas eerily. The two men's eyes made contact as the older man delicately lifted the lid off the box.

"There are seven knives," whispered Scrimshaw. "But there is space for eight. I think the missing one is the murder weapon. The police must be informed," said Scrimshaw.

"And we'll get the reward money too," added Thomas.

"Thomas, money is not our Lord. We must do what is right and ensure this Swedish monster is brought to book. However, the money will be greatly received. I shall split it 75/25 with you," said Scrimshaw with vigour.

"But sir, surely it would be fairer to split the reward down the middle?" Thomas implored.

"Firstly boy, I am your employer, and as such would be entitled to the entire amount, so I believe I am being extraordinarily generous. Just imagine what you could do with £25. Secondly, I will be the one going to the police and putting my reputation at risk if we are wrong."

"Yes, sir. You're right, of course," Thomas submitted to his elder.

"Of course, I am. Now, put the tag on my office desk, then fetch some brown paper and string and tie the box up. I shall take it to the police station immediately. You can mind the shop. You can do that, can't you?"

"Of course I can, sir," Thomas replied.

As soon as the box had been wrapped, Scrimshaw, with coat and hat in place, put it under his arm and took it to the police station, not 500 yards up the road.

Scrimshaw returned an hour later. Thomas ran to greet him like an excited retriever dog at the shop door.

"Well, what did they say?"

"They were very grateful for the evidence and are going to arrest this fellow. They now know where he lives, thanks to me. He lives close to the unfortunate woman, and they believe that along with the eye-witness reports, my information and the kitchen knives, they'll get a conviction," explained Scrimshaw.

"And what about the reward?" Thomas feverishly asked.

"That'll come our way in good time, boy. They'll have to hang the fiend first. However, something tells me that won't be too long in coming," answered Scrimshaw like a theatre villain. "Now, we must let the law take its course and try and return to normality. We shall go to church tomorrow and pray for the soul of the poor woman and also pray for the capture and quick conviction of her killer... for all our sakes."

Monday morning arrived, and before Thomas turned up for work, a police officer visited Edward Scrimshaw, requesting his presence to give evidence in court. Thomas entered the shop at 8:30, and as the previous two workdays had the daily newspaper with him. This time the headline was huge and spread across the entire width of the newspaper. "'New' Ripper Caught – Swede Arrested.' They've got him," read Scrimshaw out loud with high intensity. "Police got a swift confession, and the case is due to be heard in court today. Of course, I know all this, because I am expected to give evidence at the Old Bailey today. In fact, you'll be coming with me. We'll have to close the shop, but with the publicity and goodwill we'll receive afterwards we will make up our lost earnings threefold. I may even buy you supper when the proceedings are over." With that, Scrimshaw went to fetch his hat, and they left the premises together and hailed a taxi cab.

Earlier than usual, Scrimshaw and Thomas arrived at work the following day. Thomas followed his employer into the office. Scrimshaw sat heavily into his chair while Thomas stood in the doorway.

"I must say, I never believed a case of this magnitude could have concluded so quickly," said Scrimshaw, pulling his watch out of his waistcoat pocket. "I like to think that had a lot to do with us and the evidence we very public-spiritedly, provided. Then there was the knife found in the accused's garden."

"Indeed. And of course, the police getting a confession," Thomas added. "And even though his lawyer insisted that no confession was ever made as he understood so little English, with the weight of evidence, Ericsson was done for. A cut and dried case if ever I heard one and at nine o'clock, justice will be served, and he'll be dead."

"That's the desperate play of a desperate man. The guilty will say anything to get them off the hook, and just about now, he'll be viewing his final glimpse of daylight through the bars of his cell before being led to the gallows," said Scrimshaw staring at his watch. The police knew it was him, and the English judicial system can work miracles if everybody is reading from the same page if you understand me?"

"We were lucky he was a foreigner, I suppose," Thomas concluded.

Scrimshaw put his watch away and out of the corner of his eye saw the tag that was once attached to Ericsson's box of knives. He picked it up and noticed something he hadn't observed before.

"Hold on; this looks like your handwriting, Thomas. It

looks similar to mine, but this is not from my hand." Thomas stepped forward to have a closer look.

"Oh, so it is," he replied.

"But I always handwrite the tags myself. How come you did this one?"

"I don't know sir. You must have missed it out," replied Thomas.

"If I had, and that would be very unlikely, you would not have written one out. Let me have a look at the ledger." He barged past Thomas and went to the safe to retrieve the book. He placed it on his desk, sat down and opened it up.

"There you see," Thomas said, pointing at his entry. It was messy, but it was clear enough to see. Scrimshaw, put on his spectacles to have a close look.

"Yes, I see it, but what I also see a week earlier is my entry for the same thing, but there is no indication that the item was redeemed. So, what we have is the same thing entered twice, a week apart, but not actually leaving the premises?" Scrimshaw took off his spectacles and stared intently at Thomas.

"It must have done," protested Thomas.

"No, Thomas. What you've done and there's no need to forgive me if I'm wrong because I don't believe I am; you entered the pledge again on the 12th July, two days *after* the murder, when in fact it was brought in on the 3rd July, two days *before* the murder. You replaced my tag with one of your own – clever. But you failed to redeem the original pledge – foolish. That means the complete set of knives, lost a component while in our care."

"I don't understand, sir," said Thomas.

"What I'm suggesting Thomas, is that you took one of the knives, re-pledged the item did the dastardly deed, thus framing an innocent man."

"Sir, that's nonsense," protested Thomas.

"Is it? I very much doubt it?" replied Scrimshaw.

"But what would be my motive?"

"Greed, probably. As soon as the reward money was mentioned, your interest was piqued. The girl was from wealthy stock, and inevitably, the family would have put up a reward for the killer's capture. They invariably do. Was it just for the money, Thomas? Come on; I've discovered the truth. You might as well confess. Thomas was about to open his mouth and tell another lie, but he quickly closed it realising that the old man had the measure of him.

"I met Mary two months ago at a party. I wasn't invited myself; I was delivering the food for my previous employer. I caught her eye, and she smiled. We exchanged a few pleasantries and happened to come across an empty room where we spoke for a while. She told me that she grew tired of her strict upbringing and wanted to do something rebellious and not at all in keeping with what was expected of a daughter of a wealthy politician. We had a few clandestine meetings, and I began to love her. And then one day, out of nowhere, it was over. She informed me that the whole thing had been a 10 shilling wager between her and one of her rich friends. She said she could find and 'have relations' with an inferior and that's precisely what she did. I was devastated, and she just laughed. I swore revenge, and that's what I got. I have always been fascinated with the Whitechapel Murders, and I knew that papers would link a similar murder to him, so I knew what I had to do. When Ericsson bought the knives in, it occurred to me that if I used a customer's item, not only will I not run the risk of somebody seeing me buy a weapon, but if I hid the murder weapon on his property, the police would be in no doubt about to who it belonged. I knew from our records that the Swede lived close to Mary so he would play the killer. When her body was found, I wrote an anonymous note to the police as an eye-witness, describing Ericsson and telling them where he lived, which they acted on very quickly. However, I do regret making such a mess of Mary's body, but I did what I had to do. She deserved it; I killed her." Thomas's demeanour changed from one of downtrodden shop boy to a confident braggart.

"You did what you had to do? She deserved it? You utter monster!" screamed a sickened Scrimshaw. "I'm going to the police. There's been a miscarriage of justice, and an innocent man is about to be hanged."

Thomas blocked his way with an outstretched arm. "You're going nowhere, old man."

"Cease this insubordination and clear my way," Scrimshaw yelled.

"No, just sit down, and I'm going to tell you what will happen," Thomas calmly informed him. "Firstly and lastly, you're going to do nothing. These are the ramblings of an old man who suddenly found a conscience. You'll be changing your accusation from one man to another. They won't even do anything. You saw how quickly they wanted to nip this whole case in the bud. They got their foreigner; poor innocent Ericsson. And now the case is closed. After losing the public's faith after The Ripper, the police knew a quick resolution would be all that is required to regain it. London is safe again."

"I'll take my chance," continued the resolute Scrimshaw.

"With what evidence? What can you present them that will change their minds?"

"I have the tag and ledger that proves the knives were here all along."

"Ah, the knives which you swore under oath were pledged *after* the crime and the tag that may or may not be in your writing. It was a long day; you were tired and wanting to get home – your writing wasn't as neat as usual. And what about your reputation? You said yourself that the good publicity you'll receive would be a real benefit to your business. Even If the police believe you, you had hired a murderer for your assistant. That revelation would be very damaging to your business," explained Thomas without any shame.

"An innocent man is about to hang," pleaded Scrimshaw. The clock in the shop struck nine o'clock and chimed.

"An innocent man *was* hanged," replied Thomas, pointing over his shoulder to the clock on the wall.

Scrimshaw walked back to his chair and slumped into it. "What are we going to do now?" he asked meekly.

"Well, I'm happy to become your partner," replied Thomas. "And once the reward money is presented to us, 75/25, but in my favour now, we can buy an expensive bottle of single malt whiskey to toast our new union. What do you say, Edward?"

"Such impertinence," spluttered an enraged Scrimshaw, but was quickly subdued when he realised his impossible position.

Thomas put his hand out to Scrimshaw to shake. The older man, broken and docile, slowly moved his hand to meet Thomas's.

"I will enjoy working alongside you as my equal, Edward and picking the bountiful fruit of profits. Today is indeed a good day," Thomas pontificated.

Scrimshaw just stared at his hand as he withdrew it from Thomas' grasp. The deal with the devil was now done and was unbreakable, and the two would from that moment forward prosper from an innocent man's death.

Luck Be A Lady

Managing to perfectly position his rental SUV in between the white lines of the parking space, Daryl Cornell, a 31-year old singleton from North London had just been made redundant from his accountancy job due to 'cost-cutting measures', so with a little bit of money to his name and not having to answer to anyone, he had decided that a few days' vacation in Las Vegas was the best course of action for him. It was a venue he always dreamt of visiting but had never been.

Pulling a modest piece of luggage behind him, Daryl headed to the exit and into the night air. For such a small case, the rattling sound that the wheels made on the ground reverberated loudly around the low-beamed car park. All that was on his mind was the lure of the casino and the promise of untold riches. It was early evening, and he imagined the floor would be pretty active.

Within a few minutes, he was checking in and being given the key card to his Deluxe King room at the Golden Nugget Hotel in Downtown Las Vegas. It was almost midnight, but he could barely hold back his excitement as the distant shrill of slot machines and the whooping and laughing of successful gamblers irresistibly tempting him to join them in their fortune.

A brief shower and change of clothing later, Daryl strolled the tastefully decorated walkway towards the casino entrance. The cacophony grew louder, and his heart beat faster. He stopped in his tracks; the vision of a million flashing coloured lights and the aroma of cigarette smoke filled his nostrils. A pretty waitress with a small tray of drinks brushed past him.

"Oh, I'm sorry, honey," she apologised profusely.

"It's okay. My fault," he replied, sounding even more apologetic. The waitress smiled sweetly at him and carried on her journey to a nearby poker table where she stopped to supply a group of young people their drinks. She gratefully accepted their tips and walked off around a corner and out of view.

Daryl surveyed the area in front of him like a lion evaluating his prey on the Savannah. He put his hand in his trouser pocket and gripped his wallet tightly. What would he sample first? The slots or the tables? He decided on trying his luck on the slot machines first as he could no longer escape the lure of their melodies and the seemingly constant ka-ching of money being won. $20 bill after $20 bill slid into a variety of film and TV-tie in machines, as these were the most eye-catching with their promise of spectacular bonuses. At first, Daryl rode his luck and gratefully cashed out the printed vouchers only to insert them into the next machine. Within an hour, which could have been 10 minutes in Daryl's world, a small profit had quickly turned in to a significant loss of over $300. At that point, most people might have walked away as 'tomorrow is another day' but not Daryl. He had caught the gambling bug. There was a sure-fire way of making his money back – the roulette table.

"Oh yeah! Come to daddy!" a loud voice boomed from a nearby roulette table. Daryl turned in the direction of the voice and spotted a tall, well-upholstered man in a light grey Stetson hat and matching three-piece suit. The other players around him whooped in agreement and congratulated him wildly on his win. Daryl walked over to the table in time to watch the croupier present him with a massive pile of coloured chips.

"That's gonna keep my ex-wives happy for a while," he broadcasted in his loud Texan drawl. Everyone else at the table appeared to be eating out of the palm of his hand. "And that's for you, honey," he flipped black chip to the pretty female croupier who caught it. She delightedly thanked him for the tip before dropping it into a box beside the wheel.

The player sitting to his right shook his head, stood up, and left the scene. The luck was undoubtedly not rubbing off on this fellow. Daryl immediately sat down in the vacated seat and pulled out his wallet. He placed $300 in one hundred dollar bills on the table, and the croupier promptly collected the cash and exchanged it for three piles of purple chips.

"You feeling lucky today, son?" hollered the gregarious, middle-aged Texan without even glancing to his right. He was far too busy placing towers of chips, taller than Daryl's total collection, on his selected numbers.

"Err, I hope so," replied Daryl hesitantly.

"Speak up, son. You're being drowned out by all the noise in here," the American spoke, glancing down at his neighbour's meagre stack, before continuing to place massive bets all over the green baize. Some of the other participants were following his bets, albeit with much smaller stakes.

"I hope so," the Englishman reiterated.

"You'll get nuthin' by hoping. You have to believe it. Believe that that little white ball will land on your number."

A hesitant Daryl played it safe by placing a small

smattering of single chips on two and four-way splits. After the American sat down, he pushed a pile of chips on to "red."

"You sure know how to live life in the fast lane, boy," laughed the American. The other players chuckled in agreement. Even the croupier smiled. They weren't mocking Daryl, but he felt belittled by their actions.

Once all the bets were laid, a silence fell over the table as the ball slowed down on the wheel. It bounced and spat up from the ridges separating the numbers. Finally, it dropped into its home.

"Seventeen, black," announced the croupier.

"Yeahhh! Oh, baby!" screeched the smart Texan almost losing his hat in the process. The croupier began counting his chips as well as most of the other players who'd followed their leader. A few moments later, she began paying everyone out with large piles of chips. However, nothing came Daryl's way. None of his modest bets was successful.

"I told you. You have to be bold," said the Texan as he scooped another vast amount to his already heaving stack.

"Didn't say that," Daryl mumbled under his breath.

"Man, I love this place. Vegas is like a second home to me. Win or lose; I always have a good time in this town. When you're as rich as I am, it's all just good fun. By the way, the name's Jarrod," the Texan spoke, holding out his hand to Daryl.

"Daryl."

"Pleased to meet you," Jarrod replied, shaking his hand.

"Likewise," Daryl said, keeping his answers to a

minimum.

For the following two spins, Daryl repeated his bets, and on both occasions, he lost. However, his compadre won both times. He could hardly lose with all the numbers he'd covered. Daryl was considerably down, and it was only a couple of hours into his vacation.

Again, he watched the big gambler spread his chips about the table and placed one single $1000 chip on "black." On this occasion, Daryl decided to follow everyone else, by laying his chips down on some of the same numbers but not placing anything on black.

The croupier spun the ball, and after a flurry of late activity, the ball bounced from number to number before finally resting.

"Thirty-five, red," the croupier announced solemnly. It was one of the only numbers not covered by anyone.

"Ah damnit," spluttered the Texan. "Oh well, you can't win them all," he said before once again preparing for the next spin. The croupier pushed a single $1000 chip to a black rectangle. This small win barely registered with him. The always cheery gambler picked it up along with his original bet and dropped them on to his still impressive stack. One bounced off the top and rolled over to Daryl. Daryl picked it up, his intention to inform Jarrod of his carelessness. The Texan didn't look like he was aware that he'd lost his chip as he laughed with the flirty woman to his left. No one noticed, not even the croupier. Daryl figured that Jarrod certainly wouldn't miss the money. $1000 was an insignificantly small amount to someone of his wealth. Carefully, Daryl palmed the chip and slowly lowered his hand under the table and slipped it into his pocket. With that chip, he had wiped out his losses, and it even put him up.

All Daryl wanted to do was leave the table, but he didn't want to look guilty. An exaggerated stretch and a yawn alerted the table to his apparent fatigued state.

"You're not leaving yet are you, son?" asked Jarrod, grabbing Daryl's arm.

"It's been a long day," Daryl replied nervously.

"My Daddy said, 'Never leave a table on a loss,' and I never have," said Jarrod, his philosophy not making much sense to Daryl.

"I'm almost out of money," replied Daryl.

"Almost?" replied Jarrod still clutching Daryl's arm. "Come on, have a drink with me. Drinks all round," he cried, bringing whoops of delight from all the players. A waitress appeared from nowhere and took the drink order.

"I'll have a small Scotch and water, please," he timidly told the waitress as he re-took his seat.

"And a large, *neat* Scotch for my English friend," Jarrod corrected him. He slapped Daryl on the back. It was with such enthusiasm it caused him to choke.

"Cough it up, son. It might be a gold watch," said Jarrod loudly to the delight of his minions. "That was something else my Daddy used to say."

It was quite evident to Daryl that he wasn't going to be allowed to leave his current surroundings for some time, so alongside the knowledge that he had wiped out his losses, he joined the ranks of the performing sea lions around the table and bathed in the over-exuberant glory of his Texan host. Free drinks were plied, and even a little money won back before Daryl was satisfied that the invisible grip on him was loosening.

"Right, it's been a long day for me, so I'm going to have to leave the party," announced Daryl after another successful spin for Jarrod. It was past four in the morning. He stood up, making sure he was well out of grabbing range and offered a modest wave.

"Goodnight, son. I guess I'll have to keep on winning without you," offered Jarrod with optimism that Americans loved, but stuck in the craw of Daryl's reserved English constitution.

"Yeah, you keep doing that. Thanks for the drinks," said Daryl backing off gingerly.

"My pleasure. No doubt I'll see you around again, son?" he asked, sounding more like a threat than an enquiry.

"I guess you will, Jarrod," replied Daryl, turning around, not waiting for any further bombastic diatribe from the boastful Texan. He then hot-footed it as fast as he could, out of the casino, past the lobby and towards the guest elevators. Daryl pressed the call button, and he waited patiently for its arrival. He put his right hand into his pocket to check that the chip was still there. It was. Daryl smiled. Then a doubt entered his head. What if the chip wasn't for $1000 after all? What if he picked up a single Dollar chip? Maybe that was the reason why Jarrod wasn't at all bothered by its disappearance. The elevator doors opened, and Daryl stepped inside, pressing the gold '9' button for his floor.

He went to remove said chip from his pocket, to check, but much to his disdain, as the doors were closing, they re-opened for another male guest. Daryl released the chip and removed his hand from his pocket. His fellow elevator passenger also pressed the '9' button. He smiled and nodded generously at Daryl. Daryl forced a grin in receipt; this small inconvenience annoyed him greatly. Maybe it was an English thing; but whenever somebody enters *your* hotel elevator when you had happily prepared for a solo ride, then has the audacity to reside on the same floor as you, it was like a personal invasion of privacy. He'd now have to wait a few more minutes to check on his bounty. The last thing he wanted to do was for the man to see his chip and start a conversation with him about what game he won it on. No, that wouldn't be at all acceptable. The elevator reached its destination, and the guest left the elevator and turned left; as did Daryl. Once out of the elevator lobby, he turned right; as did Daryl. Keeping a five or six-feet distance, Daryl continued to walk in the man's slipstream down the long corridor. As his room was approaching, all Daryl could think was, 'Keep walking, keep walking.'

He finally arrived at number 956. He placed the key card in the slot, and as quickly as he could, he opened the door and walked into his room. After closing and locking the door behind him, he went over to his bed, sat down on it next to the bedside table and took a deep breath. Then he reached into his pocket and took out the chip. Without looking down, he brought his hand up to his chest, opened his fist and looked to see what was inside it. To his relief, it was indeed a chip for $1000. He drew a sigh of relief and placed the chip on the table. For a few minutes, he just stared at it with a great deal of satisfaction.

The night wasn't a comfortable one for Daryl. His conscience, due to his deception, provoked all kinds of disturbing dreams. His sleep, when it came, was rudely interrupted by one final dream which involved an army of fat Texans frog-marching him to the bank demanding payment. It was light outside; in fact, it was after 3 pm. A protracted sleep pattern and jetlag had taken a firm grip.

"I've got to give his money back," he groggily mumbled to himself as he manoeuvred himself around to sit on the edge of his bed. Barely awake, he hunched over the bedside table which still featured his ill-gotten gains staring up at him, chastising him for his dastardly deed.

"But what if I don't see him again? But, if I do, how will I manage to get it back to him?" Daryl questioned. Even though his conscience was weighing heavy, the plan to return the chip was proving even trickier. "Perhaps, I should keep it. He doesn't need it," he juxtaposed. His thoughts continued to and fro until he came up with a solution that satisfied both the angel and devil who had set up camp on his shoulders.

"If I see him today on my way out of the hotel, I'll slip it into his jacket pocket. But if I don't, then it was meant to be, and I'll cash it in," he said this out loud as if he needed to hear a verbal approval of his decision. He was happy that this plan was an adequate solution for both sides of his conscience.

Once washed and dressed, Daryl made his way down to the hotel lobby. He paused for a moment before slowly making his way to the bustling casino. No loud Texan "yee-haw-ing" pierced the general hubbub. This was a good sign. He made his way to the cashier cage and placed the roulette chip on the counter. The cashier took it without saying a word and reached into his till. Ten $100 bills slapped down one after the other in front of him, and Daryl gratefully collected them. The cashier thanked him and the transaction was complete. The gentle saunter of his entrance to the casino changed to a determined stroll towards the natural light of the exit. The closer he got to the sanctuary of Fremont Street, the more Daryl believed that he'd been exonerated from any wrongdoing.

Concluding a late lunch/early dinner in a nearby eatery and suitably stuffed, and heading back on the street, Daryl noticed an illuminated sign alerting him to a comedy show at the hotel across the road. He decided that it would be just the tonic for him and went in to buy a ticket. The hour or so waiting for the show inevitably was spent in the casino. Although he stayed away from the lure of the roulette table, he could not resist the attraction of the lights and sounds of the myriad of different slot machines. After sampling the delights of many of them and paying for the privilege, once again, Daryl's resources had taken a massive hit. The vast majority of the $1000 he had procured had disappeared. He only had a couple of hundred dollars remaining, and with another five days of the holiday to go, he would have to be very careful, which was easier said than done when spending time in Las Vegas.

The comedy show did little to improve his downward-spiralling mood, and at the show's conclusion, he sauntered back to his hotel without even engaging in the gaming atmosphere he loved 24 hours before. As is typical with all Vegas hotels, he had to walk through the Golden Nugget casino to get to the hotel lobby. Daryl was still feeling rather sorry for himself.

"Hey boy, I was hoping I'd see you again." His run of bad luck taking another hit, Jarrod had spotted him. Daryl looked up, as he inadvertently walked straight past Jarrod's lucky roulette table. He made eye-contact with the Texan, so couldn't pretend he'd not heard him. Jarrod's eyes drew him in like a tractor beam.

"How's your luck, boy? You winnin'?" asked Jarrod, in a similar but darker coloured outfit to the previous day, again with a hat to match. One thing that hadn't changed by the look of things was his good fortune. He had what looked like even higher towers of chips than he did the previous evening. Daryl stood behind Jarrod as he had no intention of gambling any more.

"Not so good today," admitted Daryl. "My luck has not been in at all."

"Ah, that's too bad. Roulette again?" replied Jarrod. He broke off to squawk in delight as "17 black" came in again. Daryl stared in disbelief. "Well, you're certainly lucky for me. That's the first time my number's come up all day." Daryl found that hard to believe as he watched the Texan's chip collection grow by another three towers.

"Tell you what, son, I'm a big believer that people can be lucky charms. And you, Daryl, are my lucky charm. I'd like to thank you." He called Daryl in close and whispered, "Make your way to the registration area, and as soon as I've cashed out, I'll be over to see you. I have a gift for you."

"Gift for me?" asked Daryl, taken aback.

"Yeah. I'll be a couple of minutes," confirmed Jarrod as he pointed in the direction of the lobby. Daryl did what he was told. He couldn't believe his luck. Not only did he get away with stealing from Jarrod, but he was going to be rewarded for it.

Daryl stood on his own, wondering what would be his gift. Cash? Chips? A free dinner? Whatever it was, he and his conscience had been absolved. Jarrod approached, pointing and laughing raucously as he gazed upon his lucky English charm waiting for him as instructed.

Jarrod put his arm around Daryl and clasped him close. " I'm going away for a night on business, and I'd like you to have the use of my penthouse suite here. You can order room service as much as you like and please take advantage of all the amenities. It's all on me. I even have a pool table. Mind you; you will need someone to play with. Perhaps I can help you out there too. I know a few young lady players who know how to sink a few balls, and I've arranged for one to meet us up there. I'm sure you catch my drift." Daryl just stood in disbelief, only a smile giving a clue to his delight.

"You like?" asked Jarrod with a beaming grin, his arm still holding Daryl close.

"I like," replied Daryl cheekily. "I'll need to get a change of clothes and some things."

"Of course. I'll come with you, and then I'll take you up to my penthouse. Is that alright?"

"Sounds good to me," replied Daryl. Jarrod laughed loudly and released his prey, and the two men made their way up to Daryl's room. He took no time in picking up some clothes, but collecting his toiletries from the bathroom took a little longer as he wanted to pick the right things to enable him to look and smell just right for his 'pool partner.'

"You nearly done in there? We don't want to keep anyone waiting now, do we?" asked Jarrod from the bedroom.

Daryl exited the bathroom slightly flustered, holding his toiletry bag. "Yes, I'm ready." He picked up his clothes and followed Jarrod out of the room and to the elevator lobby. The private elevator took the pair straight to the penthouse level. Daryl could not believe his eyes as Jarrod showed him into his palatial domain.

Around the corner where a bar was situated, slinked a

tall, brunette lady in a short white dress.

"This is Cherie. Cherie, meet our friend from England. His name is Daryl. Make sure you take real good care of him, won't you?" said Jarrod as the woman made her way over to shake Daryl's hand and kiss him on the cheek.

"Oh, I will. Have no doubt of that," Cherie replied sexily.

"Hell, I know you will," laughed Jarrod. "The key is on the bar if you need to leave the room, although I doubt if you'll need it. Anyway, you two kids have fun, and I'll see you tomorrow." Jarrod laughed again and left the room.

As soon as the door shut, Cherie took Daryl's hand and led him into the master bedroom. The following few hours would be unforgettable for the 'unlucky' Englishman.

"Wakey, wakey, sleeping beauty. It's 10 am, and the maids want to fix the room," yelled a loud voice disturbing Daryl's slumber.

Daryl slowly opened his eyes, at first, not remembering where he was. Two half-full glasses of champagne on the bedside table reminded him.

"Come on, we haven't got all day," boomed the voice again. Daryl shuffled around and sat up in bed.

"Oh, good morning Jarrod, I didn't hear you enter."

"That is evidently true," replied Jarrod, having lost the bonhomie of the night before. Cherie was standing next to him, dressed in a black tracksuit with her hair up.

"I'm going to have to ask you to leave now. I'm afraid I need the room. So, if you'd like to pay Cherie her thousand bucks, you can be on your way."

"What thousand bucks? I thought… I thought it was all free," replied a stunned Daryl.

"Oh, no. The room was free, even the use of the pool table, but I never said the player was, did I?"

"But I don't have a thousand dollars," Daryl responded now crestfallen. Jarrod moved closer to Daryl.

"Don't you? Well, you certainly did a couple of nights ago when you palmed my money. You honestly thought that I didn't spot your deception, you damn fool?" enquired a furious Jarrod. "Just hand over that $1000 chip you stole from me. Sure, I could have informed security, and they could have dealt with you, but I don't do business like that. I like to conclude matters in my way. As I'm a nice Southern gentleman, and as you did indeed bring me some luck, I'll forget about your dirty deed, and you can leave with my blessing as soon as you settle your debt."

"It's gone," mumbled Daryl.

"Pardon?" Jarrod pretended not to hear.

"It's gone. I've spent it," admitted Daryl, trying to avoid Jarrod who had just walked over to stand right beside the bed.

"That's a real pity because Cherie needs to be recompensed for her excellent service, and she needs to pay me my 'commission.' Now, if I don't get paid, I get very disappointed, Daryl. Very disappointed, indeed."

"I can't. I don't have it anymore. I cashed it in and lost almost all of it," bleated Daryl feeling very uncomfortable with only a thin sheet covering his modesty.

Jarrod stepped back and shouted, "Vernon." A tall, thin craggy-faced man in his 40s, wearing a black suit and tie, entered the bedroom. "Ah, Vernon," continued Jarrod, "We have a little situation here. This gentleman isn't able to pay his debt, so he's electing to work it off. I know you're a very busy man, so Daryl has kindly volunteered to taxi our ladies around for a few days. He's in town for a while and can't leave as I have this." He took out Daryl's passport from his inside jacket pocket and flicked through it, "Not a particularly flattering photo."

"How did you get that?" asked a flabbergasted Daryl.

"You spent that long getting your things together in your bathroom, that I could have forged a new one. Besides, rooms have safes in them for a reason. I suggest you use one in the future and not leave your valuable belongings casually laying around," explained the Texan and slipped the passport back in his jacket. "When I'm satisfied that you've paid off your debt, I'll give you your passport back, and you can buzz off back to 'Merrie ole England'."

Jarod walked over to a chair in the corner of the room and picked up Daryl's clothes which were liberally strewn over it and threw them at him.

"Get dressed," he sneered. "And the next time your sticky, Limey fingers pick up something that's not yours, think good and hard about handing it back to its rightful owner. He's all yours, Vernon. Come on, honey, we're done here." Jarrod squeezed Cherie's backside playfully, and she responded with a wink and a smile. They departed the room together and left Vernon standing at the window, watching a panicking Daryl clumsily put his clothes on in preparation for his day's work. He was about to learn three precious life lessons – don't steal; remember that nothing in life is free; and don't accept gifts from people you don't know, however tempting they may seem.

Saturday in The Park

On a pleasant late summer's day, university lecturer, Oliver, was taking his regular Saturday sabbatical around the glorious greenery of his local park. Deciding to rest his legs for a while, he sat down on a park bench and enjoyed the typical scene of children playing football and folks walking their dogs. Once such dog walker, an old lady dressed in a tweed skirt and matching hat which topped a pure white head of hair, stopped at the bench. Somewhat out of breath, she sat down, taking a rest from her labours. Both parties sat quietly for a few seconds until the lady's pet, a chocolate Labrador, decided to jump up on Oliver, licking his face frantically.

"Bertie, no! Oh, I'm most dreadfully sorry about that," pleaded the woman as she pulled at the leash, castigating the dog. Suitably chastised, the canine sat down quietly at his owner's feet.

"That's alright. I like dogs. He's a lovely fella," replied Oliver with a chortle. He beckoned the dog to him and was delighted to pet the animal who responded to his request.

"Even so, I must apologise. He's normally very calm and obedient," said the woman.

"So am I. But even I get excited sometimes," Oliver jested. The lady laughed, relieving the awkward moment.

"He must like you. Bertie is my companion and keeps me safe. By the way, my name is Barbara," said the elegant lady with an outstretched gloved hand.

"I'm Oliver. Pleased to meet you," he replied as he took the lady's hand, shaking it gently.

"Do you live locally?" asked Barbara.

"Yes. Just over there behind the line of trees, there's a row of townhouses. I live there with my wife and children," said Oliver pointing into the distance.

"That's nice. I live on the other side of the park. I live alone," replied Barbara, halting as if the revelation upset her somewhat. Averting an uncomfortable silence, Oliver began to tell the lady about his life and his job of being a university lecturer. Barbara was fascinated and listened intently.

"So, you were the first student in your school to go to Cambridge?" she rhetorically asked him. "Your mother must have been so proud of you."

"She was. Both of my parents were. And now I'm a university lecturer at UCL."

"You look too young. I've always pictured university lecturers to be old fuddy-duddies like me. I'm always being accused of being old before my time," quipped Barbara.

"No, not at all. I'm 35, and there is plenty of staff younger than me, I can assure you. Besides, I'm sure you're not a fuddy-duddy," said Oliver charmingly.

"You flatter me, young man," Barbara returned the compliment. "How come you're not out with your family today?"

"Saturday afternoon is my time to relax and clear my head. Most weeks my wife takes the kids to see her parents in Northampton, and I'm happy to rest on my own, either chilling out on the sofa in front of the sport or taking a stroll in the park. After a week trying to teach assorted classrooms of young know-it-alls about the different properties of neutrons, protons and electrons, I need a bit of *me* time. I love visiting the park alone to find peace and solace. I even leave my phone at home."

"What if your wife needs you?"

"She knows I'm either at home, in which case she'll call the house phone, or I'm here, in the park. Besides, I'm only ever out for 90 minutes or so."

"I see. So, how many children do you have?" Barbara leaned in, showing great interest.

"Three. One of each," Oliver quipped. Barbara laughed.

"I have one. Or at least, I *had* one," the old lady admitted, looking up to the sky.

"Oh, I'm sorry to hear that," Oliver sorrowfully mouthed.

"No, he's not dead. At least I have no reason to believe he is. You see, when I was a young woman, I had a bit of a fling with a man, a married man, and inevitably, I became pregnant. Of course, this fellow didn't want anything to do with me from then on, and he dropped me like a stone. I hid the truth from my parents for as long as I could, but nature caught up with me and eventually, I had to come clean. My mother and father were throwbacks to the Victorian era, and although I didn't expect them to be exactly delighted with my revelation, they were shocked and disgusted by it – my father in particular. He was very well thought of locally, a former mayor. In fact, had it got out, such a scandal would have ruined his reputation. They didn't even ask who the father was. To them, the pregnancy was *all* my fault.

"They gave me a choice – give the baby away or leave home. Well, I couldn't give up my child, I really couldn't, so I left home. I stayed with a more liberal-thinking old aunt for a while when Charlie was born, but the flat was small and not suitable for a new-born. For the next eighteen months, I stayed with kind friends, and eventually, I found a little job as a seamstress which allowed me to afford rent on a bedsit and some childcare. It was tough, especially when Charlie developed whooping cough and was hospitalised for a while. I had no choice but to crawl back home and hope my parent's attitude had changed. I hadn't contacted them in all the time I was away. I convinced myself that as I was their only child, and with the length of time I was away from them, their Victorian attitudes would have mellowed slightly, but I was wrong.

"They agreed I could come home, but I had to have my child adopted. I had no choice. They allowed me a few days to arrange matters with the authorities and the adoption agency but insisted I stay in an attic room and not to be seen out. I was a total embarrassment to them. Anyway, not long after that, Charlie was adopted. All I know is that a young couple took him in, and I believe they lived around London, but that was it. I didn't have any more children, and I didn't get married. I was close a few times. I got engaged three times but never made it to the altar.

"I got the house when they died, so that was something. No, that's cruel. It's no consolation, but it is what it is. So, that's my life in a nutshell. I'm a lonely old spinster rattling around a big house with only my canine companion for company. I hope you don't mind a stranger telling you her life story. It's not something I normally do."

"No, not at all. Your story is fascinating but so sad," said Oliver, patting Barbara's hand in a gesture of consolation. A slightly uneasy silence took over, with only the distant sound of children playing.

"It was a long time ago, and one learns to live with the pain. Life has to go on," responded Barbara bravely. "Let me show you this. I keep this with me, always."

Barbara unbuttoned her coat, put her hand down her chocolate brown polo neck sweater, and pulled out a locket on a chain. She carefully opened the locket and showed Oliver what was inside.

"There. That's the only baby photo I have of my little Charlie." Oliver leaned in to have a closer look. "It's tiny, and a bit faded, but I've kept it around my neck for all these years. And on the other side is a lock of his hair. Look."

"That's sad," Oliver sympathised, still staring at the tiny photograph.

"It is, but at least I have it, and this way he's always close to my heart."

"I don't want to talk out of turn, but have you ever tried to find him?" Oliver asked cautiously.

"I have, and I thought I came close once. Anyway, I know I'll see him again, one day. I never lost faith in my belief." With that, Barbara snapped the locket shut and placed it back inside her jumper. Oliver stood back up straight.

"It's turned a bit cold, hasn't it?" said Oliver noticing her shuddering.

"It has. These old bones are beginning to feel the cold, even on a pleasant Summer's day. Come on Bertie, it's time to go," said Barbara struggling to get to her feet.

"It was nice meeting you," said Oliver standing up, as any chivalrous Cambridge university graduate should do when a lady was about to leave the scene.

Barbara stood for a moment, appearing a little unsteady on her feet and with a pained expression on her face. "Let me walk you home," Oliver offered.

"It's alright. It just takes me a while to get going nowadays. I've had arthritis since my forties. Every day is a struggle. I'll be fine but thank you so much for the kind offer. You've worked hard all week; this is your time."

"No, I insist. I've come out for a walk, after all," Oliver asserted.

"Well, that would be lovely. Thank you, young man," Barbara relented.

Oliver took Bertie's lead, and Barbara held on to his arm. "I told you that he liked you," she said, nodding in the direction of her pet. Oliver smiled. They shuffled slowly towards the park's southern gate and onto the main road.

"It's just down the road, not more than 500 yards away," gestured the old lady, pointing the way.

"Are you as good as this to your mother, Oliver?"

"I like to think so. There's a lot to be said for good manners. Our parents brought us up to be respectful," he replied modestly.

"You say *we*?"

"Yes, me and my brother. Actually, h*e* was adopted. My parents didn't think they could have any more children after me, so they adopted Ben. Even though she's not his birth mother, Ben looks to her as his real mum. If a child is loved and cared for, it doesn't matter who his birth parents are. I'm sure your son, wherever he is, feels part of his family as Ben does to mine," said Oliver. Barbara went silent. "Oh, that came out sounded unfeeling. What I meant to say was…"

"It's okay," Barbara interrupted. I know what you mean, young man. Did your parents find out what happened to Ben's birth mother?"

"I don't know, to be honest," replied Oliver.

"Has he ever tried to find her? Did he ever want to know why she put him up for adoption?" Barbara continued. Oliver took a moment to think. "I'm so sorry. I'm just trying to look at things from the child's point of view. Ignore me."

"No, it's alright. I don't mind you asking. I have to say that when Ben was younger, I remember him asking questions about who his birth mother was and why she 'abandoned' him. However, he soon realised that my parents are his real parents. And although he may not be blood, he doesn't feel any less theirs."

"That's nice. I'm sure they feel the same about him too," said Barbara resolutely. "You're a good boy and a good brother. I know I'd be very proud if you were my son."

"Still, it must be difficult for you," he offered.

"It was a long time ago, and one learns to live with the pain. I have it all – physical and mental. Life has to go on," responded Barbara with a forced laugh.

"I had better get you home, I suppose," he said, changing the subject.

"You have. This is my house here," replied Barbara. A big smile beamed across her face.

In front of them was a large, imposing Edwardian property with wrought iron gates and a sweeping drive.

"Wow. It's massive. You live here? On your own?" Oliver gasped.

"I do, indeed. It's the old family home, and as I'm the only one left in the family, it's mine and Bertie's too, of course." Bertie began wagging his tail and barking, keen to get back inside.

"You will come in for a cup of tea, won't you, Oliver?

"How could I say no?" Barbara entered a code to the security pad outside the gates, and they slowly opened inwards. They walked in, shoes crunching in the gravel driveway. The house had a pair of impressive double doors that looked too heavy for a slight, arthritis-ridden lady, but Barbara unlocked the door and opened it with ease.

"Come in. Come in," Barbara beckoned in her new friend. Bertie bolted inside without giving anyone a chance to take his lead off.

They walked down the long hallway, footsteps echoing noisily on the stone floor until they reached the kitchen.

"Sit down." Oliver sat down at the table and Barbara filled the kettle. "Let me guess — a splash of milk and three sugars?"

"How did you know?" asked Oliver, shocked.

"Call it women's intuition, young man. You should try cutting down on the sugar. It's no good for you, you know." Oliver bowed his head in agreement but didn't say anything.

A few minutes later, Oliver was sipping his hot tea, and Bertie was in his basket happily gnawing on a bone.

"Aren't you having one yourself?" he asked.

"I will, but I'm just going to change out of my outdoor clothes. I won't be too long. Let me show you into the sitting room," said Barbara as she walked out of the kitchen. Oliver followed her.

They reached a big oak door which opened with a creak. "Please," she said, gesturing to Oliver to enter the room. "You make yourself comfortable while I pop upstairs for a minute or two."

Oliver walked into the room. The late afternoon sun streamed through the windows and highlighted the enormous amount of dust particles that filled the whole space. The door closed behind him with a solid thud. Standing alone in the middle of the room, Oliver couldn't help but notice the number of ornaments and knick-knacks from all around the world that had been liberally scattered on every conceivable shelf, table, and flat surface. Models of The Eiffel Tower, Taj Mahal, The Sphinx, The Sydney Opera House amongst others along with photos of Barbara standing in front of the very same landmarks festooned around the room.

"She's certainly been around," Oliver mumbled to himself as he perused the treasure trove of globe-trotting paraphernalia. He began feeling a little faint and assumed it was the lack of fresh air in the room. "Let's open a window," he said to himself. He tried to open the large sash window; the low beams of sunlight almost blinding him. The window was stuck rigidly. He stood clapping the dust off his hand, when out of the corner of his eye, to the right, he spied a small photo in an ornate frame on the bookcase. As he drew closer to it, his heart skipped a beat. It was a graduation photo of him.

"What the hell is she doing with a photo of me?" he muttered as he picked the frame up to take a closer look. His eyes were then drawn to the wall beside the bookshelf, and what he saw shook him to the core. There hung a half a dozen framed photos of him and his family. Two of them were taken in the park on the same bench he sat at not half an hour earlier. There was one snapped at the university, and even one of him, with his wife and his children getting into the family car outside their house. In one frame was an old cutting from the local newspaper with the story about Oliver's admission to Cambridge University. He felt very unstable and leant heavily on the bookcase. Just then, the door opened, and in walked Barbara. She had changed her clothes; the twin set and pearls look, and flat shoes had been replaced by a smart black trouser suit and expensive-looking black shoes with three-inch heels. Not only her clothes were different, but her hair. The neat white coiffured mane was now a dark auburn bob. Bright lipstick and mascara gave her a much more youthful appearance. Oliver stood statue-like, unable to move. Barbara locked the door with a large key and slipped it in her trouser pocket.

"I knew I'd have you back one day, my darling. I knew my Charlie would come home," she confidently announced in a much deeper and confident voice than before.

"Charlie? You're insane. I feel… It was the tea. You drugged the tea," Oliver breathlessly concluded. The room began spinning. He tried to figure a way out, but it was no good; his mind was addled and his body limp.

Barbara walked purposefully towards him, not

shuffling as she did earlier, but strolling with steady, upright strides. She appeared half a foot taller and 20 years younger than she did just a few minutes previous.

"Come and sit down my son," Barbara insisted, helping Oliver over to the chair. He slumped down into it. "You're home, and Mummy will never let you go again. Ever. It's time for your afternoon nap now, Charlie." She sat on the arm of the chair and stroked the head of her son's head who was beginning to fall asleep. She reached out and grabbed a blanket which was folded neatly on the sofa and covered him up snuggly.

"It was me and not Ben, who was adopted?" he breathed.

"You were both adopted, but you were *sold*, for want of a better word, to your parents. What we did was illegal, but I had to do it, and they wanted a child. My father didn't want the shame, so his solicitor sought out a couple who were willing to pay in order to skip the paperwork and red tape. It was the best solution for all involved," Barbara confessed.

"What do you want from me?" whispered Oliver, almost unconscious.

"I want nothing from you. I only want us to be together like we always should have been, Charlie. Just me and you. Mother and son. No one else. It's just us now, Charlie. Mummy will make everything alright again. I promise." Oliver's head flopped on to Barbara's chest, and as he breathed deeply in slumber, Barbara repeatedly stroked his face, whispering, "You're home now. You're home now."

A Cabbie's Tale

Geoff was a London black cab driver and had been for over thirty years. Over the last couple of years, he'd struggled to make a living due to the rise in the public's use of Uber and other minicabs, with finances becoming increasingly tight due to the impending wedding of his only daughter, Lucy, and all the expenses that came with it. However, he recently had a stroke of good fortune – a sizeable amount of money had come into his possession at just the right time. With it, he had paid for the wedding and also a luxury honeymoon for his daughter and her intended, of which she had no idea.

Lucy, who was already living with her fiancé, Nick, had come home for a couple of days before the wedding. It was the first time she'd spent a night in the family house since before her university days almost ten years prior. On the night before the wedding, Geoff and his wife, Barbara, sat in the living room watching television.

"I'm just going to pop upstairs to see if Lucy is alright," he said.

"I'm sure she is, dear," replied Barbara. "She wants an early night. After all, she's got a big day tomorrow."

"I know, but I just want to make sure and tell her the good news before she goes to sleep," said Geoff already standing up from the sofa. Barbara nodded her approval.

He climbed the stairs, turned to his left and knocked on the door of his daughter's room.

"Are you decent?" he asked.

"Well, I'm not bad," was the flippant reply. "Come in."

It was a cold night, and Lucy was lying down with the duvet up to her neck. Geoff sat down on the edge of the bed.

"It's been many years since your mother or I came in to tuck you in," he said, looking around the room that hadn't changed in the intervening years.

"I know," Lucy sighed. "It feels like such a long time, but seeing you sat there on the edge of my bed, makes me believe it was only yesterday. Do you remember telling me ghost stories? Mum would always tell you off for doing that." Geoff smiled and nodded.

"You were a strange little girl. For most children, listening to ghost stories before bed would keep them up all night. For you though, they acted as a sleeping aid, and you'd nod off straight away," Geoff reminisced joyously.

"I'm the same now, but with movies. I love a good horror film before bed," said Lucy with a giggle.

"You're weird," Geoff told her, before changing the subject. "We hope so much that you'll be happy in your new life."

"I know you do Dad, and I will be. Nick's a great guy, and we've got a nice home," Lucy replied.

"I so wished I could have given you the honeymoon you wanted," Geoff continued.

"Dad," Lucy chastised him. "I keep telling you, that's not important. We'll have a holiday when we've got enough money to afford one ourselves. You and Mum have already spent so much on the wedding, and I know things haven't exactly been easy for you over the last couple of years."

"It's true that things have been a bit difficult and I've been wasteful with money. However, things have changed recently; very recently, in fact," Geoff spoke cryptically.

"What do you mean 'recently'?" asked a curious Lucy.

Without saying another word, Geoff reached into his trouser pocket and took out a folded piece of paper. He opened it up and presented it to his daughter. Lucy began to read what was on it and immediately sat bolt upright, stared at Geoff and continued to read. It was a confirmation letter for a 10-day all-expenses-paid vacation for two in the Seychelles.

"Dad, when did you..? How can you..?" spluttered Lucy, before flinging her arms around her father.

"Let's just say I had a little piece of good fortune," he replied.

"On the horses? Football? Lottery? Not a loan? Please tell me you haven't taken out a loan, Dad?" enquired Lucy, eager to find out how a cabbie with money problems could suddenly afford such a fantastic holiday.

"No, I haven't been gambling, and I haven't put myself into debt. Something happened a few weeks ago, and it's a bit of a strange one, to be honest. I haven't told anyone, but lie down, and I'll tell you a spooky bedtime story," explained Geoff. Lucy smiled excitedly and did what she was told. She placed the letter on the bedside table and eased her way down on the bed again and lifted the duvet.

Geoff began, "As you know, I have quite a few regular customers, and one of them was an old lady called Mrs Robson – Edna Robson. Every couple of weeks for the last year or so, I would pick her up from outside her house in Hendon and drive her to Finchley cemetery. She'd always be waiting in the same coat and hat with a bunch of flowers. I would wait for her for 15 minutes or so, before driving her back home. Sometimes I would get out of the cab and watch her walk up to a grave quite close to the entrance. She'd stand motionless for a while before placing the flowers down by the headstone, and then she'd walk around the grave, take one last look and walk back out of the cemetery. The routine never changed. Mrs Robson was certainly a creature of habit. The old dear never discussed who she was visiting; I assumed it was her husband or her parents. I thought it would be insensitive to ask. The funny thing was when I dropped her off she'd always wait outside her garden gate and wave me off. She never went inside until I left. And my cab was always left smelling of lavender. I'm not sure if that was from the flowers or her perfume. Old ladies love a bit of lavender. As I said, her routine never changed. Never. She never tipped either, but I probably would have refused as she was a pensioner."

"Ah, Dad, you're all heart," Lucy giggled.

"Anyway, about six weeks ago, I had just dropped off a fare in Finchley, and I had a bit of time to kill for an airport job. It was a lovely sunny day, so I thought I'd go for a stroll around the cemetery."

"That's morbid," said Lucy.

Geoff continued. "I re-traced Mrs Robson's steps toward the grave she always visited and what I discovered shook me to the core. My eyes were drawn to the name on the stone – *Edna Robson*. Underneath, the simple inscription read, '*Beloved mother and grandmother. May you rest in peace for eternity. 3rd September 1939 – 18th August 2017.*' I stood, rooted to the spot."

"Perhaps it was her sister," reasoned a spooked Lucy.

"With the same first name?" replied Geoff firmly.

"So who was the female passenger?" asked Lucy.

"Well, that's what I wanted to find out, and why was she using a dead woman's name?" said Geoff. "A few days later, I decided that the only way to find out was to pay her a visit at her home. She'd done nothing wrong, but I needed to satisfy my curiosity, and in any event, I wanted to see how she was as I'd still not heard from her. So, the next morning, I drove to her house in Hendon. I parked up across the road and walked up to the front door. I waited for quite a while after ringing the bell and was about to leave when someone opened the door. It was an old lady, but not *my* old lady," Geoff paused.

"So, who was it? I'm on tenterhooks, here," urged an impatient Lucy, leaning into Geoff.

"I asked the lady if Mrs Edna Robson was inside. She looked perplexed, so I described her as well as I could. She didn't answer me immediately, but gave me the once over, looking me up and down.

'*Are you Geoffrey?*' she asked. That surprised me as Mrs Robson always called me Geoffrey; never Geoff. 'And you're a cab driver, I think?'

"How did she know your name and occupation?" asked Lucy.

"That's what I'm about to reveal," Geoff told her. "I said I was and the old lady asked me to wait a moment, while she shuffled off into the living room. She reappeared a minute later with a small brown envelope.

"I have something for you," said the lady. "Mrs Robson was the name of the woman who lived here before me. I bought the house from her daughter. You see, Mrs Robson died just over a year ago, and after I completed on the house, the daughter popped round and gave me this.

She told me that it was one of her mother's final wishes that she deliver this envelope to me with the express instruction that if a cab driver called Geoffrey ever came to the house looking for her, I was to give it to him. And here you are, so I guess this is yours.' She then handed over the envelope to me. There was something other than just a letter in it, I could feel it. However, I still couldn't get my head around what was happening and who the lady was that I used to take to the cemetery if it wasn't Mrs Robson."

"So what was in it?" asked Lucy.

"Well, I thanked the woman and went back to my cab. I opened the envelope and read the letter. It said, *'Dear Geoffrey. Thank you for your kindness. I hope this gift will make up for all the times I didn't tip you. Use it wisely. Affections, Edna Robson.'* Also in the envelope was a small silky pouch with a pop fastener keeping safe the object inside. I opened it and couldn't believe my eyes; it was a ring set with an enormous diamond. At first, I wanted to take it back, but who would I take it back to?"

"So if Mrs Robson left that to you before she died, who was the old woman you took to Finchley every fortnight?"

"Here's the thing. I couldn't understand what was going on, but something drew me back to the cemetery. I went to the grave again and leaning on the headstone was a fresh bunch of flowers; the same flowers, that *my* Mrs Robson used to take. All of a sudden, a beautiful serene calmness came over me. I couldn't help but smile to myself. Before I left, I put my hand on the headstone and whispered 'Goodbye.' When I got back into the cab, I could smell Mrs Robson's perfume again. Now, I'm not saying I was ferrying around a ghost for almost a year, or that the woman was an imposter, and not called Edna Robson, but when you put everything together, something otherworldly was going on. And as for the ring… well, I sold it, and now you have a wonderful honeymoon to look forward to."

Lucy was speechless and tearful as she gave her Dad a huge hug. "Wait, can you smell that?" Lucy asked, breaking the embrace.

"I can, darling," replied Geoff. It was the unmistakable aroma of lavender. Out of the corner of his eye, he could see his cab outside below the room in the driveway. The 'For Hire' sign lit up, before darkening again. He didn't mention it to Lucy.

"And thank you, Mrs Robson," offered Lucy. Geoff smiled.

"Goodnight Lucy. You have a big day tomorrow," said Geoff. "You need to get some sleep."

Lucy nodded and made herself comfortable before turning off the light. Geoff left the room and closed the door behind him. He went downstairs to resume his seat at the other end of the sofa to his wife.

"Did you give her the holiday confirmation?" asked Barbara muting the volume on the 10 o'clock news.

"Of course," replied Geoff.

"And you told her the 'Mrs Robson' story?"

"Yep, she lapped it up. Who would have thought that the dear departed old lady could be involved in such deception?" said Geoff triumphantly.

"Yes, I'm sure she'd be horrified to know that if she were still alive. Still, it was a bit of luck, that endowment policy maturing just in time for Lucy's honeymoon, eh?"

said Barbara. She passed a packet of chocolate digestives to her husband who took one out of the packet and started munching on it.

"You can say that again," laughed Geoff with biscuit crumbs flying out of his mouth and down his shirt. "By the way, Babs, how did you manage the lavender smell in her room to come and go and then the 'For Hire' sign coming on in my cab? That was a nice touch."

"What? I never did that. You must have imagined it," said Barbara convincingly.

"Oh, come on. I didn't imagine it. It must have been you. Stop kidding around," Geoff demanded.

"I promise you, Geoff. It wasn't me. I've been sat here all this time," Barbara insisted.

"Then who or what caused it?" he asked Barbara who just stared back at him blankly. An eerie silence enveloped the room until Geoff piped up.

"Wait, can you smell that? he asked apprehensively.

"Lavender?"

"Yes, lavender."

"Perhaps the late Mrs Robson is having the last laugh," suggested Barbara nervously.

"You're not helping, Babs. No one's laughing," said Geoff. At that moment, and quite inexplicably, the television volume rose, and the sound of a woman laughing came from the speakers, before silencing immediately. Both Geoff and Barbara jumped up in horror. They stared at each other, shaking in horrified disbelief. It seemed that someone indeed had the last laugh, but it wasn't the cab driver or his wife.

The Future's Not Ours To See

Cassie and Dohna had been close friends since high school, and they found themselves continuing their higher education at Brighton University. Cassie was particularly pleased with her choice of university as she spent many family summer holidays in the popular south coast resort. It was late August, and the two girls are due to share their student accommodation with two other 18 year-olds, but initially, it's just the two of them in the four-bedroom semi, not ten minutes' walk from the seafront. However close the friends were, their ideologies were poles apart. Cassie was studying chemistry, and her scientific mind always had a logical and reasonable answer to every life problem. Dohna, on the other hand, was artistic and free-spirited. Although brought up as a Buddhist, she didn't particularly follow her religious guidelines. However, she believed that whatever religion a person followed, it can still have great relevance for them even in modern society. Because of her great interest in it, Dohna's chosen subject was Theology and religious studies.

One Friday evening, the two girls were in quiet study in the living room of the house. All of a sudden, Cassie yelled, "There it is again!"

"Jeez, you scared the life out of me," shrieked Dohna almost dropping her textbook.

"I'm sorry, but I keep getting déjà vu episodes. Is that what you call them; 'episodes'?"

"I'm not sure of the exact phraseology, Cassie, but was it essential to almost give me a heart attack, because of it?"

Dohna questioned, shutting her book.

"They seem to be getting longer. I've had a few in the last couple of weeks since I arrived down here," said Cassie.

"And what in particular are these 'episodes' repeating?" asked Dohna, genuinely interested.

"Nothing in particular. They're normally quite dull. I can be washing up or getting dressed, or maybe something happens in EastEnders, and I think I've seen it before."

With EastEnders, you most probably *have* seen it before. Everybody has; many times," Dohna playfully added.

"Oy, don't you diss the 'Enders,' mate," Cassie chastised her friend.

"Sorry, go on."

"On this occasion, I just turned a page in this book and on a picture of the periodic table, a smudge of tomato ketchup covered rhodium, palladium, iridium and platinum. The thing is, I knew it would be there. At least I think I did," she explained.

"Is that it?" asked Dohna.

"I did say they were all mundane incidences, but the point is, they keep on happening and I don't know why. You're a Buddhist, what do you make of it?"

"Firstly, thank you for informing me of my religious heritage and thank you too for having enough faith in me and my beliefs to think I could answer your question in a couple of palatable soundbites." Dohna momentarily silenced her excitable friend with a large dollop of sarcasm. Cassie gave her a forced smile but didn't respond. "Okay, there is something I can suggest – Buddhists believe that what we call 'déjà vu' is an interval between death and the next rebirth."

"I get quite a lot of these, so unless I keep dying and coming back as the same person, the same age and doing the same thing, I think I must be caught up in a time loop," countered Cassie.

"I only told you what Buddhists believed in answer to your question. Religion and even science can't provide answers to all of life's mysteries," explained Dohna maturely.

"I guess you're right. However, I do think the scientific fact is far more palatable to the woman on the street than religious doctrines," said Cassie putting her case forward forcefully.

"Oh, please don't start all this science v religion stuff again. There are no winners. And for your information, 'religious doctrine' is a phrase mainly used around the Christian religion in its many forms," said Dohna laying the law down.

"Sorry, I'll drop it. Still, it's a mystery, eh?" conceded Cassie.

"Yes. Life is a mystery, my friend. Now, be a love and fetch us a can of something cold from the fridge, will you?" asked Dohna. Cassie nodded and went into the kitchen to get a can of pop from the fridge, but as she opened the door, it happened again. Déjà vu struck when she 'saw' three cans – two Diet Pepsis and a Fanta before she even set eyes on them.

"That's twice in five minutes," Cassie said to herself as she picked out a can of Cola. She also reached for her final can of Smirnoff Ice. Cassie delivered the drink to Dohna without saying another word and pulled the ring on hers.

She realised that perhaps speaking to someone more akin to her scientific mind might offer a more logical reason for this phenomenon and could satisfy her curiosity. She looked at her watch. It was 8:45 p.m., and she deliberated for a moment if it was too late to call her Mum. She knew her mother would be able to unravel the mystery. She had answers for everything. Cassie left the room, shut the door and went to sit on the second step of the stairs with her phone in her hand. She dialled her parents' phone number and took a couple of generous gulps from her can.

"Hi, Mum. How are you? I hope it's not too late to call?" she said as her Mum answered the house phone.

"Hello, darling. No, it's not too late as I don't live in a care home and your father hasn't yet imposed a post-watershed telephone call curfew," her Mum replied. Cassie smiled. She loved the fact that her mother was as sarcastic as she was and always appreciated her quick wit.

"I have a question for you," said Cassie before her mother could get in the, 'How's your studying and Are you eating enough?' double whammy.

"Go on, Cassie," said her Mum, intrigued.

"What do you think about déjà vu?" asked Cassie bluntly.

"Okay, there's no need to ask twice," replied Mum.

"But I only asked… Oh, very good," conceded Cassie.

"Sorry, I couldn't resist it," Mum replied.

"Déjà vu? I have to say that given a choice of odd questions, I probably wouldn't have gone for that. Why do you ask, Cassie?"

Cassie went on to explain the repeated phenomena she'd been experiencing of late and listen intently to her mother's answer.

"It's all about the brain's reaction to the senses. You see, we believe all our senses send messages to our brain at the same time, but they don't. For instance, and forgive the example, but say you're in a lecture and you slap your arm with a ruler, I have no idea why you would and I'm already regretting my choice of analogy, but you will see the event a split-second before you feel it. You probably won't realise you will, but that's what happens. Now, this is what I believe, and I'm not saying it's a bona fide fact, but it makes sense to me. The messages your eyes are sending your brain are delayed a fraction, so what you see will perhaps feel like a memory, rather than what is happening at that very moment. Do you understand what I mean?"

"I do Mum, and it makes perfect sense to me," Cassie gratefully replied.

"Of course it does. Everything I say makes perfect sense, ask your father. Everything can be explained by science if you think about it logically. Just be thankful it was me who answered the phone and not him. He'd have you believe it was all to do with the spirit world and such claptrap."

"Thanks, Mum. I'll let you get back to whatever you are doing," said a satisfied Cassie.

"Oh, I was enjoying ironing your father's shirts. We're going away for a few days, but we'll be back on Wednesday. Your call was a nice distraction, however brief it was, but que sera sera." said Cassie's Mum. That was her favourite phrase. Without picking up on her mother's subtle hint, and not even asking where her parents were heading, Cassie said goodbye and ended the call. She marched back into the living room with a smug smile plastered all over her face and sat herself down on the armchair with her can in her left hand and legs stretched out in front of her.

"You look happy with yourself," said Dohna, who was still studying hard.

"Sometimes, you just need your mother's words to satisfy your curiosity," replied an indignant Cassie.

"Yes, I suppose you do, especially if you chose to be very closed-minded on certain subjects," offered Dohna before burying her head into her textbook once more. Cassie ignored her and switched on the television with the remote which was handily placed by her right hand. She made sure to immediately reduce the volume as she didn't want to disturb her friend further.

The following day was a Saturday, and as students rarely study on Saturday, it either meant lying in bed all day or, if you were lucky enough as Cassie was to reside in a seaside town, taking a stroll down to the seafront and take in some salty sea air. At 9:30 am, Cassie left Dohna sleeping in her bedroom and left the house to make the pleasant downhill walk to the beach. Walking was challenging for Cassie as she was born with a slight hip deformity which gave her a pronounced limp. She had learned to live with it, and it was nothing that gave her any great concern, although pain would often flare-up.

It was nearing the end of the season, and the weather promised to be warm, so Cassie enjoyed her walk before the crowds of city dwellers laid siege.

Feeling quite peckish and approaching The Palace Pier, Cassie decided to buy what any self-respecting student would choose for breakfast — a big bag of chips. She had forgotten all about the left-over Chinese in the oven, which would have proven a most nutritious meal. Digging into her bag of chips, she stopped to admire two seagulls in mid-flight, fighting over a wooden lolly stick. Just then, she felt an object knocking into her from behind.

"Oh, I'm most dreadfully sorry," spoke a late-middle-aged lady. Cassie spun around and saw it was a wooden A-board advertising, *'Madam Savannah. Palm reader and fortune teller.'*

"You never saw that happening, did you?" said Cassie sarcastically.

"If I had a pound for every time some smart arse fed me that line," mumbled Madam Savannah still adjusting the A-board. The lady was in full Gypsy fortune-teller garb; white blouse with puffy sleeves, a multi-layered, multi-coloured full length flowing skirt with a sash around the waist, a headscarf and big earrings. She also had a gold initial 'S' on a chain around her neck.

Cassie was still admiring the costume when the fortune-teller gasped, "It's you?"

"Me?" asked Cassie, making eye contact with the woman for the first time. Madam Savannah stared at her for a moment.

"No, sorry. My mistake. I thought you were someone else. I do apologise."

"That's okay," said Cassie.

"Student?" asked Madam Savannah.

"Yes," replied Cassie.

"Hmmm. The sciences. Chemistry?"

"Yes, you're right. How did you know?" asked a

surprised Cassie. Madam Savannah tapped the top of the A-board, which made Cassie laugh. Madam Savannah followed suit and giggled sweetly.

"Come inside, young lady. I'll give you a quick reading if you like. No charge. I know you students don't have a lot of free time unless it's for Jeremy Kyle and Loose Women. I'm afraid I haven't got anything to drink apart from tea. No Smirnoff Ice – your favourite tipple, I think? Anyway, you can share some of your chips with me if you like," she said.

Cassie reeled back slightly in amazement and followed the fortune-teller into her booth. It was a wooden kiosk which was placed in between an ice cream concession and a whelk stall.

"It's not so bad in the morning, but by five o'clock, it can get a bit whiffy if the wind blows in the wrong direction. Please take a seat." Madam Savannah ushered Cassie to sit opposite her.

"Where's your…"

"Crystal ball? It's right here," pre-empted the fortune teller, as she reached down and placed the orb on its stand in the middle of her dark cloth-covered circular table. "The tourists love the crystal ball, but it's not essential to my craft."

"How long have you done this?" Cassie enquired.

"A few years now," answered Madam Savannah vaguely. "I come to Brighton during the summer months, but I do readings for people at events and even do personal readings at their houses all year round. Of course, in my civvies then – a pair of jeans and a T-shirt will do for me. I'm not what you would call 'a victim of fashion.'"

Cassie smiled. "I'm Cassie, by the way."

"I know," replied the older woman.

"How did you know that?" an amazed Cassie replied.

"You have a namedropper around your neck that says 'Cassie,'" Madam Savannah replied. Cassie smiled again, even wider. She liked the older lady.

The two women sit devouring Cassie's chips and engaging in small talk, which mainly encompassed local council rent charges and living away from home.

"Now, I suppose I'd better get on with telling your future as I'm sure you have other things to do today," said Madam Savannah before disposing of the chips wrapper in a close-by waste bin.

"I haven't got much on, to be honest, but I'm sure *you* have," Cassie replied.

Madam Savannah nodded politely, wiped her hands on a towel and adjusted her headscarf. She was now ready to go into full fortune-teller mode. She stared into the crystal ball and began to do her thing.

"You're very logical, and may I say, somewhat cynical in your approach to life, love and friendship." Cassie just sat, stony-faced, trying not to give anything away. She always believed, as her mother did, the whole world of fortune-telling, palmistry, psychic readers and the like to be poppycock. Yet already Madam Savannah had surprised her, if not amazed her, by the presentation of her persuasive psychic abilities.

"I have to say, Madam Savannah…" said Cassie.

"Call me, Savannah. I think the prefix 'Madam' sounded like I should be running a bordello, but its part of the territory I suppose," Savannah interrupted. Cassie giggled and continued to speak.

"Well Savannah, I have to say that I wouldn't ordinarily visit a psychic. I believe that…"

"Science and logic will provide answers to all of life's mysteries?" Savannah once again interrupted.

"Yes, that's right. Word for word," answered a somewhat surprised Cassie.

"And this would come from your parents, no just your mother?"

Once again, Cassie was surprised at the lady's forethought. "However, I have to be honest with you; you could just be guessing all of this. I don't wish to be rude, but body language and the inflexions of someone's speech can offer so much information, and perhaps you exploit it; perhaps."

"There's much to be said for that, I will concede. Look, I'm not here to convert you or change your whole outlook on the paranormal, but I will tell you that not everything can be explained by evidential science. I was like you when I was young. My mother was logical and cogent, and she became cold and distant because of it. As you grow up, cynicism can blinker you and harden you and believe me; you don't want that. I had a friend when I was young. She was calm, open-minded and kind. We were so close. Eventually, my ultra-logical, calculated character forced a wedge in between us. I couldn't accept her outlook and beliefs and started to resent her. We drifted apart, and although I did well for myself, I always regretted losing her. Unfortunately, it wasn't until an incident later in life that I mellowed and looked at the world in a fresh and more tolerant manner. I realised that not everything could be explained and that is good. A clear, logical mind is not a bad thing, but an open and curious mind is, in my view, better. Don't be too much like Mum. It's the mystery of life that keeps us alive. Do something reckless and silly on occasion. Take a chance. Have a gamble. You know, not everything is as it seems and time is relative. Anyway, here endeth the lesson." Savannah stood up and smiled widely and generously at Cassie.

Cassie listened intently to Savannah's word, and far from being dismissive of them, they began to resonate. She thought of her friend, Dohna, and how laid back and calm she was. Nothing much phased her, and she had probably been a better friend to Cassie than she deserved. A large stoned, cheap-looking ring on the middle finger of Savannah's right hand caught Cassie's eye. It didn't look that out of place with her whole outfit, but the band seemed too small for her finger. She also noticed that the stone had a chip taken out of it. Why it interested her so much, she didn't know.

"Anyway, I've taken enough of your valuable student time up," said Savannah, which broke Cassie's mesmeric gaze.

"I suppose I better get back and do some studying," confessed Cassie solemnly.

"Ah, que sera sera," said Savannah, with a long sigh.

Cassie laughed. "That's what my mum always says." Savannah smiled as she adjusted her headscarf.

"Listen, if you're free tomorrow pop by for a cuppa. I'll be here at the same time."

A delighted Cassie agreed and left the kiosk to walk back to her lodgings. A few yards away, she noticed the sun was high in the sky. She looked at her watch; the time was almost 1:00 pm. "That's impossible!" Cassie exclaimed to herself. Surely, she'd only been talking to Savannah for 20 minutes at the most, but the best part of three hours had elapsed. During her stroll back, she remembered Madam Savannah's words, *"Time is just relative."* Could she have spent all that time with her?

Not long later, she arrived home. The house was filled with a beautiful aroma of cooking. "That smells nice!" she shouted as she hung up her coat.

"I thought I'd make you a Sunday roast," Dohna hollered back from the kitchen. Cassie walked to the kitchen. Dohna was standing by the stove, with her back to her.

"But its Saturday," said Cassie. Then it happened again.

"So, sue me," they both said at the same time.

"Déjà vu again," said Cassie, as she sat down at the table with a concerned expression on her face.

"You've had it before. Why do you look so worried?" asked Dohna.

"It's not worry. It's just that I've never 'predicted' speech before, only situations." She paused before shaking her head to clear her mind, "Anyway, how was your morning?"

Dohna spread her arms, revealing a pinny, liberally splashed with gravy and with a large meat fork in her right hand.

"Ah, of course. You're a good friend to me, and I don't deserve you sometimes," Cassie admitted. Her mind returned to Madam Savannah's words again, especially the part about her friend that she lost contact with.

"Blimey. What's brought this on. Where's the real Cassie?" joked Dohna.

"Sit down a moment," replied Cassie. Dohna did what was requested, and Cassie told her of her meeting with the mysterious lady.

"My old cynical friend, Cassie, visiting a fortune-teller? I would never have believed it. You always thought it was all a load of nonsense. You've said that so many times," said Dohna joyfully.

"I didn't make an appointment. It was a chance meeting. However, some of what she said made sense to me. Sort of," Cassie explained.

"Did you mention the whole déjà vu thing with her?"

"No. At least I don't think so. It's all a bit odd. Anyway, I'm going back to see her tomorrow. Perhaps I'll mention it then," answered Cassie, still unsure of what happened earlier in the day.

The following morning and after oversleeping for half an hour, Cassie left the house and made her way to the seafront. It was another bright morning, and in a good mood, she was very much looking forward to spending some more time with Madam Savannah. When she reached the kiosk, it was shut. Not only was it closed, but it was boarded up, and the sign about the entrance was peeling away. The ice cream stall next to it was open, and she approached the seller.

"Where's Madam Savannah and what happened here?" asked Cassie, pointing at the abandoned kiosk.

"Madam Savannah? Oh, you mean Sandy? She packed up a few years ago. How do you know her? You look too young to be one of her clients," he said, opening the lid on a new tub of mint choc chip ice cream.

"I was here yesterday. *She* was here yesterday. We spoke," reasoned Cassie.

"You can't have, love. I'm telling you, she's not been operating here for years. No one has. Look at the state of it," the ice cream man said, pointing at the kiosk just as Cassie had done a moment earlier.

"But that's impossible," Cassie protested in disbelief.

"I'm sorry love, but I can promise you she hasn't been in town for years," confirmed the man.

"Wait a minute, you said 'Sandy'?" asked Cassie.

"Yes, Savannah was just her 'stage name.' if you like. I knew her as Sandy. It's short for Cassandra."

"That's my name," said Cassie, picking off some flaking paint from the deserted kiosk. The ice-cream man just stared at her for a moment before continuing to replenish his stock.

Cassie walked off, disconsolate and confused. Nothing made any sense. She walked back along the promenade, halting outside an amusement arcade. *"Take a chance. Have a gamble,"* thought Cassie, remembering Savannah's words. Even though she assumed it was a metaphor for life, Cassie took it at face value. She walked into the sparsely populated arcade and felt drawn to the penny drop machine. It wasn't exactly Las Vegas, but she wanted to give it a go. On closer inspection, the machine took 10p pieces and had the bonus of a few scattered watch and jewellery boxes wrapped in £5 notes to swell the punter's interest. Some primary school-aged children congregated around one side, and as soon as they lost all their loose change, they ran off to get some more money from their parents. Cassie changed a couple of pounds up using the automated change machine and proceeded to place the 10p pieces into the slot.

"Waste of bloody money," Cassie said to herself as her pocketful of loose change rapidly diminished. Four coins to go; three to go; two to go and with her final 10p and with a five-pound note wrapped box teetering on the brink, she gave it one more go. The coin cascaded down the vertical backdrop before lying flat on the top level. The step withdrew, and it pushed off the coin, which landed flat on the lower step. The last shove with the final coin proved the lucky one. Down dropped the box along with about two pounds worth of 10p pieces. Cassie quickly scooped up her booty and pocketed the lot before leaving the arcade.

The morning's mystery was still very much on her mind, and a nearby bench looked like a good place to sit and try and make sense of matters. She sat down and looked over the calm sea, which glistened magically as it reflected the mid-morning sun. She reached into her pocket and pulled out the square ring box and took off the elastic band which attached the five-pound note to it. The cash was placed into her purse before Cassie opened the box. Inside it was a ring – a very familiar looking ring. It looked identical to Madam Savannah's, although it looked brand new and was quite shiny. She pushed it on her finger; it was a little tight, but it fitted. After admiring it for a minute, Cassie pulled it off, but lost her grip, causing her to drop it on to the concrete floor. Cassie picked it up, and what she saw shocked her. The hard drop caused the stone to chip. The missing facet was precisely the same as on Savannah's ring. There was no doubt about it. The outside world drew silent, and all Cassie could hear was the thump, thump, thump of her rapidly beating heart.

It all started to make sense. The unnerving look

Savannah gave her on first laying eyes on Cassie; the knowledge regarding her degree subject, her favourite drink and the whole story of the friend she lost contact with; that was a warning for her to change her ways. Then there was 'que sera sera' and perhaps most tellingly, the same name. Cassie had seen her future. She didn't know how or why, but logic and science could not possibly explain it, but undoubtedly her future self had entered her timeline in an attempt to change the course of her history.

Cassie carefully placed the ring back in its box and out of the corner of her eye noticed a figure in the mid-distance to her right. She didn't see her face, but it was a woman dressed in a long colourful skirt turning away and starting to walk in the opposite direction back towards the amusement arcade. She had a pronounced limp. The woman stopped and drew a breath, before disappearing into a crowd of people. A tear came to Cassie's eye. She had been shown a vision of the future, and it was a future that she was able to shape. She looked down at the ring box, opened it and took out the ring and placed it on her finger once more. It didn't matter that it was too tight for her; it would never be off her finger again.

Driver Seven

There was nothing Robin liked doing more on a Friday evening after a week's hard graft than to unwind in his local with a couple of jars – just him and a newspaper. It was August 1990, and the papers were full of worrying reports of the impending conflict with Iraq. The written and television media had been filled with little else for weeks. President Bush was becoming more and more impatient with Saddam Hussein, and troops were being prepared for battle, it was an inevitability that war would break out. However, world events took a back seat as Robin sat thumbing through his local rag in search of a second-hand car to buy.

"That's the one. Silver *1987 Ford Sierra. 48,000 miles. Clean interior. Electric windows. Sunroof £3,200 ono,*" he muttered to himself, before standing up to walk over to the payphone on the wall.

Robin dropped 10p into the slot and dialled the number. A gruff man answered the phone.

"Yes?"

"Hello, I'm calling about the Sierra you have advertised."

"It's gone, man. Went this afternoon," said the man at the other end.

"Oh, I see," replied Robin mournfully.

"You're alright. Ta-ta," said the man and then hung up. Robin did the same and walked back to his table to finish his pint and continue his search.

Just then, in front of him appeared a tall, slim man. He wore a black suit and a tie and sported a 1950s D.A. hairstyle and sideburns. Robin looked up from his newspaper.

"I hope you don't mind me saying, but I overheard your conversation on the telephone just now, and I understand you're in the market for a new car?"

"Yes, that's right. Well, not a new car, but a new car for me, if you see what I mean," Robin answered.

"Of course. I may have something for you. Can I take a seat?" asked the man.

"Go ahead," he replied, gesturing that the stranger takes the seat opposite him.

"By the way, the name is James."

"I'm Robin," he put his hand out for the stranger to shake, but the gesture was rebuffed.

"I've got a cracker of a motor for you," James enthused. "A 1963 British Racing Green MG Roadster. It's a beautiful sporty number, soft top, fantastic condition. Just been taxed and MOT'd."

"To be honest, I was looking for a family saloon, like a Ford Sierra, so it's not for me, thanks," explained Robin, feeling a little put-out.

"Ah, you're a family man?"

"I'm not married, and I live on my own. I don't even do a lot of mileage, as I work within a short walking distance."

"Well, why do you want a stuffy old man's car like that? Surely, a man of means with a free spirit such as yourself deserves a bit of excitement and class in his life. What's your budget, old chap?"

"About £2,500."

"Well, I only want two grand for mine. Others are going for well over £3000, and they aren't in half as good condition as my little beauty," explained James, who was doing a fantastic job in selling the attributes of his vehicle. "I'm only selling it for this knockdown price as I've got a job starting abroad next month and I have to flog everything."

"Oh, I don't know. The price sounds good, but it's not the sort of car I'm looking for," lamented Robin. "Then again, you only live once."

"So they say, although I'm a firm believer in reincarnation," said James with conviction. "Tell you what I'll do – I'll bring her around here tomorrow at 11 a.m., and you can take her for a spin. If you like what you see, she's yours." Robin agreed, and they shook hands before James left the pub.

The following day at 11 a.m. on the button, a beautiful, green British sports car came screaming around the corner and parked up outside the pub where Robin was standing waiting. It was a lovely sunny if not crisp morning and the roof was off.

"She's a stunner, isn't she?" shouted James over the roar of the engine. "1800cc; six cylinders; twin carburettors!" Robin struggled to hear what he said, so James turned off the engine, then got out of the car. Curiously, he was still wearing the same suit from the day before. It wasn't a workday, and a black suit and tie was hardly the typical garb for a petrol head.

"Come on, get in and take her for a spin around the block," enthused James before getting back into the car on the passenger's side. Robin happily did what he was being urged to do. The interior like the exterior was immaculate and at £2000, he knew it was a snip.

With the circuit around the block complete, Robin couldn't take the smile off his face. He examined the engine and had a good look in all the nooks and crannies of the bodywork, and it was indeed in tiptop condition. James helped him pull the soft top over.

"Well, what did I tell you?" said James.

"I have to say; I love it. It's…"

"Perfect?" interrupted James.

"Well… yes," admitted Robin, still unable to relax his grin.

"And it's only done 78,000 miles. For a 28-year-old car, that's fantastic. All her owners have really looked after her.

"*All* of her owners?" asked Robin. "How many has she had then? "

"Including me… six," James confirmed.

"Six???" blurted Robin. "How come it's had so many with such low mileage and is in such good condition?"

"It's a Summer car. You only really take her out for pleasure jaunts. You said yourself you don't need a car to commute. Just imagine taking her down windy country roads or opening her up on the M23 on a day trip to Brighton. That's what all the previous owners did, I bet. Why would she want just one careful lady owner, when there have been six careful and loving gentleman owners looking after her for almost 30 years?" explained the expert salesman. "And then, there's the classic car insurance, so that won't be another big expense for you. She's been fully serviced too. You've even got a new stereo/cassette. What's not to like?"

"A Summer car? Hmmm. It *is* August, I suppose." Robin paused for a moment. "However, you're making it very difficult to refuse. And funnily enough, my mother lives close to Brighton," said Robin, with the smile returning to his face. James just stood, arms crossed, nodding.

Robin walked around the vehicle again, giving it a thorough once over. "Go on, then; you have a deal."

James laughed loudly. "Excellent. I have all the paperwork here with me." He pulled out a wad of documents from his inside jacket pocket, "Here's your MOT, V5 ownership document and service records. It even has the original manual in the glove box."

Robin pulled out a wad of fifty-pound notes from the back pocket of his jeans and handed it over to James, who took no time in counting them. "That's all fine. Here, let me fill out and tear off the green slip, and you're away," said James. Once completed, he handed him all the paperwork and gave Robin a satisfied nod. The satisfied seller walked away up the road, leaving Robin looking admiringly at his new purchase for a few lost moments. Eventually, he got in and took it for a brief run, before returning home. After a final visual examination, Robin locked the car door and walked inside his house.

The following weekend, Robin decided to visit an old friend, who he hadn't seen in ages and just happened to live a fair distance away in Kent. He probably wouldn't have bothered if he hadn't just purchased his magnificent

British sports car, but Robin wanted to show it off, which he duly did.

The return journey was at night and not a particularly pleasant one at that. High winds rattled the framework of the soft roof, and the engine noise sounded uncharacteristically loud. Robin leant over to the glove box to select one of the two tapes he put in their earlier on – Queen and Supertramp were the favoured artistes. He picked one out – *Queen's Greatest Hits*. Before he could play it, he drove in a small pothole in the road and dropped the tape. It bounced off the base of the gearstick and fell into the space underneath the driver's seat. Robin slowed down slightly and carefully bent down to pick the tape up, all the time keeping a careful eye on the road. Fumbling around for a moment, he located the tape and pushed it into the slot on the stereo. After a few moments of silence, instead of the strains of Bohemian Rhapsody, out of the speakers came the voices of a boy and girl singing. Immediately, Robin ejected the tape. It was an orange BASF cassette that he'd never seen before. Unwilling to start searching around for his desired tape and with curiosity aroused, he pushed the tape back into the player. The two people on the tape began talking about taking a day off college for the Queen's upcoming Silver Jubilee celebrations, which immediately aged them in their late teenage years and the recording from 1977.

"How long has this tape been in this car?" Robin asked himself. Bearing in mind, the superb condition and cleanliness of the vehicle, it seemed inconceivable that the cassette, which was so easily located by the driver, for 14 years could have been overlooked. The voices suddenly went silent, and Robin fast-forwarded it a couple of times to find some further recording, but to no avail. So, he ejected the tape, flung it on the passenger seat and turned the radio on instead. Hey Presto – Queen. That made him smile, and his mind turned to music rather than the mystery of the recordings on the old tape. Within twenty minutes, Robin was home, and with the car safely locked in the garage, he spent the rest of the evening in front of the television, watching a more comprehensive coverage of what was now officially called *Operation Desert Storm*.

After a long and challenging working week, Saturday morning couldn't arrive soon enough. Robin planned to go and visit his mother who lived in Hove, and as luck would have it, the weekend began warm and bright. Although not "roof down" weather, the trip down to the south coast was an enjoyable one. He allowed himself to open the MG on the M23, and she didn't disappoint. Whether purring at a junction or roaring down the motorway, the car performed like a thoroughbred. Robin couldn't believe his luck at the series of events that occurred to enable him to buy such an exceptional vehicle.

The visit to see his old mum mainly consisted of him listening to tales of her youth and his late father. Although he'd heard them dozens of times before, he always tried to make it appear like it was the first time. At several points during the day, he did try and interrupt her constant flow with a tale of his own regarding his new car, but his mum was far too involved in her distant memories for him to lever it into the conversation, so he gave up.

By nine o'clock, with a stomach full of tea and Victoria Sponge cake and ears almost bleeding from the telling and re-telling of a dozen stories of his youth and "wassername" next door, Robin decided it was time to leave. It was beginning to get dark, and the weather had changed for the worse.

Upon bidding her son farewell, Robin's mother, standing on her doorstep piped up, "Oh, you've got a new car. Why didn't you tell me?"

"It must have slipped my mind, Mum," her son replied, not wishing to explain to her how many times he tried to bring up the subject throughout the day.

The wind had picked up, and a fine misty rain filled the atmosphere. Reports of tailbacks on the motorway prompted Robin to take the A23 back to London. Even though in mileage terms, the trip was longer. If there was one thing that Robin hated, it was traffic jams, so the A road was the only viable option. Not fifteen miles into his journey with the weather conditions worsening further, he hit traffic. Being unfamiliar with the locality of East Sussex, and without a roadmap at hand, Robin didn't want to take a chance and deviate from his route, so he reluctantly elected to stay in the tailback. The hard rain produced a cacophony of noise on the soft top. With both the Queen and Supertramp exhausted, he decided to try the radio for company. He turned it on, but there was so much interference on every station, bar one – a news station. Inevitably the topic of conversation was the impending Iraq war. Fed up with the whole situation, but with no other option, he continued listening to the discussion.

"Bloody noise," shouted Robin, frustrated by the weather and the traffic.

"You can't blame the car for that," spoke a voice. Robin stopped in his tracks. Unquestionably, it must have come from the radio. The traffic began to move but ground to a halt, suddenly forcing the driver to slam on the breaks.

"Why is there so much traffic?" Robin questioned loudly.

"You decided to come this way." It was the same voice. Robin felt a cold shiver run up his spine. "It's alright. It's just your imagination," Robin spluttered out loud. He turned up the volume on the radio.

A while later, with the traffic starting to flow again, and with the only radio station still available continuing to talk about the war, he remembered the tape he found the previous week. He leant over to the glove box and reached for it. He slipped it into the stereo and fast-forwarded it for a few times searching for more recordings. After a few failed attempts, there it was, the two youngsters once again talking and laughing about nonsense, mainly consisting of parties, the monarchy, and even a quiche recipe. Throughout, they were continually giggling. By this time, the road was completely clear of traffic, but the rain was relentlessly giving the windscreen wipers a challenging job.

"War or giggling idiots? What a choice," Robin voiced. The recording paused momentarily but started again. The subject matter had turned to a more sombre one. The giggles had stopped, and the mood changed.

"Tell me, as I'm curious; how would you like to die?" asked the male.

"Jimmy, what a question to ask," replied the female.

"Go on; tell me."

"Well, I haven't given it much thought, but I'd like to die painlessly, at a grand old age in my bed, surrounded by my loved ones, thank you very much," replied the woman in a matter-of-fact fashion. Humouring her friend, she asked the question, "What about you?"

"I'd like to die in a car accident like James Dean. It's

such a cool way to go," the male enthused.

"Dying like your hero? You're so morbid sometimes," the girl concluded.

Jimmy just laughed. The laugh sounded familiar to Robin as it grew louder and louder before the tape stopped and got trapped in the mechanism. He tried to eject the cassette, but it was stuck. It couldn't play, rewind, or fast forward, and no matter what he attempted, Robin couldn't release it.

"He's right, you know, it's a good way to go, the best." It was the voice again, but more defined than earlier. A glance into the rear-view mirror provided the spectral image of James, the man who sold the car to Robin. The shimmering image began to laugh, just like the youth on the tape.

"You!" shouted Robin, eyes transfixed on the figure in the mirror. James kept laughing. Robin turned his head to look behind, but no one was there. There wasn't enough space for a person anyway. A loud horn sounded from ahead forcing Robin to turn around abruptly. The raised headlights blinded him. Violently swerving to avoid the oncoming vehicle, he lost control of the car. The car hit a divot in the road, and the MG bounced into the air before rolling over twice and landing into a ditch by the side of the carriageway. The impact was so enormous that what was an immaculate piece of machinery had instantaneously transformed into a crumpled heap of metal and glass. The oncoming car came to a measured halt just a few metres away. There were no other vehicles on the road.

A man stepped out of the car, a silver 1987 Ford Sierra, and casually walked towards the wrecked MG. A barely conscious and rapidly fading Robin watched his advance.

In his condition, nothing made sense to him, but there was a familiarity about this approaching menace. He was quite tall, wearing a dark suit and tie with hair in a D.A. style. "It can't be," Robin spluttered to himself. It was. It was James.

"Why?" Robin choked, with barely enough breath to speak. There was no doubt it was an apparition. He could see through the smashed windscreen, the man who sold him the car.

James stopped a few yards away and reached into his jacket pocket to pull out some papers, one of them being a green V5 registration document. He then took out a pen and ticked it with a flourish.

"That's driver seven. Now to find number eight," he chuckled with sinister delight before slipping the paperwork back into his jacket. He then turned around and walked away, past his car and into the distant night.

It didn't seem real, but at this point, nothing did. The cruel scene was the last thing Robin observed before everything faded away into eternal blackness.

A Dime to Change History

It is November 1973, and lifelong friends, Ken and Pat from London were partaking in a long-planned road trip around the Southern states of the USA. Following a lengthy drive through the night, the pair arrived in Dallas, Texas, their final destination, where not long after checking in at a cheap hotel, their hunger pangs dictated a search for somewhere to eat.

"I'm ravenous. I fancy a hotdog or burger and plenty of fries. Something terribly unhealthy and terribly American," said Ken.

"Yes, it's not like we haven't eaten anything like that over the last couple of weeks, is it?" Pat replied sarcastically.

"I know, but I'd like it from a 50s-style diner, served by a waitress on roller-skates," Ken added.

"Whatever floats your boat, I suppose," giggled Pat.

After a few hundred yards walk, they spotted across the road a 50s-style diner with roof signage gleaming in the November sunshine, beckoning them in.

"I don't believe it. How's that for luck? That'll do nicely," announced Pat joyfully, pointing at the restaurant.

"That'll do very nicely indeed," agreed Ken excitedly.

They crossed the road and walked into the restaurant. Pat took his sunglasses off and dropped them in his shirt pocket. He looked around in amazement. It's just as he'd imagined a retro American diner to look like – a long bar with red leather-topped stools with beautiful turned chrome finishing to all the countertops and tables. Photographs of 50s icons such as James Dean, Marlon Brando and Jayne Mansfield alongside black and white prints of various American football and baseball players adorned the walls. In pride of place, was a photo of incumbent President Richard Nixon. A middle-aged man, resplendent in a pristine white shirt and black bow tie with a white soda jerk hat, wiped down the bar top. Topping off the creation next to the restroom door was a stunning, authentic Wurlitzer jukebox.

The waiter offered the two Brits, a cheery welcome. "Good morning. Take any table you gents prefer." Ken and Pat chose a table at the rear of the restaurant close to the jukebox.

"Well, there's no roller-skated waitresses, but this has everything else I wanted. Do you think it's too early for a hotdog with onions, relish and mustard, and a massive portion of French Fries?" asked Ken perusing the menu, his eyes lighting up at the choice of edible Americana.

"This is America. It's never too early to get those arteries nice and clogged-up mate," replied Pat, salivating at the prospect enjoying something similar.

This is just the sort of place my intended would love," announced Ken, looking around lovingly at the spotless, but surprisingly empty diner.

"Perhaps you should suggest that you convert one of her parent's garages into one?" Pat jokingly proposes. "I bet you can't wait to move in there. Shoes off in the hallway; in by 10 pm; church every Sunday."

"Oh, don't," pleaded Ken.

Pat takes out a photograph from his wallet and stares at

it. It's of him, Ken and his fiancée, Patricia, on a boat trip on the Thames. "We've all been friends for quite a long time, haven't we? You're a lucky guy, Ken. If you hadn't have seen her first, she'd have been mine," Pat teased him.

"Yeah, right. You wouldn't have stood a chance with her. She likes the more sophisticated man, not a common oik, like you," Ken replied playfully.

"I would have snapped her up straight away. Seven years and you're still to be wed. What's keeping you?"

"I don't know. At least Patricia's parents are happy for me to move in now. It's taken years," said Ken.

"Good luck with that," Pat returned.

"Look, you look so happy. We all look happy. I wonder how long it will last?" said Pat, showing Ken the photo.

"It'll last, don't you worry," Ken admonished his friend. "Anyway, our living arrangements are only temporary. We'll get our own place soon enough," Ken replied. His eyes catch the selection of milkshakes on offer, and he changes the subject quickly. "Who would order a *lime* milkshake?"

"I guess some people would; otherwise, it wouldn't be on the menu. Go on, give it a try. I dare you," said Pat.

"Very well. You only live once," said Ken and placed the menu down. Just then, the waiter approaches their table with notepad and pencil at the ready.

"Have you gentleman made your decisions?" he asked politely with a cheery smile.

"Yes, I'll have the hotdog and fries and the lime milkshake, please. Oh, and everything on the hotdog," said Ken.

"A lime milkshake?" asked the waiter, somewhat surprised by the request. Ken and Pat gave each other with a quizzical look. "You gentlemen are British, yes?"

"Yes, we're from London," confirmed Ken.

"We always like to welcome our friends from England here. I'd love to visit *Lahndan, but oi ave to look after this place,*" said the waiter, trying to effect a Cockney accent. The two visitors laugh sympathetically, unwilling to upset their host. The waiter chuckled generously, delighted with his effort. "By the way, my name's Billy. And you sir, what would you like?" he asked, turning to Pat.

"Oh, I'll have the double quarter pounder cheeseburger, fries and… a root beer, please?" answered Pat. The waiter nodded and wrote down the order and went away to prepare the food.

"A root beer? Do you even know what root beer is?" asked Ken.

"Yes, a root beer and no, I don't know what it is, but it's an American favourite. You've got your lime shake, and I've got my root beer," replied Pat.

"Okay. Fair enough," replied Ken. "Here, let's pick a record from the jukebox." The two men stood up and headed towards the Wurlitzer. They spend a good minute or two browsing the options before Pat pipes up.

"Eddie Cochran – Summertime Blues," suggested Pat.

"I was going down the route of 'Roy Orbison – In Dreams," said Ken.

"We'll flip for it, then," suggested Pat, picking a shiny dime out of his pocket. "Heads or tails?"

"Heads," chose Ken as Pat flipped the coin in the air before catching it in his right hand and slapping it down on the back of his left. Ken revealed the reverse side.

"Too bad, mate. He pushes the coin into the slot and made his selection. "Now then, let's see… C6," announced Ken triumphantly before selecting his chosen record. The arm of the jukebox slid from left to right before grabbing a 45 and turning it, dropping it onto the turntable.

'They asked me how I knew; our true love was true…'

"This isn't 'In Dreams'," complained Ken.

"It's not even 'Summertime Blues'," countered Pat.

"Nobody picked 'Smoke Gets in Your Eyes by The Platters'. Stupid machine," said Pat. He aimed a kick to the base of the unit. The jolt caused the record to jump and begin to emit a strange whirring sound. Just then, a brilliant flash of light emanated from the centre of the jukebox which temporarily blinded the men. It disappeared as quickly as it appeared and left Ken and Pat rubbing their eyes.

"You okay?" asked Pat.

"I think so. What on earth happened there?" replied Ken.

"I don't know, but I think we should leave the jukebox alone and get back to the table," Pat apologetically said.

They both turned around, and to their surprise, the diner was now well-populated and vibrant. The pair sat down at their table, still unable to comprehend what had happened. As soon as they did, the waiter brought over their order.

"There we go, gentlemen," he said cheerily, and placed the plates of food down on the table. The drinks were already in situ.

"Thank you," said Ken, looking up at the waiter.

"You're welcome," he replied and walked away back behind the counter.

Looking shocked, Ken asked, "Is that the same guy? He looks sort of the same, but younger somehow."

"Perhaps he's moisturising," replied Pat playfully before ravenously biting into his burger.

"Hold on a minute," said Ken looking around. "Wasn't there a picture of President Nixon on the wall behind the counter when we came in?"

"Yes, why?" replied Pat taking another massive bite of his meaty treat.

"So, why has it been replaced with one of JFK?"

Sure enough, in the same frame was a picture of John F. Kennedy where Nixon's grinning face once beamed.

Ken tentatively took a nibble of his burger, all the time trying to figure out the small changes to the interior. He watched the waiter behind the bar turn on the television in the corner of the diner with a broom handle. The TV, tuned to the local news channel, appeared to be re-running some old footage of the Governor of Texas preparing to greet Mr and Mrs Kennedy the following day.

"Did you notice the TV there before, Pat?" he asked.

"No, I can't say I did," replied Pat with a full mouth, without taking his eyes off the remains of his hotdog.

"Why is the news channel showing this about Kennedy?" asked Ken.

"I guess because it's ten years since his assassination. I assume it's a documentary," explained Pat. Ken nodded in agreement, and for a moment, his thirst for answers slaked.

Ken took a larger bite of his burger and a sip of his lime milkshake, the taste of which made him wince slightly. He looked up at the television again, and his moment of satisfaction was swiftly aborted.

"Then why does it say '*LIVE: 21st November 1963*' at the bottom of the screen?" Ken put his burger down and looked around at the busy diner. Not only had the place mysteriously filled up with customers and Billy miraculously de-aged significantly, but all the patrons were wearing fashions aligning to the early 1960s. He turned again to face Pat.

"Somehow, and I don't know-how, we appeared to have gone back in time, mate."

Pat, more interested in finishing his meal, put down his fork on to the empty plate and laughed at his friend. "Yeah, sure. The jukebox/time machine has spirited us back ten years in the past. I think the lime milkshake has gone to your head."

"Okay, so who is that guy sitting on his own at the end of the bar staring at his coffee?" said Ken.

Both men turn to look at the solitary figure shuffling slightly uncomfortably on his stool.

"Oh my God," said Pat, unable to take his eyes off the stranger.

"Exactly. *Now*, do you believe me?" asked Ken.

"It can't be him. It just can't be. That's... that's Lee Harvey Oswald," Pat declares.

"It is. And somehow, we have been blasted back to 1963 and tomorrow that man, over there, will be arrested for killing the President and in two days he'll be dead. It was a set-up, and I have to warn him," said Ken.

"Don't be silly. You can't do that," said Pat forcefully.

"But he didn't do it. He was a patsy. He's innocent," maintained Ken.

"No! No, you can't," exclaimed Pat, grabbing hold of his friend's arm. "You are such a conspiracy theorist. Most people believe it was him, but in any event, you can't say anything to him as it will change everything, and if I've learned anything from my science fiction novels, it's that any slight action can change the course of history, let alone something of this scale. The history of the world will change significantly. You can't say a word to him. In fact, you mustn't even make eye contact. Come on, let's settle the bill and get out of here." Pat stands up to leave.

"You forget one thing, my friend – we are in 1963 now. Where are we going to go, and what are we going to do?" says Ken. Pat sighs deeply, re-takes his seat and takes another sip of his drink. The unusual taste makes him wince once again. The two men sat in silence, trying not to be too conspicuous although some patrons were beginning to take a keen interest in them. "Why are they looking at us?"

"It's 1963, and we're wearing pastel flares and floral shirts. I have a handlebar moustache, and we've both got long hair. We probably look like aliens from outer-space to them," explained Pat in a quiet voice. "Listen, I have an idea. Just keep yourself to yourself while I pop to the gents. When I get back, we'll go to the jukebox and do precisely what we did when we came in. Perhaps, that'll reverse the time jump, or whatever it is."

"That's your brilliant plan?" spluttered Ken.

"It's all I've got. Anyway, I didn't say it was 'brilliant'," Pat replied. "Just stay put and don't make eye contact with anyone, especially Lee Harvey Oswald, over there," he added cautiously. "I can't believe those words just came out of my mouth," he mumbled as he stood up and left the table. Pat disappeared through the doors to the restrooms and as he did a man sitting at a table opposite walked over to Ken who was eyeing the dessert options on the menu.

"You ladies must be from out of town?" the man jibed in a robust Texan drawl, before taking a drag of a cigarette.

Ken somewhat surprised answers, timidly, "Er, we're from England."

"Well, that would explain it. You Limeys are a strange breed indeed. Just be careful. There are folks around here that don't care too much for homosexuals." He looked Ken up and down, shakes his head before re-joining his party at his table.

"Homosexuals?" Ken whispered to himself. He looked over at the 'murderer-to-be' again who was still sitting by himself all alone looking forlorn. "It's not right. It's just not right," he repeated to himself.

In the gent's restroom, Pat unlocks the cubicle door and steps over to the basin. He turned on the tap and splashed cold water over his face, taking a long stare at the wet, dripping reflection looking back at him, trying to work out what the hell was going on. "It has to be a dream," he said to himself. From the adjoining cubicle, there was a flush, and an older man opens the door, washes his hands in the adjacent basin, looks at Pat and gives him a wink. Saying nothing, he wrings his hands and leaves the restroom. Unwilling to create questions, Pat waits a while before opening the door to re-join his friend at the table.

"I think they think we're…"

"Queer? I know," interrupted Ken. "Look, I'm just

going to take a leak myself, and we'll do as you said. We have to get back to our own time.

Pat looked around and got several strange looks again. There is one difference – the stool where Lee Harvey Oswald was sitting was now vacant. Feeling increasingly uncomfortable and not willing to wait any longer, he stood up and stepped over to the jukebox which was now silent. He reached into his pocket and pulled out another shiny dime. He flips it, and it lands on tails. "So far, so good," he said to himself, pushing the coin in the slot. "Now what number was it? Ah yes, C6," he answered to himself. A few moments later, once again, instead of 'In Dreams by Roy Orbison, the opening bars of 'Smoke Gets In Your Eyes' began to play. As before, Pat kicked the base of the jukebox in the same place he had aimed at earlier. Mirroring previous events, the record jumped, and the jukebox began emitting the strange whirring sound again. He shut his eyes but could still see the flash of bright light burst from the machine through his closed eyelids. He waited a few seconds before daring to open his eyes, and when he did, he gingerly turned around to see if his actions had taken him back to 1973.

The first thing he realised was the diner was as empty as it was when he and Ken entered it. The waiter wiped dry a milkshake glass had aged and looked out through the windows at the front of the establishment, and Pat noticed people walking along wearing flares and flowery shirts, sporting long hair. He drew a huge sigh of relief and sat down at the table. Smiling in satisfaction, he picked up the menu again, feeling very pleased with himself.

The door to the restroom opened.

"I did it all by myself," Pat said. "I couldn't wait for you."

"Oh, that's thoughtful of you. What did you order, darling?" spoke a woman's voice.

Pat looked up at the figure sitting down opposite him.

"Patricia? What are you doing here?" he questioned loudly.

"Well, I just went to the ladies – remember? You look like you hadn't seen me in years. I've only been gone a few minutes," she replied with a confused look on her face.

Pat paused for a moment. "Yes, of course," he replied none too convinced of his sanity. "And we are?"

"On holiday, Pat. Really, what is wrong? Have you received a bang on the head in the time since I left you?"

"Pat and Pat?" Pat said wistfully as he looked at the beautiful woman sitting opposite him.

"Yes, have you just realised that? We've only been married for seven years after all."

Pat reached in his trouser pocket for his wallet. His heart began pounding like a jackhammer as he carefully pulled out the photo, fearing what he might see. The photograph only featured the happy smiling faces of him and Patricia. Ken was gone. He took a moment and feeling a little bilious, looked around the diner again. His eye caught the Presidential photo on the wall. It wasn't of Kennedy anymore, but it wasn't of Nixon either. He stood up and walked over to the counter to try and get a closer look. "Who is that?" he asked Billy, the waiter.

"Sir, that is President Humphrey, of course," answered the waiter, slightly aggrieved at the question.

"What happened to Nixon?"

"Strange question. Well, when he lost to Kennedy in

'60, and again in '64, that was it for him, or at least everyone thought. He disappeared into the political abyss, before coming back and losing again in '72. If you look 'loser' up in the dictionary, you'll see a photo of Richard Milhouse Nixon," laughed Billy.

"I'm sorry, I'm a bit rusty on American history," said Pat softly. "What happened to Kennedy?"

Billy looked at him like he was an idiot, but unwilling to be rude to a patron, he gave Pat a brief history lesson.

"Kennedy came to power in 1960 and at the start of his re-election campaign, came to Dallas in November 1963 when the secret service prevented an assassination attempt. Some weird kid from New Orleans teamed up with one of your countrymen to kill the President. Interestingly, they were picked up by the police just outside this diner. Anyway, the Mob got to them both a couple of days later, so we'll never know why they wanted Kennedy dead, although there are plenty of conspiracy theories. Kennedy won the '64 election with a landslide victory. Lyndon Johnson won in '68, but only wanted to serve one term. Hubert Humphrey beat the old loser Nixon and here we are in 1973 with President Humphrey."

"Ken and Oswald?" said Pat to himself. "And what about Vietnam?"

"What *about* Vietnam?" asked Billy, looking befuddled.

"Watergate?"

"Water-what?" Again, Billy looked confused. "I've gotta say, you Brits are very strange. I hope you don't mind me saying, sir." Pat nodded at him and re-took his seat opposite his 'wife'.

"So, what happened to Ken?" he asked Patricia.

"Are you sure you're alright. You're acting like you've forgotten the last ten years of your life," she replied.

"I know. Humour me. What happened to Ken?" insisted Pat.

"That's one reason why we're here, isn't it? You're laying some ghosts to rest. I never even met him, but I know he had a big impact on your life. It's been ten years since…"

"Since what?" demanded Pat.

"Since Ken was killed. He and Oswald were gunned down two days after their arrest, weren't they? Look, I know you don't like talking about it, and I can only assume you've completely blocked it out of your memory, but somehow, and we still don't know how he got caught up with the conspiracy to kill Kennedy – him and that Oswald bloke. I didn't even know he was a Communist."

"A Communist? Ken, a Communist? He wouldn't even re-join the local Labour Party because they wanted to charge him postage to send him a replacement membership card. He wasn't mixed up with Lee Harvey Oswald," said Pat loudly. Patricia looked over to Billy, who had been alerted by Pat's outburst.

"Shhh. Keep your voice down. Anyway, how did he get himself involved with Oswald? You've never said," asked Patricia.

"He warned him. I told him not to, but he warned him. The stupid idiot," Pat mouthed to himself, ignoring his wife's question.

"What did you say?" asked Patricia.

"Nothing," said Pat sombrely.

"That's always been the problem with you. You won't

say anything about Ken, but now you're asking questions about him. What is wrong, darling?" asked the worried Patricia, taking Pat's hands in hers.

"I don't know. Sorry, I think it's just being back here again. It's doing strange things to me. I'm not sure it's been a good idea."

"Come on, let's pay and go back to the hotel. "It's our last day, and I don't want you getting all miserable and morbid." Patricia stood up, placed a kiss on Pat's head and walked over to the front door and exiting the diner. The winter sun was very bright, and she donned a pair of sunglasses.

Still very confused and unable to quite fathom the situation, Pat went over to Billy and gave him a $10 bill which more than covered the check and a tip.

"Thank you, sir," said Billy happily. "I hope you and your good lady wife have a safe journey home and if I may offer some advice to you – Don't spend too long living with your wife's folks. A young couple need their own space."

Pat looked perplexed and thanked Billy before joining his wife outside the building.

"Patricia?" he asked as they started to walk up the road towards their hotel.

"Yes, darling?" she replied.

"When are we going to get our own place?" asked Pat, hoping that the information just bestowed on him by Billy was incorrect.

"Soon, I hope. My folks aren't that bad, are they? After seven years, they're just about getting used to you."

Pat gulped, took his sunglasses from his shirt pocket

and grabbed his wife's hand. She smiled at him, and they walked hand-in-hand up the road into the bright early afternoon sunlight.

and grabbed his wife's hand. She smiled at him, and they walked hand-in-hand up the road into the bright early afternoon sunlight.

The Wolf Who Cried Wolf

"Oh, why don't you just get a life, mate?" Laura shouted down the phone before ending the call abruptly.

"Him again?" asked Cindy, one of her colleagues and long-standing friend.

"Yes, it's the third time this week, and somehow he knows my name now. For heaven's sake, it's only Wednesday," said Laura angrily.

"Tuesday," corrected Cindy.

"Of course; Tuesday. That makes it even worse. It's getting tiresome. And why does he always ask for me?"

"Perhaps he's drawn to your calm, easy-going demeanour, Laura," Cindy suggested sarcastically.

"Hey, that's enough of that. A lot of people appreciate my no-nonsense approach," Laura responded aloofly.

"Tell that to the legions of people you've fired," added Cindy in the same vein.

"Look, if someone isn't doing their job correctly, they're out. Besides, it's more like half a dozen, than 'legions', Cindy. However, the one I'd like to get my hands on is this 'Wolf' character; and I use that word advisedly. What's with all the voices?"

"And the police can't find him?" Cindy replied, answering a question with a question.

"No, they think he's a lunatic; and in any event, he always calls from phone boxes and the calls don't last long, so they can't trace him," explains Laura, who heads the local news department.

Laura and Cindy work for the Canterbury Advertiser, a newspaper based in Kent. Laura is the assistant editor, and Cindy reports local events. A man, known as Mr Wolf has been calling the newspaper's office for several weeks, threatening all sorts; from setting off smoke bombs in department stores and kidnapping members of the Royal Family, to even jumping off Canterbury Cathedral. His calls are always short, and he often asks for someone to be sent out to interview him, although, of course, he never reveals his whereabouts. Recently, his calls had become more frequent and demanding.

"Can't we do anything about him?" asked Cindy.

"If the police can't, what chance have we got?" replied Laura. "Anyway, we have enough on our plate, and it's that time of year again when the local school palms us off with their most desperate job experience kids. And guess who's been asked to take him under her wing? Yes, muggins here. Although, Cindy, would you mind..?"

"Er, no. I have work to do too, you know. Why are you so cynical? I know it's difficult for you to be anything else, but give it a try," Cindy bit sternly.

A sports reporter, Phil, walks up to the ladies. "Laura, there's a young man here to see you. His name is Jason."

Laura looks at her watch. "Great, he's early," she hisses with disdain. "Okay, Phil. Tell him I'll be with him in a minute or two. Or three. Or four."

After making a phone call which lasted for 10 minutes, Laura walked over to the youth who was sitting, hands clasped together in between his knees and staring to the ground.

"You must be Jason?" she said.

He looked up, "Yes, I'm here for my job experience," he replied timidly.

Jason was 15 years old but had the appearance of someone a little younger. He was timid and introverted, but well-mannered and polite, so the school thought it would be beneficial for him to experience life in a working office environment. As the Canterbury Advertiser had taken on students in this capacity from the school in the past successfully, they thought it an excellent opportunity for Jason.

"You're prompt. That's a good start. Would you follow me?" Laura told him like a strict school teacher. "Come and sit down at this desk. Let me introduce Cindy. She'll be 'looking after you' for want of a better phrase for the rest of the day." Cindy gave Laura a confused stare. Laura mouthed 'sorry.'

"Hello, Jason. I'm Cindy, but you already knew that," said Cindy nervously as she held out her hand. Jason shook it limply and smiled.

"Would you like a cup of tea, Jason?" asked Laura. "It might be the only one you don't have to make yourself here."

"No, no, thanks," the lad replied.

"Good, then I have work to do. We'll catch up later on. Cindy, it's over to you," announced Laura before walking off but not before Cindy afforded her another stare; this time a little more scornful.

Cindy spent some time explaining her job and how a local newspaper works before her phone rang. She picked it up.

"Just put those papers in the filing cabinet over there, Jason. 'Hello, Canterbury Advertiser. Oh no, not you again… Really, Mr Wolf?… No, Mr Wolf. We won't be sending a reporter out to you. Because, Mr Wolf, you haven't kidnapped anyone, have you? No, you haven't, Mr Wolf. I must go now. I have a job to do. Please stop calling us." With that, Cindy, very deliberately, put down the receiver. Jason looked at her curiously.

"That was a call from a gentleman called Mr Wolf – but I'm sure you guessed that. The guy keeps phoning the paper telling us he's done or about to do all sorts. One time he threatened to jump off a building, then he was going to chain himself to a school bus and the next day he threatened to drive his car off a cliff. A cliff… in Canterbury."

"Haven't you called the police?" asked Jason.

"Oh yes, many times, but they think he's a local nutter – not their words, but mine. He only wants publicity. He's just an attention seeker, and he's not getting it from this newspaper," she added defiantly.

Most of the morning centred around making tea and coffee for staff members and watching Cindy type up stories she'd written about a local garden show and the plans to build more council homes on the outskirts of the city. Just before midday, Cindy had to leave the office for a short while, leaving Jason on his own at her desk. The phone rang, and there was nobody else free to answer it, and believing it could be some sort of test, Jason picked it up.

"Good morning, Canterbury Advertiser. Jason speaking."

"Oh, good morning," said the surprised male caller.

"Are you new?"

"I'm just here doing my job experience," Jason naively divulged.

"Oh, I see. I bet you're doing a good job, Jason."

"I've just been making teas and coffees mainly, but I want to do more."

"Of course you do. I expect you'd like to be a reporter and a good one at that. What you need is a scoop. Something that'll make them sit up and notice you."

"That's right. No one notices me."

"Perhaps I can help you there. You see, my name is Mr Wolf, and I'm trying to be noticed too. People think I'm crazy, but I'm not. I like to have a bit of fun, but I'm getting bored. I think I've been annoying the folks at the newspaper, and I want to say sorry, but no one will listen to me." Jason took notice, intently. "I have an idea. How about we meet up for an interview? You can ask me some questions, and I'll give you some answers. Then you can take the interview back to the newspaper, and they'll run it as a local interest piece. You know, the plight of the everyday ignored or something. They'll be so impressed with you."

"I'd like to do that," said Jason excitedly.

"Don't tell anyone, as they might want to do it themselves and take away your chance. Besides, you sound like a nice fellow. I think I can trust you. I'm not sure if I could trust anyone else there, especially Laura. She sounds like a right snooty cow." Jason laughed, and Mr Wolf followed suit.

"Tell me, Jason, are you working tomorrow?"

"No, I'm at school tomorrow, but I'm back here on

Thursday and Friday."

"That's perfect. Why don't we meet after school tomorrow and you can take the interview back with you to the newspaper on Thursday morning? Now, I'll give you my address. It's 42 Lansdowne Road. Do you know where that is?"

"Yes, it's close to my school," the youth replied as he wrote down the address on a scrap of paper.

"That's convenient. You can visit me during your lunch break instead," Mr Wolf said. Now, don't tell anyone else about this, okay? I don't want anyone else stealing your thunder. Shall we say oneish tomorrow, then?"

"Yes, I'll be there."

"And don't forget your pen and paper."

"I won't. See you at about 1:00 pm tomorrow."

"Excellent. Until tomorrow then. Tata," said Mr Wolf before the line went dead.

Jason carefully put the phone down. He noticed a Dictaphone at the edge of the desk and thinking that it would be a better idea to record the interview rather than write everything down, he picked it. After looking around to check if anyone was watching, he slipped the device into his trouser pocket.

The remainder of the day went by pretty much as the morning did, but all Jason was thinking about was the next day and his interview with the notorious, Mr Wolf.

As the bell went to signify the end of the last lesson before lunch, Jason told his friend that he had something to do and if he wasn't back by afternoon registration, he was to sign in on his behalf. It was a regular occurrence in Jason's form for anyone wanting to play truant afternoon lessons as Mr Beaumont, the form tutor, was partially blind and very scatty. No one ever checked the register anyway.

Jason slipped out of school without anyone noticing and ran around the corner. He waited for a short time and took the Dictaphone out of his blazer to check that everything was working fine. It was, and he continued his short journey down the road and into Lansdowne Road. He walked down the street, searching for number 42.

"36… 38… 40… 42. Oh," Jason said to himself. He stood outside a dilapidated property in stark contrast to the well-kept semi-detached houses on either side. He looked up and down the road; it was tranquil with no one about, so he slowly approached the front door. It was white with paint flaking off and was slightly ajar. Jason took a deep breath, pushed open the door and walked in and down the wooden-floored hallway. It creaked loudly.

"Hello!" Jason shouted. There was no answer, so he repeated himself. A creak at the top of the stairs alerted him to a man standing on the landing.

"Oh sorry, Jason, I was just upstairs," spoke a well-groomed man in his early thirties wringing his wet hands. He was wearing a white shirt under a V-neck sky blue jumper and light stone-wash jeans. He slowly descended the staircase. Jason stepped back, observing the shabby interior. There were no pictures or personal effects to be seen. A thin layer of dust over the paintwork and a musty aroma suggested that the house had been vacant for some time. Jason felt a little uneasy, but his thoughts were interrupted by the man.

"This is not mine," said Mr Wolf gesturing to the ceiling and walls. You see, I obviously couldn't invite you to my home, and we couldn't speak in public, and I don't think I'd be welcome at the newspaper office. I knew this house had been empty for a while, and I thought it would be an ideal neutral place to conduct our interview." Jason remained rigid and silent.

"Look, if you're worried, I will certainly understand if you wanted to forget the whole idea and leave. It's your decision. I don't want you to feel uneasy or get in trouble at school."

"It's okay. I'm alright, and someone will mark me in as present if I'm late getting back," answered Jason.

"Clever boy. Let's go inside and sit down." He breezed past the lad and went straight into the front room. The room itself was sparse with only two wooden chairs and a glass coffee table furnishing it. There was a crumpled piece of old tarpaulin in a heap in the corner, but that was it. Mr Wolf sat down on one of the chairs and Jason followed him, sitting opposite him. He pulled out the Dictaphone from his pocket.

"Ah, what an ingenious idea. And here I thought you'd forgotten your pen and paper, but that's much better. I can tell that you are a lad with brains."

Jason smiled. He rarely received any praise and certainly not for the use of his brain. "They think you're a nutter," he blurted out.

"Do they?" uttered a giggling Mr Wolf. "Mind you; I don't suppose I can blame them. I do say some rather 'nutty' things in some strange voices."

"So, why do you do it, then?" Jason asked curiously.

"That's a good question and one for the interview," Mr Wolf curtly answered. "Anyway, let me get you a drink. You must be thirsty. Fanta or Pepsi?"

"Fanta, please," replied Jason.

"Manners too. Excellent. Excellent," said Mr Wolf as he exited the room. He returned a few moments later with the can which he opened for his guest. He handed it to Jason, who took a couple of gulps of the lukewarm drink before placing it down on the coffee table. Mr Wolf sat down opposite, watching him cross-legged and cross-armed waiting for the questioning to start. Jason paused.

"Why don't you place your recorder on the table, and we can begin the interview?"

Jason did what he was told. "So, why do you keep making phone calls to the newspaper?" Jason asked bluntly.

"No, no, no. And we were doing so well, Jason. You can't open up with a question like that. You have to 'befriend' me; coax me into a relaxed state before… *boom!*" Mr Wolf slapped the top of the coffee table, causing Jason to jump and the can to gush some of its carbonated orange content onto the glass. "…you ask the killer question."

Jason sat and thought for a moment. "Right. When did you start thinking about making hoax phone calls?"

Mr Wolf stares at him in disappointment. "That's pretty much the same question, Jason. Switch your recorder off for a moment. I have something in the kitchen that may help us," suggested Mr Wolf. He stood up, straightened his clothes and wandered out of the room. He first turned left, and Jason heard him bolt the front door, and then he walked past the doorway and to the kitchen.

Jason just sat looking ahead and realised that the windows had been boarded up; something he hadn't noticed before. He was beginning to feel a little uneasy and thought about leaving the house, but he got the feeling that Mr Wolf would see and may try to apprehend him. He had to do something. Cupboard doors could be heard opening and shutting in the kitchen. "Where is it? Where is it?" bellowed Mr Wolf to himself. "I won't be a minute," he shouted to Jason who was beginning to feel very uneasy. He wanted to leave the house immediately. What Jason didn't hear was Mr Wolf re-entering the room. All of a sudden, he felt a rope thrown around him and the man's left arm across his throat, making him unable to move or shout. Round and round the rope went, tying Jason tightly to the chair. Jason struggled to free himself, but he was no match for a fully-grown man. Then a handkerchief was forced into his mouth and tied together behind his head, before his assailant's arm released his grip. With Jason incapacitated, Mr Wolf breathless from his activity, walked around in front of the lad and re-took his seat opposite. He calmly pulled down his jumper that had risen during the struggle and patted down his hair with his hands.

"Now that's better, isn't it, little pig?" Mr Wolf calmly asked. Jason tried to shout, but couldn't. He picked up the can of Fanta, drank what remained, before crushing the can in his hand and tossing it to the corner of the room.

"I'll tell you what I'll do. Instead of you asking me some obvious mind-numbing questions, I'll tell you all you need to know. How's that then, Jason? You won't have to do any work at all. You can rest your brain." Jason just sat stiff, staring at the man and trying his best not to cry.

Mr Wolf calmly crossed his legs and placed his hands behind his head. "What I'm going to do first is call the newspaper again and tell them I've kidnapped a boy. I wonder if they'll believe me this time." He stood up, walked over to the corner of the room where he'd thrown the can, lifted the tarp and picked up a hidden telephone which he then plugged into the wall.

"Now you be quiet, little pig… or else," he instructed the boy who nodded timidly.

Mr Wolf dialled a number and waited and waited… and waited. "It looks like we might have to wait until tomorrow, Jason. No one wants to take my call." Just then, the call connected. He cleared his throat and affected a posh voice.

"Ah, young lady. It's your friendly neighbourhood wolf here. I have something to tell you. No no, please don't hang up. You'll like this one," said Mr Wolf disguising his voice with a Scottish accent. The room was silent save for Jason's heavy breathing through the handkerchief. "I have a boy. You see, I've kidnapped him. I understand he was on work experience with you yesterday; Jason is his name. I have your attention now, don't I? Don't worry; I'm not going to hurt him. Not yet, anyway." Mr Wolf looked up at Jason and made a 'throat slit' gesture. Jason's eyes widened in fear. Wolf covered the receiver. "Don't worry. I'm just telling them that," he whispered. Jason was not put at ease and tried again frantically to free himself.

An angry Wolf shouted down the phone, "I'll call back shortly. Tata." before abruptly ending the conversation. He walked over to Jason, who had stopped struggling. "I hope you realise that your endeavours to escape are pointless. However, if you make any further attempts, I will be forced to move you upstairs and place you in a secure trunk. Now, do I make myself clear?" Jason nodded.

Back at The Canterbury Advertiser, Cindy had told Laura about Mr Wolf's latest call.

"How did he know about the work experience boy?" Laura asked fiercely.

"I don't know," Cindy replied in a wavering voice.

"Call the school," demanded Laura. "Actually, I'll do it." After finding the phone number, Laura dialled the school and spoke to the secretary asking about the whereabouts of Jason.

"So, he's definitely at school today?" Laura asked. "Good. No, no reason. It's just we thought he might be here this afternoon, but he's not… He's at school, and that's just fine. Thank you. Goodbye," she continued trying to find a way out of the situation without alarming the school.

"He's been marked as present in the register," said Laura breathlessly before slumping into a chair. There was silence for a moment before she piped up. "Hold on a minute. How did Wolf know that he was called Jason?" Again there was a confused silence before Cindy opened her mouth.

"I think that may have been my fault. You see, Wolf called again yesterday, and I picked up the phone, I may have been telling Jason to put away something in the filing cabinet," she admitted coyly.

"So, that's how he knows his name," concluded Laura. "If he phones again, you tell him in no uncertain terms that no one here is ever going to take his calls from now on. How dare he waste our time like this. I'm getting fed up with this." Laura had spoken, and everyone else had taken heed. They all went back to work.

Back at 42 Lansdowne Road, Mr Wolf strolls around the room, causing the floorboards under his feet to creak and groan. He began to tell Jason about himself.

"Firstly Jason, I'm tired of all this. My name is John, and I'll be relieved to get caught. My life is one long miserable existence, and I don't even have anyone to share the misery. I used to have a job. It was at the Canterbury Advertiser working alongside Laura. You've met Laura, haven't you? We were both junior reporters and started work there at the same time. Laura and I became romantically involved, and everything was great for a while until she got a promotion. It didn't worry me. I mean, it should have, because I had so much more investigative talent than she did, but if your face doesn't fit, then it doesn't fit. She got ideas above her station, and our relationship suffered. As time went on, she became power-mad. She was only a features editor at a crummy local newspaper, not editor-in-chief of the bloody Daily Telegraph. Excuse me for swearing, but it still irks me. I had it out with her one day. Things got very heated, and I pushed her, not hard, but I pushed her. She had me fired there and then. I tried to apologise, but she wouldn't even listen to me. She would threaten to call the police every time I tried to contact her. She hated me; all she loved was the job – she probably always did. My life went from bad to worse, but you don't want to hear all about that. The thing is, Jason, I want to let her know what she's done to me, and so I created Mr Wolf. I call the newspaper using a disguised voice trying to lure her into coming out to attend one of my made-up scenarios. However, I suppose she was always too smart for that. All I ever wanted to do was impress her. Well, now I have you, and I have a very real kidnapping. She'll have to come out now; she knows I have a real victim." He stopped walking and checked his watch. "I think that'll be enough time for them to know I'm telling the truth. Let's call them back, eh?"

He calls the newspaper again, and Cindy happened to pick up the phone.

"Hello. It's Mr, Wolf. I'll huff, and I'll puff, and I'll blow your house down," he announced menacingly before laughing like a mad man.

"Oh, it's you again," scoffed Cindy.

"Of course, it is. I said I'd call back and I'm a man of my word. Have you had time to digest my information," he asked.

"Yes and we're not impressed," replied Cindy.

"What do you mean you're 'not impressed'? I told you I have a minor held against his will, and you're 'not impressed'?"

"That's right. We know for a fact that the boy is at school this afternoon and this is another one of your ridiculous fantasies. It's the last time you'll call us here, and if you do again, you won't even get the time of day. Now go away." Cindy ended the call leaving Wolf standing holding the telephone.

Wolf casually put the receiver down before furiously pulling the wire out of the wall; he did it so violently, it took the connection box with it. He stood in silence for a while, thinking about his next move.

"Well, I didn't expect that." He began pacing across the room again. Jason's eyes fixed on his every step. "Hmmm, that's put a spanner in the works. And all because you used your initiative to ask your friend to mark you present at school, I expect. I'm right, aren't I? Of course, I am. Your smart move could prove to be your downfall. I've got three options now. Do I simply disappear and leave you here? Do I take you with me on an adventure, or do I just get rid of you? But how do I decide?" He continued pacing around, ruminating his options.

"I know. If you can impress me, as you have done before, I will let you go. As I said earlier, I am a man of my word. But, how are you going to do that, tied to a chair?" He stood, pondering while keeping a close eye on the boy.

Click. The sound came from inside Jason's jacket. It was from the Dictaphone. Wolf thrust his hand inside the jacket and pulled out the recording device.

"It was taping all the time. Mmmm, that's quite impressive. Clever, but such a pity. You nearly earned your freedom there, little pig."

Jason looked away crestfallen as Wolf started rewinding the tape and played it back at intervals. At one point, and all he could hear was a lot of banging in the background and then a voice – Jason's voice. *"This is Jason Neal. A man called Mr Wolf has taken me hostage. If anyone finds this recording, you'll hear his confession after my message. I was at 42 Lansdowne Road. Please try to find me."* Then, Mr Wolf's voice from the kitchen, *"Where is it? Where is it? I won't be a minute."* Mr Wolf pressed stop and just stood, his tall frame looming over the bound-up schoolboy. A huge grin began spreading across his face.

"Bravo! Now *that* is impressive, little pig. Well, as a man of my word, I will have to let you go. Obviously, I'll have to keep this, but you've earned your freedom. I'll make my exit first as we can't have you running off to the police before I'm out of range, can we?" Jason, breathing heavily and sweating, shook his head in agreement. "What

I'll do is loosen your bonds. I reckon a healthy young man like yourself will be able to release himself within say, five or six minutes. Yes, that's the best course of action." Wolf left the room momentarily to fetch his jacket which he put on. He then went about loosening the knots at the back of the chair. "Now, I want you to promise me you'll count to 100 before trying to loosen yourself?" Jason nodded. "I know you will. I trust you. By the time you've been to the police, I'll be long gone. When you get back to your work experience, you'll be able to tell them about your adventure. They'll get a good story and Laura will hopefully be so wracked with guilt she'll have to resign her post; that's if she's not been charged with neglecting a minor in her care or something like that. So, maybe it's all worked out for the best after all. She'll get her comeuppance, I get my resolution, and you'll get a nice story as a junior reporter. Stick with it, Jason."

With the ropes loosened, Wolf said goodbye to the still restrained boy and then exited the room, before popping his head around the doorframe. "Oh, by the way, when you've released yourself, be a good chap leave straight away. I don't want you trapesing around the place and making a pigsty out of it. I do hate to leave a mess in someone else's house. Tata." Wolf made his exit.

Jason heard the front door unbolt and open, and he was gone. Very quickly, Jason counted to a hundred before pulling away at the loosened rope behind his back. It only took him a couple of minutes to make his escape. Jason untied the handkerchief and spat it out. He stood up, rubbing the burn marks on his wrists and arms and drew a huge breath. Instead of running out of the house as he intended and ending his terrible ordeal. Once out of the room, Jason saw the open front door beckoning him to freedom, but the curiosity of a budding journalist got the better of him.

"Why didn't he want me nosing around the house and what was he looking for in the kitchen?" he asked himself. Glancing at the front door again, he walked in the opposite direction and into the kitchen. It wasn't much of a kitchen as aside from a work surface spanning almost the entire length of the room with a sink at its centre, there was nothing, apart from a swing top bin in the corner and a double-doored wall cabinet. One of the doors was slightly askew as it was hanging on by a single hinge. Jason imagined that the violent banging of the door from Mr Wolf was probably the reason for its state. He cautiously opened the door – what greeted him made him almost faint with terror. On the bottom shelf were five items – a can of Pepsi Cola, a bottle of chloroform, a tea towel, a knife and rubber face mask of a wolf. He slammed shut the cabinet door and ran out of the house sprinting as fast as he could. He daren't look back for fear that the wolf might be watching; prowling his prey once again.

A few minutes later, out of breath and tired, Jason finally came to a halt a few streets away. With his backside pressed against the white wall of an end-of-terrace house and hands on his knees, Jason drew enough courage to peek around the corner. Relieved to see that no one was following him, he straightened up and prepared to continue his journey to the police station. However, he was alerted by an engine revving of red hatchback parked across the road to him. The window of the car opened and the silhouette of a man leant over the empty passenger seat.

"Little pig… You didn't get too far, did you?"

Jason's heart sank. He was too tired to run, and in any event, he knew he couldn't outrun a car.

"I thought you'd come this way as the cop shop is just a couple of streets away. Don't worry. I've got bigger fish to fry. Fortunately, I quite like you, Jason. Oh, and don't bother reporting the car registration number, I stole this motor and won't have it very long anyway. I really am a naughty Wolf, aren't I?" he chuckled to himself. Jason, just stood, eyes fixed on his foe. "Oh and one other thing, after I watched you leave the house, I popped back in to collect my phone and my belongings from the kitchen, so no evidence, I'm afraid. Never mind. Oh, and I've been thinking – let's keep our little soiree to ourselves, eh? No need for the police to be informed. You see, I've changed my mind about getting caught. I don't want to face a barrage of questioning from the law quite yet. It's probably for the best, don't you think? Tata." The window closed, and the car drove off at pace down the road and out of sight. Jason stood rigid to the spot, unable to decide what to do. If he went to the police, would they believe him? And if he did, would Mr Wolf come after him? It was a chance that this little pig didn't want to take.

Karma Police

Bill and Steve had been best friends since high school and have shared many life experiences; from holidays, jobs, and at one point, they were even engaged to the same girl, albeit at different points in time. In their early 40s, they owned and ran their own business – a garage called Bill & Steve's Autos, which employed three other people – a full-time mechanic, named Mo; a junior, Ian; and a receptionist/secretary/filing clerk/tea lady called Lucy. They were very good at their jobs, (but not necessarily at finding an original name for their business) and have a loyal clientele stretching far and wide from their base in Banbury in Oxfordshire. Although they had been friends for a big chunk of their lives and they had similar tastes, they had quite different characters. Bill was excitable, funny, and even a little reckless, but extremely passionate about his interests and work. Steve, by contrast, was much more laid back and philosophical about life. His "what will be, will be" attitude sometimes annoyed Bill, as did their opposing political allegiances. But regardless of their divergent approaches, they were tolerant of each other's ideologies and would generally try to reach the same goals.

One day, Lucy was otherwise indisposed, and Bill picked up the phone in the office to take a call from a gentleman who wanted to bring his car in for a service. The noise from the radio outside the office made it difficult to hear the customer. The caller's voice sounded familiar to him, but he couldn't immediately put his finger on who it was or why he felt as if he should recognise it; this irked him.

"So, I've got the registration, and it's a 2014 Ford C-Max Titanium for a full service, on Monday the 7th. Is that correct, sir?" Bill asked the customer on the phone.

"Yes, that's right. I'll bring it in before I go to work, but I wonder if you can drop it back to my home in the late afternoon? I'll be home, and I'll pay you then if that's okay?" asked the customer.

"Yes, that's fine. Either one of my colleagues or I will drop it off to you. I suppose you'd better let me have your name and address then otherwise we'd never find you," Bill said with a small chuckle.

"Of course. The name is Garland, and my address is 42, Coniston Walk. I'm only about a five-minute drive away from you actually," said the man confidently.

Bill now had the name, but still, it wasn't ringing any bells with him. He wracked his brain, trying to find something, anything that would explain why Garland's voice sounded so familiar.

"Hello, did you get that?" asked the customer as the pause prolonged.

"Oh yes, sorry about that. I just…" floundered Bill. "So, that's all booked it for the 7th August then. We'll see you later. Bill ended the call and sat back into his seat, tapping the phone on his desk, trying in vain to remember how he knew the voice.

"You alright, mate?" asked Steve, who had just walked into the office.

"Yeah, I think so," replied Bill, looking puzzled. He told Steve about the custormer sounding familiar to him, but that was all he disclosed. Steve looked at him as if to say, 'so what?' Without saying another word, he walked out of the office as Lucy made her way in past him.

"Okay, Lucy?" said Bill, standing up from the desk to allow Lucy to take her seat.

"Yes, I'm alright. I just went to get my nail polish from my bag. I couldn't find it for a moment. I was rummaging around, and it was nowhere to be found, but then I remembered, I put it in the little compartment in the front. Now, I never usually put anything there, so I was surprised to find it in there. Anyway, here it is now," explained the ditzy receptionist holding up the small glass bottle of deep red polish. Bill just stood, staring at her in amazement.

"Oh, that's a relief," he said sarcastically.

"Oh, I know," replied Lucy, not picking up on Bill's tone at all.

"I think I'll go back to my job now, Lucy. Perhaps you can do the same?"

"Me? But I don't... oh, you mean in the office? I thought you meant out there with you. What am I like, eh?" said Lucy, giggling like a schoolgirl. Lucy would laugh at anything, mainly her ineptitude, but she was sweet, loyal and cheap. Bill forced a smile and left the office, closing the door behind him. He stood for a moment, shook his head and went to join Steve who was changing the brakes on a Peugeot 206.

"She's a funny girl," said Bill as he fastened up his blue overalls.

"She thinks she's the funniest person alive. *'What am I liiiike?'*" said Steve mimicking Lucy superbly. "Pass me those pads will you." Bill picked up a box of brake pads off the ground under the raised vehicle.

"Of course. I've got it!" exclaimed Bill out of the blue.

"I know, but can you hand them over to me, please?" said Steve without the same excited enthusiasm in his voice.

"No, I mean, I recognise the voice and the name," Bill replied, handing the brake pads to his friend. "I'm sure Garland was the name of the so-called pension investment expert who ripped off my poor parents off all those years ago. Yes, it was him. I'm sure it is. He made all these promises that he could find ways to increase their income and make their retirement more comfortable. You know, the usual claptrap?"

"Oh, yes, I remember you were intent on tracking him down. It was almost to the extent of an obsession," said Steve.

"I had to try, didn't I? He ripped off my folks. I tried to find him after the 'investments' went south, but the company had gone into liquidation, and there was no sign of Garland. Surprise, surprise. I couldn't find the swine, but now he's come to me. I know his name and where he lives now, and that gives me the upper hand," enthused Bill.

"What do you mean 'upper hand'?" asked Steve, pausing his brake fitting.

"He screwed over my parents, and now I'm going to get him back. My Dad is no longer with us, and my Mum has to live on the crappy state pension and what's left of her diminished savings. It's payback time, my friend. You leave Mr Garland and his car to me," replied Bill, a villainous grin developing on his face.

"Why, what are you going to do?" asked Steve worriedly.

"I'm going to right a wrong," replied Bill taking the old

brake pads from his colleague.

Steve looked puzzled as Bill walked off, whistling happily to himself.

The 7th August arrived, and as promised, Mr Garland bought his Ford in for a service. Bill made sure that he was out of sight behind a stack of tyres. When the customer left, Lucy handed the keys to Mo, who was waiting to start his first service of the day.

"I'll take this job," said Bill holding out his hand.

"It's alright boss, I can handle it," insisted Mo.

"No, I'll do this service. You see, I promised the customer I'd handle the job personally when he booked his car in, and I'm a man of my word." Mo dropped the keys into Bill's outstretched hand. "Listen, Steve will be in shortly, and we're quiet at the moment. Why don't you take young Ian down to Hudson's to fetch the exhaust for the Micra and I'll get started on the Ford?" Mo did what he was told, and Bill began the service on Garland's motor.

Bill drove Garland's car onto the ramp and lifted it for inspection.

"Hmmm, those front brake discs look a bit worn. I should probably replace them with some new ones. Mind you; it'll be more fun to replace them with some old ones," Bill said to himself. He went over to a pile of used brake pads and discs and picked a couple of old, worn discs. "Oh, yes. They'll do just fine." He looked around to make sure that no one was watching and set about replacing the worn discs with another set of worn discs, all the time with a fixed smirk on his face.

Later that afternoon, once the dastardly deed was done

and the rest of the service complete, to a proper standard, Bill drove the car, albeit carefully around to Garland's house. He wanted to deliver it himself as the satisfaction of being paid for the job and knowing that the crook who cheated his parents out of thousands would get his comeuppance excited him. Twenty minutes later, Bill found himself parked up outside Garland's house. It was a large semi-detached with a pretty garden and garage. "Bought with ill-gotten gains I expect," he mumbled to himself before turning the engine off and getting out of the vehicle. He strolled up to the front door and rang the bell. Finally, he was going to come face-to-face with the man he spent so long trying to track down. The temptation to lay one on Garland would be immense, but the satisfaction of his revenge being served up just a little bit cooler than he originally planned, appeased thoughts of a more violent retribution.

A few moments after pressing the bell, a tall, smart man opened the door. He looked at Bill, then over his shoulder, spying his car returned to his home. A beaming smile spread across his face. Bill was finally facing to face with the man he spent so much time looking for, and he had no idea who Bill was or how his revenge was to taste.

"On time as promised," Garland beamed.

"We like to stick to our word and provide an honest and transparent service," Bill replied with intent.

"How much do I owe you?"

"Including the oils and fluids… oh and new front discs it comes to £215 exactly."

"Ah, marvellous. My wife will be glad. It's her car, you see. Do come in while I fetch my wallet," Garland delighted, gesturing Bill to enter his house. Bill nodded, stepped over the threshold and walked into the living room. The sight that greeted him shocked and confused the mechanic, because amongst the family photos placed liberally about the room was photos of Garland in uniform – a police uniform. Upon spying the first one, Bill assumed that it was from a fancy-dress party, but there were more, including a framed newspaper cutting of "Detective Sargent Garland receiving his award from the Chief Constable". Bill walked over to the wall to take a closer look. Just then, Garland entered the room.

"That was a few years ago now," he joyfully pronounced. Bill spun around, slightly startled by the voice behind him.

"You're a DS?" Bill asked realising immediately how stupidly obvious the question was.

"I was at the time. I'm a Detective Inspector now," Garland replied as he walked over to the photo, picking it up in his right hand. We set up a community project in the area to help mentally and physically disabled kids. As parents of a disabled child ourselves, my wife and I thought there should be a community scheme where the children could meet and socialise together. We helped raise a fair bit of money to extend the community centre and provide staffing to make that a reality." Bill was stunned. "The photographer took a few pictures with Charlotte, my wife, included, but the paper chose this one," he laughed as he carefully placed the photo back on its shelf.

"You have a disabled child?" Bill asked nervously continuing his rhetorical line of questioning.

"Yes. Sam is now eleven years old and was born with Cerebral Palsy. He's a great lad and quite mischievous. We're fortunate that he's quite independent. Although he has the condition, it's not as severe as some cases, and we have to be thankful for that."

Although Bill listened to Garland's words all he could he think about was *'How long has this guy been a policeman?'* and *'How could he make such a moral jump of careers, and indeed, outlook?'* He looked around the room and noticed many more family photos of Garland in uniform from over the years. All of a sudden, Bill began to doubt that this man was who he thought he was. How could a dodgy pension salesman become such a respected and decorated upstanding policeman?

"How long have you been in the Force?" he asked nervously.

"We call it the "Police Service" now. At least that's what the Home Office want us to. I've been a copper for quite a while."

"What did you do before?"

"Oh, this and that. I didn't hold down any job for very long, but I eventually found my calling. There was a brief and slightly uncomfortable pause because Garland piped up, "I'm sure I've kept you for far too long. Here's your money." Garland took his wallet from his trouser pocket and counted out the cash and handed it over to Bill.

"Thank you and here's your receipt." Bill took out the previously prepared printed receipt from his inside jacket pocket and exchanged it for the payment.

With each passing moment, Bill became increasingly unsure that the man standing in front of him was who he thought he was and even if it was, the horror of what he had done to his car was beginning to register.

"I must be off myself. I need to pick up my wife and

son from the multiplex cinema across town. She's taken him to the latest superhero film that's just come out. It feels like there a new one every week or so, but Sam loves them," Garland said with a smile. Bill followed Garland to the front door all the time trying to think about how he could stop him from using his car, but nothing was forthcoming.

"Can I give you a lift anywhere?" asked Garland as they approached the car.

"No! No!" shrieked Bill in a loud and dramatic fashion. Garland looked at him curiously. "Sorry, I mean I arranged for my colleague to collect me in a few minutes, so there's no need. Thank you all the same."

"Very well," replied Garland before opening the car door and getting in. Bill was desperate to think of an excuse to stop him, but just couldn't. Garland turned the ignition, and the window descended. "No doubt, I'll see you again soon. Thanks again." With those words, he drove off up the road and away. Bill frantically took his mobile out of his pocket to call Steve back at work.

Steve picked up the call immediately. "Steve, come and pick me up. We've got a problem."

"Hold on. Hold on. What do you mean, 'We've got a problem'?"

"Just collect me from Coniston Walk, and I'll explain then," said Bill in a panic.

Less than five minutes later, Steve sped around the corner in his C-class Mercedes. He stopped beside his colleague, and he opened the passenger door and got in. "We need to go to the multiplex now!" he insisted.

"Why? What's going on?" asked Steve. He hadn't a

clue to what was going on.

"Drive. Just drive. I'll explain on the way," shouted Bill, pointing the way. Steve put his foot down and drove up the road at breakneck speed.

"I've made a mistake. A terrible mistake," confessed Bill, voice quivering with regret.

"Calm down and tell me what the hell you're talking about and why we're driving to the cinema," demanded Steve.

"You're my best friend, right?" asked Bill.

"This sounds like a preamble to a terrible confession. Just tell me," said Steve, his voice tinged with menace.

"It's Garland. I thought I knew who he was. I thought he was the guy who swindled my parents. I did something to his car."

"What?" Steve angrily asked as he screeched around a corner.

"When I did the service on his car, I changed the brake discs."

"So?"

"I changed them for old ones that were so worn down that if he breaks hard at 30mph, he hasn't a hope of coming to a safe halt. I made a terrible mistake, Steve."

"You damn idiot," spat Steve taking a right turn as the lights were turning red.

"It wasn't even him. He's a cop, a detective inspector." Steve turned to face him. If his hands weren't on the wheel, he'd have laid one on his stupid friend. "Not only that, he's a good family man with a disabled child who he's on the way to picking up from the cinema now."

"Oh, this is priceless. Absolutely priceless," yelled Steve. "What possessed you to do something so stupid? You know what, don't answer that." Steve paused and took a large intake of breath before calmly asking, "What do you intend to say when or if we catch up with him?"

"I'll say I wasn't sure if I topped up the brake fluid or something. Just leave that to me," replied Bill.

"Okay, we're not too far away now. Just calm down and work out what you're going to say while I do the driving. It's starting to rain now, and I need to concentrate on the road," said Steve.

Bill took out his phone and typed Detective Inspector Garland into the search engine. The photo of Garland shaking hands with the Chief Constable from the local newspaper came up, and he touched on it to read the entire article.

"Oh my God," he explained.

"What now?" asked Steve.

"Listen to this. '*Asked if he always wanted to be a policeman, Det. Insp. Garland replied, 'Not really. I had a few different jobs in my younger years, none of them I particularly liked. I worked as a pensions advisor for a Reading company, but after they went into receivership, I felt the lure of law and order, and I haven't looked back.*' I was right all along. It was him. Look."

Bill thrust the phone in front of Steve's face to make his point. That action caused Steve to lose concentration on the road, and he skidded across the street and unable to regain control, he careered into a garden wall. The jolt was so severe that both men lost consciousness. After a short time, Bill opened his eyes and slowly turned to his left; his neck stiff and painful. There sat his best friend, eyes still shut, with the side of the car crushed inwards incarcerating him between door and seat. Blood dripped from his nose, and he was not breathing.

"What have I done? What have I done?" panted Bill, unable to fully comprehend the situation. He looked down to the footwell, and there was his phone on the floor, face up with Garland's smiling face filling the screen. He just stared at the photo, which eventually faded until the screen went blank as approaching police car sirens became louder and louder, coupled with their red and blue flashing lights. Revenge may be a dish best served cold, but the scorching heat of karma had just burned a massive hole in the life of Bill. For his colleague and best friend, however, Bill's actions resulted in a far worse consequence.

Four-minute Confession

It is the mid-1980s and a family barbecue is not the way Kit prefers to spend his Sunday afternoon, but they were thankfully becoming rarer. As this was August Bank holiday weekend, the chances of being summoned to any more for the remainder of the year are unlikely. He sits alone, enjoying the relative peace at a large table formerly populated by his family and his brother. His wife is at another chatting with some family friends, and his four children are inside, causing havoc with their cousins. His brother, a little worse for wear following seven bottles of lager, comes back to the table with an eighth and sits down opposite him.

"Don't you think you've had enough, young man?" shouts family patriarch, Charles Manley.

"It's alright, Dad. It's all under control. Just relax," replies Russell. His father laughs and turns away back to his guests.

"It's been a good day, don't you think?"

"If you like these sorts of things, Russell; which you clearly do," says an indignant Kit.

"Well, I do. I always like spending time with the fam," Russell confesses.

"That's because you still *live* with the 'fam' in this massive house, while I have my own 'fam' and we can only afford to live in a modest semi-detached."

"What is it with you today? You've been on a downer

since you got here."

"You know I don't particularly like these family get-togethers. When we were kids, mother always put them on to show off to the rest of the clan and her Kalooki cronies. The woman never had much time for me, anyway. However, she died four years ago, and why *she* feels these things are still relevant is beyond me," Kit moans.

"*She* has a name, and I think, no, I *know* that Jenny makes dad happy and because she does, then we should be happy too. Besides, it's a tradition," argues Russell before necking half the bottle.

"Tradition is another word for 'control' in my mind," reasons Kit. He was not having a good time.

"Okay. Then, let's change the subject. Erm… What, would you do with your time if the four-minute warning siren sounded?"

"Bloody hell, Russ. The four-minute warning – where did that come from? I was thinking perhaps changing the subject to something on the lines of 'Watford's chances in the First Division this season,' not necessarily of the impending nuclear holocaust and the imminent destruction of life as we know it," says Kit exultantly.

"It's been on my mind a lot since all that business between Reagan and Gorbachev," explains Russell.

"This has been going on since the early '60s. Whether it's Kennedy/Kruschev, Nixon/Brezhnev or Reagan/Gorbachev, it's all political posturing. The real concerns are nearer to home. Now that Thatcher's finished with the miners, who'll be her next victims? Ask yourself that, brother."

"Okay, I get you but humour me a little. Let me tell

you what I would do. I'd get the nearest gorgeous bit of skirt I can find and have my wicked way with her or loot a shop. Just go crazy."

"Brilliant. So your life would end with a sex spree and robbery? Or probably both if your reputation is accurate. That's impressive. You've put a lot of thought into that, haven't you? My brother, the burgling rapist."

"Technically, it's shoplifting," intervenes Russell.

"Okay, a shoplifting rapist. I give up, I really do," mutters the exasperated older brother.

"Why does everything have to end with an argument?" Russell asks before finishing the rest of his lager.

"It's not an argument. Am I arguing with you? I'm merely making a statement of fact. You probably only asked me the question to antagonise me and create tension anyway," adds Kit.

"You've always had it in for me, ever since we were children," says Russell somewhat rattled.

"No, I haven't. Besides, you're the one who has it all," Kit retorts.

"Me – have it all? You have a job for life in the family business; a wife; the children. Then you also have the mortgage; the school fees; the expensive holidays to pay for," Russell laughs.

"It's all a big joke to you, isn't it? You're the golden boy, who gets to bum around, poncing off Dad and living rent-free in the family mansion?"

"Yeah, something like that," confirms Russell, unwilling to take his brother's bait.

"My life had been set out with military precision — the

heir-apparent to Charles Manley's kingdom. Well, I'm not, am I? Dad still doesn't trust me to run the firm, and that's why I'm still head of development and not the CEO. It should all be mine by now. Okay, I have a reasonably well-paid job, but it's not what I want.

"Wow, such greed, bro," Russell mocks.

Kit continues, ignoring his sibling. "I'm where they can keep an eye on me; making sure I do things the Manley way. I'm made to feel grateful for everything. I have no choice. And going back, I wasn't able to enjoy my formative years. You were the one who had it all, mate. Well, almost everything."

"And what do you mean by *almost* everything'?"

"Well, you had your freedom and the attention of our parents, but you didn't have your precious comic collection for very long, did you?"

"No, you know I was gutted when it was chucked out by mistake when we had the house extended."

"By mistake? Actually, Russell, it was me. I dumped the box in the skip. It was no accident. I wanted to see you cry like a baby, which you did, for days and days," teases Kit.

"What an unpleasant little bastard you are," shouts Kit, standing to his feet, albeit a little unsteadily due to the amount of alcohol he had consumed. "In that case, I've got a little secret to tell you."

"Oh, really?" taunts Kit also standing up.

"The reason Mum always favoured me was because of the incident when you pushed me down the stairs, causing this scar," shouts Russell pointing to the V-shaped scar on his forehead. "Because of that, she could never trust you and would always take my side."

"Oh, not that old chestnut again. I was five, and you were two, for heaven's sake. Whenever we disagree about anything, you bring that up," counters Kit.

"But you didn't know that she hated you for it, did you?"

"Of course, I did. And you, you were always the blue-eyed boy who could do no wrong in her eyes."

"Well, you shouldn't have pushed me, should you? Anyway, it's getting cold now. I'm going to get that jumper Mum lovingly knitted for me." He storms off into the house. It was getting chilly and after a minute or so and still fuming with rage, Kit follows suit.

Due to the change in temperature, most of the guests congregate in the vast lounge area, so Kit decides to go upstairs to continue his war of words with Russell. At the top of the stairs, he passes Russell's bedroom, and the door is open. He spies him trying to fit into the jumper he said he was fetching. It was too small, it has always been too small, but Russell liked to wear it as it reminds him of his mother. It also has the added value of agitating his brother too. Kit trots around the corner out of sight and waits for his brother to come out to continue their argument. When he eventually does, Russell realises that he's wearing the jumper back to front and goes about rearranging himself at the top of the stairs. In a fit of anger, Kit sees his chance and sprints over to Russell who doesn't see him. He nudges him in the back and Russell goes tumbling down the staircase, only stopping when his head violently curtails his fall on the marble floor at the base of the stairs. His body lies lifeless in a crumpled mass.

Realising what he had done, Kit runs down the hall to take the back stairs down and back into the garden. No one notices him walk over to his table. He sits back down and waits and waits.

A woman screams, and a crowd gathers at the base of the staircase where Russell's body is discovered. Kit rushes in and joins the back of the throng. His Dad pushes his way through the crowd to tend to his younger son, but there are no life signs. The boy's stepmother, Jenny, pushes forward to comfort her husband.

"Kit! Kit!" shouts Charles. "Call an ambulance; damn it."

Kit rushes to the phone and calls 999 while Jenny ushers the guests out of the house. The party is over.

The paramedics soon arrive, but there's nothing they can do. Russell is not breathing, and there is no pulse. Kit, his father and stepmother, who are the only ones left in the hallway stand unable to say or do anything as one of the ambulance crew places a red blanket over Russell's torso and then, carefully over his face. Kit's wife, Michelle, approaches him and puts her arm around his shoulders. All he wants to do is push her away, but he knows he has to keep calm. He murdered his brother.

Two weeks later, Russell is laid to rest in the local cemetery. There was an inquiry that concluded earlier in the week that a high level of alcohol in Russell's bloodstream was the likely cause that led to his `accident.' The funeral itself is a huge one with the great and the good of local society turning out to pay their respects to the Manley family. Kit attends alongside his wife and dutifully accepts the heartfelt condolences to the stream of people as they file away from the graveside. There is nowhere he wouldn't rather be than that cemetery. Wracked with guilt, but also still with anger, as he believed his brother forced him into a situation, he couldn't get out of. Part of him wants to run away forever, but part of him wants to tell all about his inner turmoil.

"It was he who put me in this position. If he were more grown-up and responsible, this would never have happened. Never," he thinks to himself as he catches the open grave out of the corner of his eye while nodding and shaking hands with the assembled funeral-goers.

As the mass begins to thin out, he feels an arm around him. "You've done well, this week, Kit. I'm proud of you." It was his father. "I have to say that there were times over the years that I wasn't sure you'd be up to it, but I'm delighted to say that I can see you are. You've been a rock to me over the last couple of weeks. Come, let's walk to the cars." Kit looks around to find his wife as the last thing he wants is a father/son chat. Michelle was talking to family members and unaware of her husband's angst.

"Thanks, Dad," Kit manages to muster.

"You know your mother was a harsh critic, but she always believed in you," says Charles.

Kit stopped in his tracks. "What? Mum never really had any time for me, so I doubt that very much."

"No, not at all. Your mother had trouble displaying her emotions and would keep everything inside, but I can promise you, she was a great admirer of you and what you achieved, both in education and in business. More than I was, to be honest," Charles offers.

"Well, I wish she could have shown it a bit. From what I remember, we were quite close until Russell's accident – his first accident. I know she always blamed me for pushing him," Kit awkwardly elucidates.

"No she didn't," says Charles looking his son square in the eye. "Poor Russell was always reckless and clumsy. You were both playing in the upstairs hallway. You spilt a drink down yourself, and the nanny took you away to clean you up. She was away just for a moment, but that was enough for Russell to slip and fall down the stairs. Well, sadly, history has a way of repeating itself, doesn't it?" Charles laments.

"So, it was nothing to do with me? All these years, I thought it was my fault, and that was the reason Mum hated me."

"No, son. Whoever gave you that idea? If anything, it was the nanny's fault for taking her eye of your brother. Mum never wanted to speak of the incident, because she blamed herself for hiring the nanny."

The conflicting feelings of guilt and anger are now joined in Kit's head by one of pure schadenfreude – and it was this that was quickly pushing 'guilt' out of the equation altogether. For all these years, Russell had him believe that it was he who pushed him down the stairs, giving rise to the now unfounded belief that his mother put the blame solely on him.

"We always knew Russell wouldn't amount to a great deal. He never had it in him. It feels a little unfair to say now, but your mother treated him as a lapdog – a pet. She did everything for him because she knew he couldn't be trusted to do things on his own. We all know about his addictive personality, and we've bailed him out financially after he built up many many debts. And then there was his drinking. Anyway, that's why she wanted him to stay with us. It kept him out of trouble and under our surveillance. Don't get me wrong; she loved him; we both did. We loved you equally, but I guess in different ways. I know there were times you felt we treated you harshly, but we knew you could take it. Russell couldn't. He crumbled at the signs of any disagreement or consternation. He needed to be protected. Just before your mother died, she told me I had to look after him. It was the one thing that worried her – not her illness, but Russell's safety."

Kit stands stunned by the lead car of the funeral cortege.

"Kit, I'm getting old, and it sometimes takes a tragedy like this to make you take stock of your life. I'm stepping down as CEO of the company with immediate effect, and I want you to take over. Your income will increase immeasurably, but your responsibility will too. However, as I said, I think you're up to the task. Anyway, Jenny's coming over now. I'll see you back at the house."

"Thank you so much, Dad," Kit gleams.

"Why do you look so happy?" asks Michelle as she walks up behind Kit.

"It seems like poor Russell's untimely death has made Dad realise it's time for me to take over the firm."

"That's wonderful news, but what a place to announce his successor," Michelle says before getting into the back of the second car. "Are you getting in, Kit?"

"Give me a moment." Kit trots off back up the path to the graveyard.

The gravediggers are beginning to fill in Russell's plot with earth, so Kit stays out of sight and stands in the shade of an old yew tree.

"Oh, Russell. It would seem that your inability to keep your mouth shut has not only killed you but given your brother what he truly deserves. I have the company now, and it won't be too long before Dad, and his new wife gets tired of rattling around that big old house, so I might just get that too. But, rest assured, there won't be an occasion I walk down that staircase and don't think of my poor little brother, lying at the bottom wearing that stupid tight jumper. *See ya, bro.*"

With a smirk, Kit turned around and strode away purposely back towards the car park, his waiting wife and his new life. Everything he ever wanted was now in reach.

The Bell Tolls For Thee

The beautiful, ornate and genuine 18th-century French carriage clock which stood resplendent on the centre of a teak dresser, chimed twice. For the third night in a row, octogenarian Ralph Barrington lay awake, unable to settle in the master bedroom of his empty Edwardian detached house. It was a frigid and windy December night, and icy rain was lashing against his bedroom windows, but this alone wasn't what was keeping him awake. He turned to sit on the edge of his bed, contemplating the short, cold walk to the bathroom. He was not getting younger, and in actuality, he was pretty lucky that he'd reached his mid-80s before he began suffering the repeated and urgent bladder pressure which provoked his truncated sleeping patterns. It was the second such visit of the night, and he suspected there'd be at least one more before sunrise. Ralph lived alone since his wife, Belinda, died in a car accident 25 years ago that very week. It was the only thing that he blamed himself for. He was a wealthy man if wealth could solely be quantified with money and processions, which – for capitalist flag bearers like him – it did. Spiritually and emotionally, he was a pauper. Following a lifetime concentrating on business and empire-building, the ruthless and relentless financier had reaped what he sowed – his field lay barren and fallow. Apart from the very occasional flickers of humanity, this modern-day Scrooge gave very little back to society and even less to his family.

"Every bloody night, it's the same routine," he complained to himself as he shuffled his way from his bed to the en suite bathroom. "It's not like I'm a heavy drinker;

I don't even take a glass of water to bed with me. I don't know where it all comes from."

Following his ablutions, Ralph returned to bed, but with the storm still brewing outside, he tossed and turned, unable to get back to sleep. The storm made him irritable and resentful. Thoughts of how everyone in his life had deserted him filled his restless mind.

"Those ungrateful children of mine, for starters," he elucidated, staring at the ceiling. "I provided them with the best education money could buy and what thanks do I get? None, that's what. They're far too busy with their careers and their own families to be concerned about their father. And as for my employees – I kept them on a decent wage, even when the industry was suffering, and what do they do? They jump ship as soon as a better offer comes along. Where is the loyalty? And then there are my so-called friends? They were just after hand-outs from me. They knew a cash cow when they saw one. Anyway, I don't need them. I don't need anyone. Damn them. Damn them all, I say." A sudden flash of lightning, quickly followed by a loud crack of thunder from the devil himself, gave recognition to Ralph's unfair outburst.

Even on his own with his thoughts, Ralph couldn't find a single shred of humility. The reality that it was him who created the division with everyone else didn't register with him. The weather conditions worsened as if to mirror Ralph's deteriorating mood. A loud unannounced rumble of thunder caused him to shudder violently.

"Couldn't you at least have warned me with a flash of lightning?" he shouted.

By now, he was so enraged; he was even blaming the weather conditions for his state.

As much as he tried, he couldn't get back to sleep, and as his clock signalled the hour of 3 o'clock with a trio of high-pitched tings; he'd had enough.

"Oh, this is ridiculous. I'm going downstairs."

Living on his own for so many years had induced Ralph to talk to himself and even narrate his daily routines. Often, he didn't even realise what he was doing, but when he did, he found that an audible voice, albeit his own, had a soothing effect.

He slipped on his dressing-gown and opened the bedroom door. It was pitch black, so he switched on the hall light before going downstairs to the kitchen to make a hot drink.

Once in the kitchen, he opened and slammed shut cupboards looking for something in particular. "Where does she keep the bloody hot chocolate powder?" he snarled to himself, referring to his part-time cleaner and housemaid. Inside one of the cupboards, right at the back, was a large Tupperware box full of chocolate brownies. Ralph took the box out and looked at it suspiciously. He opened the box, and the heady aroma of chocolate filled his nostrils. He couldn't resist, so he took some out and put them on a plate.

"I bet she's been using my ingredients to make these for herself and then carefully hid them so I wouldn't find out. Well, you'd have to get up very early to catch me out. Very early indeed," he repeated, catching the time on the cooker clock. "If that is the case, she can't object if I take some, can she?" He took a bite of one. "I have to say; the old girl can bake a bit. He would always refer to her as 'the old girl' even though he was of an age to be her father. He wolfed down the rest of the brownie and then another. He finally found the cylindrical container housing the hot chocolate mix and scooped three heaped teaspoons into a mug. Then he filled the kettle with water from the tap and stood watching it boil, cursing it relentlessly due to its slow progress. After what seemed like an age, but in reality, only a few minutes, he wearily took his freshly made hot chocolate from the kitchen into the lounge. He made a b-line for the drinks cabinet and picked out a bottle of brandy.

"That'll spruce it up a bit," he said and poured a generous quantity into his hot drink.

He picked up the daily newspaper, which he'd read earlier from the seat and tossed it on the floor in the direction of the fireplace; before sitting down on his favourite leather Chesterfield chair. Next to the armchair, a vase full of fresh flowers that his housekeeper bought, stood beautifully displayed on a small table.

Betty had been Ralph's housekeeper for over 30 years although her position was now just part-time. She continued her job, more as a favour to the late Mrs Barrington. Ralph was heartbroken when his wife died and initially sought comfort in one of the only people who had any time for him. Over the years, she, like everyone else, would become irritated and disdainful of her employer and he felt much the same for her, but they put up with each other. It was like a 'marriage of convenience.' Deep down, Ralph knew he couldn't get by without Betty, and in return, the dutiful Betty didn't want to desert her employer. Every year on the anniversary of Mrs Barrington's death, she would buy an arrangement of fresh lilies and place them in a tall vase in the lounge.

It was cold in the lounge, and Ralph's thin, Japanese silk dressing gown and leather slippers were doing nothing to keep the chills from his ageing bones. The cold leather of the chair wasn't helping the blood circulate either, so Ralph decided to light the logs in the fireplace to warm the arctic temperature in the room. The fire soon warmed up the area; the flickering flames danced, creating ever-changing silhouettes on the walls. Ralph stared at the leaping flames and began to think of his wife. His constant furrowed brow smoothed out as the happy memories of his early married years started to flood back. The heat from the fire warmed his cold, sallow complexion. It was a rare moment of reflection for the bitter, old man.

The Grandfather clock standing proud against the far wall chimed for 4 o'clock.

"I wish you were still with me Belinda. Perhaps, I would have mellowed instead of becoming the hard-edged bitter old man that I am now," he conceded. "Don't tell anyone I said that, though." A smile developed across his face.

"I blame myself for your death," he continued. "Had I listened to the car mechanic at the garage and agreed to get the brake discs changed, then maybe… no, surely, you would never have been involved in that accident. You were a good, kind soul; too good for me, that's for sure. Your parents told me that, as did mine. When you died, I lost my way. I had no time for the children, and now they have no time for me. I threw myself into business and craved victory in every deal I pursued. All that mattered was that I won. Now, I have nothing apart from material things. What can I do to make things better? I can't have long left on this mortal coil. Please tell me, Belinda, what can I do?" he implored.

The flames leapt higher and fiercer, and a shrill howl of wind blew down the chimney stack and drove the orange flames far and wide. Ralph gasped as the brief, intense heat forced his body back into the firm, red leather seat. It died down immediately, and Ralph simply stared at the flames listening to the crackles that gave them a voice. Maybe it was the alcohol taking effect, but at that moment, he listened intently for the answer to his woe.

"Yes, I must make amends," he slurred somewhat. "I will write a letter to my dear Belinda. I want her to understand that I was under extreme pressure and… and… oh, I had been just terrible to her. I want to ask her for forgiveness before it's too late."

What took Ebenezer Scrooge three spirits and fanciful visits to his past, present and future, took Ralph Barrington a freak gust of wind and burst of fire to realise. It was most out of character for the ordinarily belligerent old man.

"Now, where's my writing paper?" asked Ralph to himself, before immediately realising that it was in the drawer of the writing desk in the corner of the room. He marched over, took a batch of monogrammed writing paper from the drawer and sat himself down to begin the well-overdue confession to his deceased spouse.

"I won't be able to send it to you, and you won't be able to read it, but it's something that I'd like to do," conceded Ralph to himself.

Initially, with pen poised over the lined vellum, words failed to materialise, but after a while, they started to flow. He managed to write three pages of quite sentimental, but nevertheless, heartfelt prose addressed to his late wife. Once finished, he attempted to read the letter through, but with eyelids growing heavier and heavier, he didn't manage to complete it. Perhaps the combination of lack of sleep, sounds of the inclement weather and the hot, alcohol-laced drink had something to do with his personality change, but they certainly caused him to nod off at the writing desk. His pen dropped to the floor as he fell back open-mouthed in the chair, snoring loudly enough to give the violent winds outside a run for their money.

His slumber was rudely interrupted by the chimes of the Grandfather clock. Before it rang out for the fifth and final time, Ralph was standing up, peering down at the letter he had written to his wife. With the fire dying down, the room was darker, as was Ralph's demeanour. The alcohol, which influenced his unusual compassionate mood, had also become diluted. He picked up the letter.

"What a load of sentimental claptrap? What the hell was I thinking?" he said, reverting to type. "She's the one who left me, not the other way around. You left me alone, Belinda!" he angrily shouted and ripped up the letter. A piece fell to the floor, but the remainder was scrunched up into a ball before being indignantly tossed into the fire. The paper burned rapidly affecting a brief, but significant charge to the flame. Out of the corner of his eye, he caught sight of the flower arrangement again. He marched over, pulled the lilies from the vase and dropped them, heads first into the waste paper bin. Some stems bounced off the edge of the receptacle and fell to the floor. They were left where they fell, as Ralph grabbed the vase and walked over to the fire. With the water in the vessel, he doused the flame and then slammed down the empty vase on the mantelpiece above the grate. His final act was to take a considerable slug from the rum bottle and storm off upstairs and back to bed.

As Ralph tried to make himself comfortable to resume his slumber, back downstairs in the living room, a single flickering ember leapt from the smoking logs in the fireplace. It fluttered and floated up and down around and around before landing in the middle of the newspaper that Ralph had irresponsibly flung to the floor earlier on. The heat from the cinder created a small burning hole, which rapidly became larger and larger engulfing the broadsheet. The strong winds caused a draught from the ageing window frame, which in turn provoked the curtains to billow. The flame from the newspaper licked the curtain material, and in a moment, they were alight. Once the flames had caught them, it wasn't long before the fire began to travel throughout the room. In only a few minutes, the room was an inferno. The thick black smoke it created began filtering throughout the ground floor of the house and then rapidly up the stairwell and towards Ralph's bedroom.

Soon after, much of the ground floor ablaze, neighbours alerted the fire brigade, and within 10 minutes they had arrived and began tackling the fire. When under control, fire-fighters in breathing apparatus entered the charred hallway and began searching for signs of life. Due to the stone-constructed stairs and tiled walls, the fire, fortunately, hadn't reached the first floor, but smoke still filled the space leading upstairs. One of the fire-fighters located an unconscious Ralph in bed and carried him out of the smouldering residence.

Once outside on a stretcher, recently arrived, paramedics performed CPR on him. Following several unsuccessful endeavours, it was clear that all attempts of resuscitation were in vain. Ralph was dead – killed by smoke inhalation, caused by his own careless actions.

As the first sunrays of a cloudless-skied December

morning rose from the horizon, the Chief fire-fighter entered the partially burned-out building and began inspecting the water-sodden, smoky mess of what was three hours earlier a beautiful early-20th century residence. It was almost tranquil within the husk of the lounge with only the light wind, dripping of water on the wet floor and his own footsteps making any sound. Because of that, the first of the eight chimes emanating from the fire-damaged, but amazingly still working Grandfather clock startled him. He looked down and noticed something in the centre of the room – it was a piece of monogrammed writing paper, the edges were slightly burnt, but the rest of it was untouched by the fire and the water from the hoses. On top of it laid a single fresh lily. He picked up the flower in his left hand and the piece of paper in his right, and read what had been written on it –

'To my dearest Belinda,

Time is against me. It's ticking towards the end, and even with all my money, I can't stop each hour from chiming away.

I will be eternally regretful for the poor way I treated you. The fire which once burned inside me has, due to my arrogance and self-destructive path, been a long time extinguished. How I long to be reunited with you once again, my love, and for that fire to burn inexorably again…'

Take-away of Death

Sanjay worked as a chef in a large, well-established Indian restaurant in North London. He was not long out of university, where he had studied medicine, but dropped out after two years. Cooking was his passion, and he was delighted when Arjun, an old family friend, offered him a job as the head chef in his popular establishment. He was a bit of a "Jack-the-lad" character, who had given his parents all sorts of problems with his antics throughout his youth, but at least he'd settled down with a good job, although it wasn't exactly what his father had hoped. He always dreamed of his son following him into the medical profession, but that wasn't to be.

As the evening service began, in the kitchen, onions were sizzling gently, spices were carefully added to curry sauces, and the naan breads were slowly baking in the tandoor. Sanjay was in his element in the kitchen.

It was just 6.30 p.m., and out on the restaurant floor, guests were arriving, and the waiters were taking orders. Arjun was at the bar at the front, taking orders from customers who just required a take-away. One of those customers was Mr Stewart, a polite, retired officer who was always resplendent in a suit and tie, even when just popping up to collect food.

"And there you go, Mr Stewart. I hope you enjoy your meal," said Arjun to his regular customer as he handed over the large brown paper bag packed full of Indian delights.

"I always do, Arjun. I always do. See you again soon,"

replied Mr Stewart, salivating at the prospect of tucking into his favourite cuisine.

Just behind him was another lady, Mrs Spencer, who had waited patiently for Arjun to take her order at the front desk of the restaurant which was starting to fill up for the evening trade. As she began perusing the menu, a large, untidy man entered the restaurant right behind her.

"I'll have my usual," he bawled over the shoulder of the startled lady. His name was Mr Rankin, and he was another regular. He was the antithesis of Mr Stewart. He was of similar age but had none of the finesse and refinement of the ex-army man. He'd regularly come into the restaurant and demanded service regardless of how busy the staff were with other patrons, whether it was for a takeaway or as a sit-down guest with his meek wife.

"If you could just hold on a few moments, sir. I will see to you once I've finished with this lady," Arjun replied calmly. The man huffed but waited somewhat impatiently just behind Mrs Spencer.

"Er, now let me see," said Mrs Spencer nervously. "I'll have the vegetable samosas… Actually, I won't. I'll have the onion pakora instead. Er, no, I'll stick to the samosas…"

"Really?" asked the man standing not 3 feet behind her. "While she's faffing around, can you take my order? You know what it is. I always have the same thing."

"Excuse me, sir," Arjun replied.

"It's alright. Let him go first. He seems in a hurry. I've got time," Mrs Spencer timidly submitted.

"Thank you," said Mr Rankin right into Mrs Spencer's ear. This made her jump. Arjun came out from behind the counter, sat the old lady down at a vacant table and placed the menu down in front of her.

"So, you're usual then?" asked Arjun. "Chicken tikka masala, chicken madras, onion bhajee, vegetable curry, two pilau rice and two garlic naan breads." Arjun hurriedly wrote down the items on his notepad.

"Oh, yes. That's what I like about your lot. You've got good memories," replied Mr Rankin with his usual charm.

"Yes, sir. It's what *my lot* are very good at," Arjun replied sarcastically. He took the order to the kitchen and handed it to Sanjay.

"Rankin?" asked Sanjay.

"You could hear him?" Arjun questioned.

"The whole restaurant could hear him. What a horrible old git."

"He is, but he's still a customer and a regular one at that. Just prepare his food so that I can get rid of him as soon as possible, will you, Sanjay?"

"No problem," Sanjay answered, looking at the order slip.

When Arjun left the kitchen to tend to his customers, Sanjay looked around to make sure no one was looking at him. He placed his hand in his back trousers' pocket and pulled out a small plastic bag. It had several small tablets. Sanjay was not opposed to the odd amphetamine. Speed helped him get through long evening shifts and the late night/early morning partying that sometimes followed.

"One of these little beauties will bring that loudmouthed idiot down a peg or two. He placed the pill in between two teaspoons and crushed it forcefully. He put the spoon of ground down powder to one side and prepared Mr Rankin's curry. Making sure the other two chefs were busying themselves, he sprinkled the drug onto the chicken madras. After stirring it in slowly, he put on the lid and smirked slyly to himself.

A few minutes later, the food was ready, and he pressed the order bell to alert Arjan to collect it.

"There we go, sir," Arjan handed the order to Mr Rankin, taking his money.

"I hope it's as good as usual," said Mr Rankin.

"You'll not be disappointed," replied Arjan, utterly unaware of the unique element that had been added to Mr Rankin's curry.

"I'd better not be," Mr Rankin cruelly replied before leaving the premises without even a cursory goodbye.

The evening service continued in a pleasant and orderly fashion, and Sanjay was far too busy in the kitchen to pay a thought to how his extra ingredient could be affecting the unpleasant Mr Rankin.

A few days later and during a lull in activity before the lunchtime rush, Arjan was leaning on the bar, opening the day's mail. Most of the envelopes contained either bills or junk mail, but one carried something a little more engaging. He read the letter with great interest and what it contained made him run to the kitchen with delight.

"Sanjay! Sanjay!" he cried.

"What is it?" answered the chef, who had his head in the fridge.

"Listen to this," announced Arjan, opening the letter dramatically and clearing his voice. "*The Barnet Chamber of*

Commerce has selected *The Pride of India* as one of the top six Indian restaurants in the borough. We would very much like you to accept our invitation to enter our competition to find the best Indian restaurant in Barnet."

"Wow, that's great news," offered Sanjay, whose head was now out of the freezer and on its way into the clouds.

"This is down to you. Your culinary skills have really put us on the map, and now we've been recognised," Arjun generously declared.

"It's not all down to me, Arjun," replied Sanjay, noticing his young assistant looking slightly disappointed with the boss's unilateral praise.

"We'll definitely enter the competition," Arjun pointed out, re-reading the invitation to himself.

"Where's it going to be held?" asked Sanjay.

"At the Star of Bengal, up the road. We'll have to put on a good show as they'll be firm favourites, especially as the contest is on their home turf," buzzed the restaurant owner. "Anyway, you get on, and I'll get back to what I was doing," Arjun chirped as he left the kitchen as excited as he'd entered it.

Sanjay continued counting the delivery of chicken breasts when the kitchen door flung open again.

"Don't tell me, they've rescinded our invitation," shouted Sanjay with a chortle.

"No, no, no. Come and have a look at this," replied Arjun. He was carrying the local newspaper.

Sanjay joined him, and Arjun pointed at a news item.

'Local Magistrate Killed in Car Accident' read the headline.

"And?" said Sanjay disinterested.

"Read the story," demanded a straight-faced Arjun. Sanjay took the paper from his boss and read the article.

"Bloody hell," he calmly said and lowered the paper slowly.

"Yes, bloody hell. He was only here three days ago. And now he's... dead. He wasn't the most pleasant of people, but I wouldn't wish death on him. It happened the same evening he last came in. It was only around the corner in Edgerton Avenue," said Arjun solemnly.

Sanjay stood silent and ashen-faced. He immediately believed that he could well be the cause of Mr Rankin's death as the realisation of what he'd done set in.

"I never knew he was a magistrate, let alone one so highly regarded," said Arjun. "It doesn't say what caused him to lose control and plough his car into the garden wall. Perhaps he was under the influence."

"Of what?" Sanjay snapped.

"Drink, I imagine," replied Arjun, somewhat surprised at his employee's tone. "Unless you slipped a sleeping pill into his curry?" Arjun said menacingly.

"Why would you say that?" asked Sanjay in horror.

"I was just joking. Your face, honestly," laughed Arjun nervously, trying to lighten the mood.

"Oh, yes. Of course," Sanjay said more calmly.

"Anyway, you best get on," Arjun instructed before leaving a still stunned Sanjay to digest the information.

Sanjay spent the rest of the day, keeping his own counsel as much as he could, trying to make sense of the revelation. So many questions entered his head – 'Perhaps he was drunk? Maybe the brakes on his car were faulty? Or a small child ran out into the road, and he was trying to avoid him? Or maybe he was so out of his mind due to the drug-laced curry I'd prepared for him?' Regardless, he knew he had to try to put it to the back of his mind and continue his work. The coroner's report would shed more light on the full cause of death, but for the time being, that information was yet to be released.

The days rolled on, and Sanjay reasoned that as there was no knock on the door from the police, that he wasn't going to be questioned about Rankin's demise. Besides, where was the motive? However, the relief that it was becoming increasingly unlikely that he'd be accused of anything was quickly tempered by the nagging realisation that he probably caused the death of an innocent, albeit highly unpleasant man. He had to put these concerns to one side and focus on the competition.

Thursday morning arrived, and as the competition for the Indian Restaurant of the Year was that afternoon, Sanjay was happily in his own world, busy making the finishing touches to his preparations. He made sure he was using the very finest cuts of meat and the freshest vegetables and spices.

"Have you got everything ready?" boomed a loud voice behind him. Sanjay visibly jumped.

"Bloody hell Arjun, how long have you been standing there?" asked a flustered Sanjay.

"I just came in. I'm sorry I startled you. I have to say you've been a bit jumpy all week. Is everything alright?"

"Yes, Everything's fine. I guess I've just had this competition on my mind. It's crucial to me. I want to win it.

"I want to win it too, but I don't think we will," replied Arjun dismissively.

"Why do you say that?"

"Well, it's being held in the restaurant that's won it for four of the last five years. I'm sure they've given a few free poppadums to the judges if you catch my drift," explained Arjun. "I would be delighted if we came second."

"No, I want to win," insisted a resolute Sanjay.

"The only way we'll do that is if you drop something into their curry," said Arjun as he left Sanjay alone. Arjun's candid, but prescient comment shocked Sanjay. After a moment's reflection, he continued with his preparations.

With all his ingredients and utensils prepared and ready, the young chef packed everything into his backpack and joined Arjun at the front of the restaurant.

"Right then, I'm ready," he said, facing his boss.

"I know you are," Arjun smiled. "By the way, before you go, take a look at this." Arjun grabbed the latest local newspaper and opened it up on page nine. Sanjay gulped. He knew what the story would be, and he began to feel very cold. "There it is," said Arjun, smacking the newspaper with the back of his hand – accidental death." Sanjay took the paper and read the article.

"*Mr Francis Rankin, local magistrate…* blah blah, blah… *post mortem showed nothing. No alcohol was found in his blood.*' Yes! What a relief," Sanjay blurted out rather colourfully.

"Why are you relieved?" asked a confused Arjun.

"Err, I mean, for his wife. He probably killed himself deliberately. At least she knows now," Sanjay lied unconvincingly.

"I don't see how she can be relieved at the conclusion that her husband killed himself, Sanjay," Arjun concluded. Sanjay just stared at him in silence, not wishing to dig his hole deeper. "Anyway, you had better be off now. Just do your best, and great things will happen. I'm confident of that," said Arjun generously. He patted Sanjay on the back and sent him on his way.

A few yards across the road from The Pride of India, Sanjay carefully placed his backpack in the well of the passenger's seat of his car. He started the engine and expelled a large lungful of air before driving the short distance to the competition's venue.

The Star of Bengal was a massive restaurant on the other side of town. Once all the contestants had arrived, they were all shown into the expansive kitchen, and there was plenty of prep space available for all six of the entrants. Extra gas hobs had been hired out, especially for the competition. The competitors were shown to their stations by the head judge, a tall thin man, who looked like he took his job far too seriously.

"My name's Sedgewick, and I'm heading the judging panel," said the man in a very nasally voice.

"My name's Sanjay," replied the chef politely.

"I know," Sedgewick sneered back. He looked over Sanjay's ingredients and even prodded some of the packets of spices with the tip of his pen like he was a prison officer looking for contraband. Sanjay attempted to lighten the mood.

"It's like an episode of MasterChef, isn't it?" he joked to the judge who was checking off the names on his clipboard.

"I suppose so. If you like that sort of thing," replied

the judge, looking up from the table and down at Sanjay.

Attempting to ingratiate himself to the judge, Sanjay chanced his arm and tried again.

"Cooking doesn't get tougher than this, eh?"

The judge once again looked up from his clipboard, waited a moment before sneering, "No, it doesn't, and you'll do well to remember that." He then walked off to the home chef and shook him firmly by the hand and offered a hitherto undiscovered smile.

Arjun's suggestion that The Star of Bengal probably had it all sewn up started to look like a certainty. However, Sanjay was determined to put in a good show and do his very best for himself and the growing reputation of The Pride of India.

The rules of the competition were that the competitors had to provide a complete Indian meal from scratch within 90 minutes. They were required to prepare one starter, two main meals, with at least one having to be vegetarian, with accompaniments and bread, and a dessert.

Sanjay decided to make mini vegetable samosas as an appetiser, his own variation on a Lamb Rogan Josh, a Palak Paneer, Chana Dal, saffron rice with roti, and for a dessert, traditional Gulab Jamun. Precisely 90 minutes later, he was finished.

His efforts, when presented inside the restaurant, looked quite exquisite as he stood beside the pristine white linen-clad table. He could tell the three judges enjoyed what they tasted – even Mr Sedgewick seemed impressed, in the sense that the constant hard-nosed sneer has somewhat evaporated during the tasting of Sanjay's delights.

Once the judges had completed their sampling, they asked the contestants to leave the restaurant while the trio deliberated and cogitated to find their winner. Mingling with the others outside the front of the restaurant, Rahul, the favourite and head chef of The Star of Bengal, walked over to Sanjay who had just lit up a cigarette.

"Your menu looked good. I think the judges were impressed."

"Cheers. I think I did an okay job," Sanjay said humbly.

"I'd say it was more than okay. You certainly beat the pants off The Raj Mahal and The New Delhi *Craphouse* or whatever it's called," replied Rahul with a chortle. Sanjay laughed and coughed out a cloud of cigarette smoke.

"I like that. I don't even know where they came from."

"I think they took over the premises of that old Thai restaurant near the cinema. I noticed one of the judge's faces when she tried his Aloo Gobi. It was not a face that screamed *delicious*; I can tell you," Rahul continued. Sanjay sniggered and took another drag of his cigarette.

"I wasn't sure if I'd be here today," Sanjay told Rahul as he stepped on the cigarette butt.

"Why is that?" asked Rahul.

"My mind just wasn't on the task in hand. I received some rather disturbing news last week; however, it turned out that it wasn't as bad as I first thought," came back the cryptic reply.

"Well, life throws all sorts of arrows at you. Believe me, by the time you get to my age, you'll just let them fire over you. You 've got a good future in the business, I can tell — and between you and me," Rahul stepped in close to Sanjay and whispered, "I'm sure I can get you a position in my restaurant, if you'd like one, of course." Sanjay beamed and thanked him profusely but told him that he wasn't looking for a change quite yet.

"Anyway, as for as long as you don't poison a customer's food and killed them, I'm sure you'll do just fine." Rahul stepped back and giggled impishly, leaving Sanjay shocked with heart palpitations. That wasn't the first occasion that somebody had made a comment alluding to him killing someone. Although he realised that they were perfectly innocent statements, it left him cold.

Just then, Mr Sedgewick opened the restaurant door to invite, or more to the point, instruct everyone back inside. A decision had been made.

"On behalf of the judging panel," he began, "I would firstly like to say what a high quality of entrants we have seen today. Any of you could have won this competition. However, two contestants stood out. So, without further ado, I would like to award our Silver award for the runner-up, and that goes to… The Pride of India."

"Well done," said Rahul as he offered his hand out to Sanjay. The runner-up duly shook it before collecting his framed certificate. The female judge fumbled around her pocket to find her camera with which she snapped a couple of photos of the smiling Sanjay and the impassive Mr Sedgewick. As the smattering of applause disappeared, Sedgewick announced which restaurant came in first place and the announcement wasn't a shock to anyone.

"I'm delighted to announce that the winner of The Barnet Chamber of Commerce Indian Restaurant of the Year is… The Star of Bengal." Rahul gave Sanjay a crafty wink before stepping forward to collect his prize. Some of the other losing contestants looked downbeat, but Sanjay knew by now that it was a forgone conclusion and finishing second was in effect a victory.

It was the host restaurant's duty to clean up, so after the other contestants had washed and packed up their kitchen hardware, they were free to go.

Excited to tell his boss of his silver award in person, Sanjay was first to leave. He congratulated Rahul once again and skipped off to his car carrying his backpack. Without any food ingredients to be concerned about, he slung it into the boot without a care. However, the certificate took pride of place on the passenger seat.

In his eagerness to get back to his restaurant, Sanjay decided to take a short cut down the narrow back roads. As he entered Edgerton Avenue, he couldn't resist another peek at his certificate and foolishly took his eye off the road ahead. At that precise moment, from the left around the corner, drove a Vauxhall Corsa. The oncoming vehicle sounded its horn, but as Sanjay looked up, he was already on a collision course. He yanked the steering wheel to the right towards a garden wall laden with several bunches of flowers. Immediately Sanjay's car came to a halt, destroying the wall and sending the flowers into all directions. The man, driving the Corsa, jumped out of his car to check on Sanjay's condition. The front of the vehicle concertinaed from the head-on collision and eft Sanjay trapped and barely able to breathe. The other driver immediately called an ambulance, and within a few, it had arrived.

"You're a lucky boy," were the first words Sanjay heard as he slowly came to in the hospital the following evening. It sounded like he was hearing them under water. He groggily looked to his left and witnessed a doctor in a long white coat standing back to the wall, looking at him. He was one of the old-fashioned physicians, with a blue pin-striped suit underneath his coat and a pair of half-moon spectacles perched on the end of his nose.

"Another couple of inches to the left and your spinal cord would have been severed, you know," said the doctor in a very matter-of-fact way, now leaning against the wall with both hands in his pockets. Sanjay heard this a lot clearer as the fuzziness of his unconsciousness began to ebb away. He still couldn't figure out why he was in the hospital. He looked at the doctor hoping for some clarification.

"You were in a car crash, Mr Rahman. You've been unconscious and under surveillance for 18 hours. You have a cornucopia of drugs inside you, so you probably can't even register what I'm saying," he said with a world-weariness that suggested he'd seen it all before and didn't care much to see it again. He took out a pen from his breast pocket and began pointing at the plastered parts of Sanjay's body. "But, for the record, you have a broken arm, a broken right leg, and a fractured left ankle. You've suffered swelling and bruising to your neck, so I wouldn't try talking for a few days, because you've also got a fractured jaw. Sorry, I should have mentioned that first. We're feeding you from a drip at the moment, of course, and hopefully, you'll graduate to fluids shortly. You've also got severe whiplash, *genuine* whiplash, which is unusual. You can put that on your car insurance claim with all impunity. Oh, and I wouldn't try to move your head if I were you; you won't like the painful reaction." Sanjay couldn't, even if he tried, as the neck brace was quite tight. "You'll be here for a little while, I'm afraid, but you'll live to see many more days. As I said, you're a lucky boy."

"The funny thing, although *funny* is probably not the best word to use, is that a couple of weeks ago a fella crashed his car in the same place, into the same garden wall. He was brought in, but he never made it. A well-respected magistrate, he was. Anyway, and I'm only telling you this because you probably can't even process what I'm saying. Pilled up to the eyeballs, he was. He'd been taking amphetamines, and they in all probability caused him to crash, but by the time the post mortem report came out, he was clean, and it was recorded as an accidental death. Just goes to show its who you know or who you *knew* in his case."

Even if Sanjay wanted to say something, he couldn't, but this revelation made him feel even worse if that was possible.

The doctor continued, "I guess that's what power and influence can do for you. All misdemeanours are swept under the carpet, even in death, if you're amongst the elite. I know you can't even decipher my words just now, but I just wanted to vent. It does me good. Anyway, shout if you need anything. Oh, you can't. Just press the call button with your good hand, and someone will attend to you. Sleep well. I'll be around tomorrow to see how you're getting on. Goodnight, old chap." The doctor slinked out of the private room, closing the door firmly behind him. Sanjay could see him through the window sharing joke with the duty nurses before walking away and out of sight.

The room was so quiet, almost eerily so and Sanjay laid motionless, staring at the ceiling, now fully aware that his actions caused the death of another person. Just one day earlier, he was one of the area's most promising young chefs with an offer to join the crew of one of the most prestigious eateries in town, and now he lay prostrate, broken, unable to assert himself through speech and with the heavy heart of a remorseful murderer. He felt a strong urge to confess, even though no one would ever know what he did. But *he* knew – he knew what he had done and so did his maker. Taking responsibility for his actions may well give him absolution, but would also destroy his future. Sanjay had a decision to make, and he would have to justify it within the confines of his aching head and the quiet solitude of his sanitised hospital prison cell – a decision that, in whatever direction it went, would change his life forever.

Family Misfortunes

Den Hubbard and his 19-year-old son, Ross, own and operate a small family-run printers in the South Yorkshire town of Barnsley. The machinery they've used for decades has seen better days but was still in excellent working order – usually.

"Dad, if we don't modernise, we'll be in big trouble, and Mum agrees," Ross told his father across a jammed four-colour printing press.

"No, she doesn't. And don't be so melodramatic. I have been in the printing business for a long, long time as was my father before me. I have raised you alongside your mother, and we've done alright there. Just because our marriage is not exactly a blissful one, it doesn't mean to say we're not in agreement, so don't go trying to cosy up to her on this matter. Twenty-six years and two heart attacks later, I'm still with her, and we're still on the same page, pardon the pun. Now why has this damned nozzle clogged up again?" replied Den a no-nonsense Yorkshireman in his brusque Barnsley accent.

"This is exactly my point. The machinery is old. The ink nozzles are forever getting bunged up, the paper feeders are temperamental, to say the least, and as for the noise they make. Even when they work, which is becoming more and more infrequent I might add, they're slow and expensive to run. These printing presses are almost as old as you. The print industry has moved on, Dad. The modern print machines are so much quicker, easier to maintain and are far more cost-effective."

"Don't be cheeky, son. I know this industry inside out, and I know the advances made over the last few years. What I'm saying is that I don't want to risk my business, and your inheritance, by the way, by making unnecessary changes. Ah, that's it. You're alright now, Phil. She's off and running again," shouted Den across the factory floor to one of his staff, as he managed to release some dirt that was blocking the cyan nozzle. He then walked off to the office, all the time wiping the excess ink onto a grey rag which was rapidly becoming bluer in hue. His son followed behind.

"All I'm saying Dad, is that one day, these machines will pack up completely and then what? It'll cost a fortune to get them repaired, and it won't be a quick job either. Folk can get small print jobs done online quickly and cheaply from numerous sources. You're a dinosaur Dad, and you risk becoming extinct."

Den stops in his tracks and turns to his son. "Now listen here, Ross," he snarled, pointing his finger in his face with the inky rag still in hand. "You listen. I'll hear no more of this. We're doing fine. We've outlasted Wavertree's and Boyson's, and why is that? Because people know us and trust us. We provide a good service for a good price."

"Yes, but Sterry's up the road are still around, and if they continue to steal our customers at the rate they are now, modernisation or not, we'll be out of business within two years. Open your eyes, Dad," he implored.

"Now, I'm still in charge of this company, and I know what's best for it, so I'll not hear any more about 'modernising' alright? Look, I know we need an injection of cash, and we've got to maintain our machinery, but I'm trying to find a sustainable source of extra income, and that's something I'm going to do myself. You look after the day to day running of the business."

A flabbergasted Ross didn't say anything. He just stepped away from his pontificating father and sat down at his desk, leaving his father standing in the same pose, still with an outstretched finger.

"I'm going home to get cleaned up. I've had enough today. Sort out that invoice for Baker & Sons will you? This month's order is on my desk."

With his father out of the way, Ross calms down and prepares the invoice as instructed.

The phone rings, and he answered it, "Oh, hello, Mr White. How are you?" It was one of Hubbard's best customers; a book publisher from Sheffield.

"Is your father about?" asked Mr White.

"No, he's left for the day, I'm afraid. Is there anything I can help you with?" Ross asked politely.

"Well, you'll do. I'm going to have to cancel our regular order," came the gruff response.

"Oh, no. Why is that?"

"It's nothing personal, but I've had a cheaper quote — a much cheaper one. I know I've been with your company for a long time, but business is business. You understand?" Mr White explained.

"I understand, but perhaps we can do something about the price?" asked a concerned Ross.

"I doubt it. Anyway, I've made my mind up. I'm sorry," informed Mr White.

"Can I ask before you go, Mr White, did the cheaper quote come from Sterry's?"

"Er, actually it did. Yes. Again, I'm sorry." The line went dead, and Ross slowly put the receiver down.

After a few moments of reflection, Ross started sifting through a pile of papers on his father's desk.

"I suppose I'd better sort out that invoice, while we've still got a business," Ross mumbled to himself. "Hold on, what's this?" Amongst the order forms and bills was a credit statement full of payments to various online gambling companies. He sat down and perused the paperwork in disbelief. There were dozens of entries totalling over £2,000. What made matters worse was the card was a business credit card. His so-called frugal father had been spending thousands of pounds from the business to aid what looked very much to Ross like a gambling addiction. Now he had a problem of his own. Does he confront his father, knowing full well he'd receive a barrage of excuses and lies about his find which will inevitably alert him to cover up any further debts? Does he tell his mother or should he keep this information to himself, thus burying his head in the sand? After several minutes of weighing up the options, Ross decides that the best way forward was to speak to his long-suffering mother.

"Perhaps she might already be aware of it. I suppose he might have told her about his problem already," Ross told himself, trying to make some sense of it all.

Half an hour later, he returned home and, fortunately, his father was out. His mother, Vanessa, was in the kitchen cooking.

"Where's Dad?" asked Ross after he warmly greeted his mother with a kiss on the cheek.

"Gone to a Lodge meeting. He didn't even hang

around long enough to take his pills," replied Vanessa with a redundant sigh. "To be honest with you Ross, I don't much care *where* your father has gone."

"You've had another row?" Ross deduced. His mother didn't say anything; she just began aggressively stabbing a leg of lamb with a skewer before indignantly pushing through cloves of garlic and sprigs of rosemary.

"I'm not sure if I should say what I want to say, but I feel I must," Ross continued. His mother wiped her hands on a tea cloth and turned around.

"Go on, son. What is it?" she probed.

"I was going through some paperwork on Dad's desk, and I found a business credit card statement for over £2,000. Every transaction was from betting companies. I wasn't sure whether to tell you or him or to keep it to myself, Mum," Ross admitted. To his surprise, Vanessa didn't say anything. She just folded her arms and looked to the ceiling. "Mum, did you hear me?"

"I heard you. He's gambling again, eh? That stupid, stupid man. We almost lost the business, the house, the lot, once before due to his habit. That's when he had his first heart attack. It was due to stress. He was trying to keep the business afloat and keep on top of his gambling addiction, but you were too young to remember, of course. I had to take charge of all our affairs, both business and domestic. He couldn't be trusted with money. It's not like he ever won much – and when he did, he put it straight back on another horse. Anyway, I finally managed to get him to go to Gambler's Anonymous, and he kicked the habit. He promised never to walk into a bookmaker's again. Mind you, he doesn't have to anymore, not with online gambling sites."

"I never knew," admitted Ross. "We had words this afternoon again about modernising the equipment at work. He doesn't want to know, and now I know why."

"I don't think that has anything to do with his gambling addiction. Your father's a very stubborn and proud man. He doesn't like change for change's sake, even if those around him are imploring him to open his eyes. Besides, we also had words when he got home. And after what you've just told me, I know why he said what he said," Vanessa cryptically voiced.

"What do you mean?"

"He came home all chipper and smiley, and that immediately made me suspicious. When does your father ever smile? Anyway, he tried some small talk for all of 20 seconds. He asked how my day was and even complimented me on my hair. Nevertheless, you know your grandmother is coming over for dinner tomorrow night? Well, he wants me to ask her for; how did he put it? Oh yes, 'an advance on my inheritance'."

"What?" asked a confused Ross.

"My Mum's getting on and Grandad left her a lot of money in his will, and she's hardly spent a penny of it. You know that your grandmother is not the most ostentatious of people. Anyway, your father wants me to ask her for some money. He claims it's for some home improvements that he's been thinking about for a while. Well, it was the first time I'd heard about it, but now we know the real reason. I fear that the £2,000 he owes the credit card company is just the tip of the iceberg. I told him I wouldn't broach the subject with my Mum and he just got all angry and stormed out letting me know he's off to The Lodge," Vanessa explained.

"What are you going to say to him?"

"Nothing. Not yet, anyway. Look, whatever happens, you'll be alright. I'll make sure you're catered for. I thought that the one thing he truly cared about was his work. Now, there are two things."

"Mum, you sound like you hardly even like him, let alone love him. Do you even feel much for him?" asked Ross, trying to comprehend everything.

"All I wanted was for him to retire or at least take a backseat and spend more time at home, with me. He has no desire to do so; I know that now," Vanessa points out not answering Ross' question at all. I'm dreading tomorrow night now. I know he'll find a way to bring the whole money thing up again. Oh, and don't you go lending him any money. Your money is yours, and you'll need it to put a deposit on your first home when you move out – whenever that may be," Vanessa winked at her son.

Ross smiled back. He knew full well what his father was like. He felt sorry for his mother having to put up with Den's moods and decided not to persist with his questioning.

"Help me lay the table, will you?"

"Of course," Ross obliged obediently and took the stack of plates and cutlery his mother handed to him. He left the kitchen and set the dining table.

The following day Ross decided it was best to stay away from his father and spent the day out with his friends. He arrived home, and the little white car in the driveway told him that Sylvia, his grandmother, was already there. He opened the door to the living room, and she was the first person who greeted him. She was seated in Den's favourite armchair. There was an eerie silence suggesting that something or someone, someone like Den, had said something to sour the atmosphere.

"Hello, darling," she greeted her grandson.

"Hello grandma," he replied and immediately walked over and gave her a peck on the cheek.

"How have you been?" she asked.

"He's been alright. Asking too many questions as usual, but he's been working hard, just like his old man," interrupted Den. Everyone ignored him.

"I'm fine thanks, Grandma," Ross answered for himself.

"That's good," said Sylvia.

"How are you?" asked Ross.

"Oh, you know me. I'm not one for complaining." An audible sigh came from the direction of Den, who was perched at one end of the sofa, his wife at the other extreme. Ross began telling his Grandma about his day out.

"Right, that's the pleasantries out of the way. It's my turn to ask something now," grunted Den.

"Erm Den, come into the kitchen a minute. I need some help with the potatoes."

"Help with the potatoes? What do you have to do, pull them out of the ground, woman?" he sneered. His wife was not amused and walked away. Den sighed again and followed Vanessa into the kitchen, leaving Ross perched on the arm of the chair where Sylvia sat engrossed in her grandson's words.

"Don't you dare go there again, Dennis Hubbard," Vanessa said in one of those loud, angry whispers that people use; invariably more emphatic than their normal speaking voice.

"What? I've said nowt," Den protested his innocence.

"Apart from asking my mother outright for money," Vanessa continued.

"I didn't ask her outright."

"So, telling her that she 'should put her money to good use; help the family out a bit' wasn't a blatant request for her cash?"

"She brought the subject of money up in the first instance. She only mentioned it to rub my nose in it. She's fooling no one. She's a hard, uncaring woman. Always has been, always will be," he added stubbornly.

Vanessa made sure the kitchen door was firmly shut before she replied. "Will you keep your voice down? She asked about Ross, and if he's managed to find a place of his own yet. All she said was that the price of property is so high nowadays, and she'd struggle to get a foot on the housing ladder if she were Ross' age," Vanessa refuted.

"What does she want with all of her money? She never spends it, and she knows her grandson needs a few grand for a deposit on a flat. Why shouldn't the old goat put her hand in the pockets of that ragged tweed skirt and give him a few quid?"

"Give *you* a few quid, you mean."

"How can you say that? It's the boy I'm thinking of," Den replied smarmily.

"Oh, don't give me all that nonsense. You want to get your hands on it. You always have. No doubt you've got yourself into trouble again?"

"What does that even mean?" Den asked angrily, moving menacingly closer to his wife.

"Oh, I don't know," Vanessa backtracked. "No doubt you've got yourself into financial strife again," she reasoned before turning away and getting the condiments out of a cupboard. Den went quiet, and she busied herself feeling her husband's eyes burning a hole in the back of her head.

Next door in the living room, the small talk between Ross and Sylvia continued with the background of what had become a very audible argument coming from the kitchen.

"Are they always like this?" asked Sylvia, cutting Ross' tale of his friend's near motorcycle accident short.

"It seems to be more and more regular," he replied, sadly.

The words in the kitchen continued and became even louder.

"You're always getting at me. I've worked so hard trying to provide you with everything – a beautiful house, holidays abroad, two wardrobes; not one, but *two* wardrobes full of expensive clothes."

"Expensive-*looking* clothes. Most of them are market knock-offs. Do you think I don't know that? And thank you, master, for allowing me space to hang them in," she continued sarcastically.

"Those dresses I bought for you when on business in Milan. That's Milan, not Macclesfield, sweetheart – do you think they were knock-offs too?"

"No, I'm not saying that. All I'm saying is…" Vanessa

admits before being interrupted.

"A trip you were very keen on me going on, I might add."

Vanessa, feeling that a full-blown argument was brewing and didn't want to alert her mother and son in the adjoining room. However, she didn't know that they were all too aware of what was being said in the kitchen. Nevertheless, Vanessa tried to defuse the situation by reducing the volume of her voice.

"Den, I'm not saying they're all hooky, and I'm grateful for what you've bought me. All I'm saying is that you can't keep trying to get money from my mother. She'll think that inviting her here was a trap and I don't want my mother feeling uncomfortable in her our house."

Not in any mood to calm matters down, Den kept on the attack. "Oh, come on. She's only here to rub my nose in it. She's never liked me. I was never good enough for her only daughter. No wonder your poor Dad died young. He couldn't bear the thought of living through to his dotage in the presence of the Queen Bitch."

Vanessa hit the Formica work surface with the ladle she had just picked up to stir the soup.

"I'm so sorry. I'll go in there and tell them to cool it," said an embarrassed Ross to his Grandma.

"No, don't Ross. Let them finish what they've started. If you intervene, it'll only fester over dinner. That's if we're going to get any dinner," Sylvia reasoned.

Ross nodded before standing up from the arm of the armchair to sit opposite her. "It's just so unnecessary," he said forlornly.

Before Sylvia could answer, a tremendous clatter of

plates crashing to the floor could be heard from the kitchen followed by a piercing scream. Ross jumped up and rushed over to the kitchen door, pushing it open with force. Before him lying on the ground was his father and he wasn't moving. His mother stood over him with the ladle in hand.

"He fell against the table and just collapsed. He went for me, but stopped rigid and fell to the floor," Vanessa bleated.

"What do you mean, he went for you?" Ross asked as he knelt down to check if his father was still breathing.

Sylvia appeared at the doorway and leant on it calmly. "Third time unlucky," she casually muttered. Her daughter looked at her, not knowing what to do.

"Call an ambulance!" shrieked Ross. "Will one of you call a bloody ambulance? Oh, I will. Try to revive him, Mum." Ross stepped over his father's apparently lifeless body to the house phone and made the 999 call.

"I'd hide that if I were you. Might be considered evidence," said Sylvia nodding at the soup ladle in Vanessa's hand.

"I didn't hit him, Mum. He just collapsed," protested Vanessa desperately. She placed the ladle into the soup pan and turned off the gas. Sylvia stared down at Den. Her sweet old lady demeanour had vanished, and it was replaced by a woman bereft of feeling for her possibly dead son-in-law.

"You'll be able to live your life now, Vanessa."

"Shhh, Ross will hear you. Besides, he might not even be dead."

"Oh, he's dead, alright. He's gone the same shade of

white that your Dad did when he keeled over and died. They're cut from the same cloth, those two. My father always told us, 'what you reap, you sow.' Now *he* was a good man," said Sylvia calmly.

"They'll be here in five minutes. We've got to try something," a returning Ross panted frantically. He once again checked to see if Den was breathing. He wasn't. He gently turned his fallen father on to his back and began a crude attempt at CPR. Vanessa knelt too, watching her son attempt to revive his father, all the time glancing up at her mother who still leant up against the door frame, expressionless.

Ross' efforts proved fruitless, and as the distant two-tone sirens of an ambulance increased in volume, he knew that there was no hope. Vanessa went to open the front door as the ambulance pulled up. Two paramedics entered the house and tried to revive Den. They knew, as did everyone else, that any attempts were futile. Den was dead. The paramedics wheeled in a gurney, and they lifted his lifeless body onto it. Ross and his mother followed them out of the house.

"Wait a moment, Vanessa," said Sylvia barring her daughter's passage out of the house.

"What is it?"

"Are you still seeing that Sterry fella?" she asked in a hushed tone.

"Not now, Mum?" replied Vanessa urgently.

"Are you?"

"Yes, I am."

"And is he still keen on buying the company?"

"Yes. Very."

"Then all's well that ends well. Oh, and I'll help Ross get on to that ladder. Go on. You'd better be with your husband," said Sylvia. "You don't want to look 'uncaring.' I'll stay here. Perhaps we'll get a takeaway in later."

Vanessa smiled with quiet satisfaction. She caught up with Ross who was standing impatiently by the open doors at the rear of the ambulance. Before she clambered aboard, she turned back to the house to see her mother stand watching, arms folded. Sylvia blew her daughter a kiss, went inside and closed the door behind her.

It's Your Lucky Day

Vic was in his mid-twenties and worked in a jewellery shop in a busy seaside town. It was by no means his ideal job, but his chosen path of becoming a rally car driver ended with a severe crash a couple of years earlier.

One bright Monday morning, an old lady came into the shop and approached Vic, who was standing at the counter, waiting.

"Hello, young man," said the woman, reaching into her handbag.

"Hello, old lady," replied Vic, just softly enough to be sure the customer couldn't hear him properly.

"I have something here, and I wonder if you could look at it for me. An aunt left it to me a few years ago, and I'm sure it isn't worth very much. Probably paste stones, but I'd like to sell it as I live on my own and I'm a little short."

"You can say that again," mumbled Vic gazing at the lady's five foot nothing frame.

"I'm sorry?" she clarified.

"I said, 'well, let's have a look at it then'," said Vic, covering his tracks.

The old lady presented him with a white stone set cluster ring. Vic's eyes lit up. It was indeed set with an array of clean diamonds. After looking at it with his jeweller's eyepiece, said to the lady, "Well, you're correct, they're just paste stones, so it's not worth a great deal, unfortunately, as you suspected, but I can give you £25 for it."

"Oh, that would be wonderful," beamed the lady. As quick as he could, Vic walked over to the till checking to make sure the customer couldn't see him and reached into his back pocket to pull out his wallet. He took a twenty and a five out of it, opened and shut the till, and handed the cash to the lady who thanked him profusely with a huge smile as she made her way out if the shop. As soon as she was out of sight, Vic examined the ring again, which he had previously secreted in the palm of his hand.

"Nine, ten, eleven, twelve, quarter carat stones. It's going to be worth a few quid alright. Dozy old mare," he said cruelly to himself. He deliberately did the poor woman out of a sizable amount of cash and was delighted by that fact.

An hour later, Vic called out to his boss, who would spend most of his day playing online chess in his office. A solitary grunt signalled to Vic that it was okay for him to leave the shop, so he grabbed his jacket and hot-footed it down the road to another jeweller's shop. The owner, Ted, was well known to Vic as he would occasionally sell bits and pieces of jewellery he'd procured from other unsuspecting customers. Ted was also a little shady and never asked too many questions. So, when Vic brought in his "Grandma's ring" to sell, Ted took Vic's words with a pinch of salt. Ted's eyes lit up as he examined the piece.

"Wealthy lady, your grandma, was she?" he asked.

"She had a few bob, yes. Mind you; she inherited a lot of jewellery from her mother," Vic lied.

"Of course, she did," replied Ted unconvinced. "Now

let me have a close look."

Ted took out his loupe and scrutinised the stones, making sounds of affirmation as his eyes leapt from one to another.

"It's a nice piece. A very nice piece, indeed. I'll make you an offer," said Ted, as he put the eyepiece back into his waistcoat pocket. Vic's eyes lit up in anticipation. He didn't say a word deliberately building the anticipation. Finally, Ted made his bid.

"I'll give you two thousand for it."

"Two grand?" asked Vic, barely able to dampen his excitement.

"Yep. Will cash be acceptable?" asked Ted, knowing that he'd at least double his money.

"That'll be fine. Cash is king, eh?" he said with a chortle. Ted gave him a sideways glance before heading out of sight to his office to fetch the cash.

"Two grand… Two bloody grand," Vic repeated to himself, a little louder than he thought.

"Yes, two grand, old boy. More than you expected, eh?" shouted back, Ted, still out of sight.

"No, I thought it would be somewhere around that amount," Vic lied. Ted returned with a handful of crisp £50 notes and began counting them out in front of Vic. "One hundred, two hundred, three hundred…" Vic's heart beat harder and faster as every hundred pounds was placed on the counter.

Once the cash had been laid out, Vic gathered all the notes up into a neat pile before slipping the wad of cash into the inside pocket of his jacket. He bade Ted a farewell and left the premises. He couldn't wait to spend some of his ill-earned moolah. Across the road from Ted's shop was a betting shop. Vic's big green eyes lit up with greed, and he skipped over the road. Once inside, Vic perused the raft of television screens for the next race on which he could bet. One particular runner in the 1.30 from Catterick took his eye. "Haha, perfect," he squealed and walked over to the counter.

"Fifty quid to win on "Give Me a Ring" in the one-thirty at Catterick, please."

The clerk searched for the odds on her computer and gave him a funny look. "Give me a Ring is twenty-five to one, sir. Are you sure you want to put £50 on the nose to win, sir?"

"Oh, yes. £50 to win," said Vic, already imagining collecting his £1300 winnings to add to his booty of ill-gotten gains. He knew nothing about horseracing, but he did know about greed and how to waste money. He reached into his jacket and peeled off a single £50 note and slid it to the lady on the other side of the glass. She happily accepted his gamble and printed out his betting slip.

A couple of minutes later, the race began. Vic's eyes glued to the monitor showing the race. Within a minute, one of the horses pulled up as it approached the first fence.

"That's your race done. That was 'Give Me a Ring,'" called the clerk from behind the glass.

"Oh well, easy come, easy go," announced Vic as he made his way out of the betting shop and back to his store. Before he reached his workplace, Vic slipped into the newsagents, two doors away and bought twenty-five £2 scratch cards.

"You must feel like it's your lucky day," said the

shopkeeper.

"It's my lucky day, alright," replied Vic, folding up the small rectangles of card and running out of the shop.

Five minutes later and Vic sat staring at the pile of frantically scratched and non-winning cards in front of him in his shop's staffroom, Vic muttered to himself, "Not one winner. Not a single pound. How can that be possible? That's one hundred pounds wasted in just 10 minutes." Looking around to check that no one else was behind him, he pulled the remaining £1900 out of his jacket pocket and counted the notes again. He nodded, realising that there was plenty more fun he could have with the remaining cash. He set about making a few phone calls to his mates to hastily arrange a poker night, which they all quickly agreed on. Vic was not a good poker player and had lost hundreds of pounds gambling in the past. Then he phoned his fiancé, who was also on her lunch break.

"Hello, babe. You know that posh steak restaurant you like, but is a bit on the pricey side? Well, don't eat any lunch on Friday, because we're going there for a slap-up dinner in the evening."

"What brought this on? You know we can't afford their prices, Vic," replied Caroline, his long-suffering, American other half. "Don't tell me you've borrowed more money from that lunatic down the pub? You surely remember what happened last time you didn't pay him back? I don't need to take any more time off work to visit you in the hospital."

"No, no, Caz. This is all legit. I got a bonus at work and who better to spend it on than my lovely fiancée?" Vic responded without a pause.

"Well, in that case… Hold on, how much did you get?"

"A couple of hundred."

"Okay, but we'll skip starters. I don't want you to spend the lot on a meal. Thank you. It's your lucky day, I guess," Caroline conceded.

"It is. Oh, and by the way, I'm going out with the lads on Thursday night. Just for a couple of jars. Okay?"

"I can hardly deny you since you'll be paying for a perfectly prepared medium-rare filet mignon the following night," giggled Caroline.

"Lovely. I'll book it now. See you later on, babe." Vic ended the conversation and made one last call to the restaurant to book a table. On completing the call, he clapped his hands and rubbed them together villainously. Finally, he took his jacket off, picked up the cash and put it in his back pocket and returned to work.

Friday night arrived, and at the restaurant, Vic and Caroline were shown to their booth by a smartly dressed waiter.

"A booth, just as you requested, sir," simpered the waiter. They sat down and momentarily received their menus. Vic just stared at it blankly.

"What's up, Vic. You've been very jittery since you came home this evening. What's wrong?" asked Caroline.

"Nothing babe. Just a hard day at work," replied Vic trying to fashion a smile.

"If we do not have starters, does that mean we can have dessert?" asked Caroline, poking Vic's menu with hers.

"Er, if you want to. I'm not sure if I will, but you can."

"Oh, why not? You love a dessert, Vic," said Caroline.

"Well, we'll see," said Vic, still not looking at all comfortable.

The waiter appeared to take the drinks order. Caroline elected to have a vodka and orange, and Vic ordered a pint of lager. They sat in silence, perusing the entre options.

A few moments later, the waiter returned to take the couple's order.

"I'll have the filet mignon, sauté potatoes and the selection of vegetables please," announced Caroline.

"Would madam care for a sauce with that?" asked the waiter.

"Yes, the bleu cheese, please," said Caroline.

"And what about sir?" asked the waiter to Vic who was beginning to fidget uncomfortably.

"Er, I'll have the eight-ounce rump and chips. Medium. No veg," answered Vic.

"The rump; medium. No vegetables," repeated the waiter snidely as he wrote down the order on his pad.

Caroline looked at Vic with a quizzed expression. "You always have the filet or at least the ribeye."

"I just fancy the rump tonight, Caroline," said Vic with just a hint of menace in his voice. Caroline shifted back in her seat, suitably chastised.

"And a sauce with that, sir?" the waiter asked.

"Just ketchup," said Vic sharply.

"Steak and chips with ketchup," the waiter condescendingly muttered as he walked away from the table with the menus in hand.

"I know there's something wrong with you today. What is it?" demanded Caroline.

"I told you, it was just a bad day at work," Vic snapped.

"You said it was a *busy* day, not *bad*. We hardly ever go out for a nice meal, and I hope you won't spoil it by being Mr Grumpy," said Caroline snapping back. "I'm going to the bathroom, and when I come back, I hope you're in a better mood. With that, Caroline stood up and walked away.

"*I'm going to the bathroom*," muttered Vic mimicking his girlfriend in a bad American accent. "She must think she's in New York, not New Haven." Looking over his shoulder to make sure Caroline was out of sight, he reached into his trouser pocket for his wallet. He opened it up to make sure he had enough money to cover the meal. Aside from being a liar and rip-off merchant, Vic was notoriously bad at gambling.

Along with his racing and scratchcard losses earlier in the week, the previous night's poker losses amounted to over £1800. Vic's friends weren't averse to taking him to the cleaners, and because of his folly, he could barely afford the evening out. The only saving grace was the Caroline didn't know how he came about his money, how much he had, and thankfully, how much he lost. However, he also knew that unless he pretended that everything was right, she would dig and dig until she found out.

Vic did his best to disguise his disappointment throughout the meal and made an effort to appear as if everything was fine. Concluding a reasonably expensive, but delicious meal, the bill was presented to Vic and to his relief it came to just under £65. When the waiter came to collect the money, Vic stood up immediately; putting the waiter in no doubt that he'd been left a pretty miserly tip. The waiter sniffed and ushered the two diners to the door. Caroline thanked him profusely, while Vic did his best to avoid eye contact.

It was not a comfortable night's sleep for Caroline, who was up most of it with a stomach upset and sickness, taking numerous trips to the bathroom, which upset Vic's sleep pattern. Her discomfort put her in a foul mood. Unfeelingly, he poured fuel to the fire by attributing the illness to the bleu cheese sauce that Caroline had liberally plastered onto her steak. "You should have had ketchup like me, love," he said before one particular emergency bathroom run. Caroline's reply was short and to the point, which left Vic in no doubt that he'd be best off sleeping the rest of the night on the uncomfortable sofa and that was precisely what he did.

Due to his disjointed night, Vic was late in getting up, and the knock-on effect was that he was late in getting to the train station for his morning commute to work. Lack of sleep always left him in a bad mood, and that mood disintegrated further when he ran into the station only to see the last of the passengers step from the platform and into the carriages. He knew he had to catch that train or he'd be very late for work, so he attempted to jump over the ticket barrier. In his haste, Vic tripped and was picked up off the floor by a burly ticket inspector, who had no desire to listen to Vic's excuses.

"Get your hands off me," Vic screamed, struggling to free himself while watching his train crawl away from the platform.

"I don't think so. You're coming with me," said the inspector gruffly as he tried to subdue Vic, who was trying everything he could to release himself from the firm grip. Wriggling violently, like a trout trying to release itself from an angler's keepnet, he managed to free his right arm, and with one swing, he punched the inspector square on the jaw and bought his liberation from his oppressor. He jumped to his feet but was immediately confronted by two members of the transport police who'd just arrived on the scene. There was nothing Vic could do to talk himself out of the situation, and within minutes, he was being loaded into the back of a police van and driven down to the police station where he was charged with grievous bodily harm.

During the following weeks leading up to the court trial, Vic found himself going from one disaster to the next. His actions caused his boss to let him go, and due to this, he and Caroline could no longer afford rent on their flat, which in turn led to her moving back home with her parents. Vic had been taken in, like a stray animal, by one of his poker buddies, where sleeping on a sofa had become a nightly occurrence. His and Caroline's relationship unravelled somewhat, but they remained a couple. She was very loyal to him and attended court to support her man.

Vic turned up at court in his suit and clean-shaven. Vic wanted to proclaim his innocence because, typically, he still believed that a smile and a good suit could still get him out of any situation, especially if the magistrate was female. However, the advice from his solicitor finally sunk in. Due to the overwhelming evidence, a not-guilty plea would almost certainly land him in prison. His only chance was to plead guilty and hope the magistrate took mercy on him. The trial was brief but intense, and following a reluctant guilty plea, the sentence was delivered. Fortunately for Vic, it was a non-custodial one, which meant he was still a free man – albeit, not totally.

"One hundred hours community service – unpaid," Vic moaned to Caroline outside the court building.

"Come on. Learn to take your punishment. You were very fortunate. Surely, you must realise that? Like the magistrate, herself said, 'It's your lucky day that I've decided not to send you to prison.' Oh, and nobody gets paid for community service. It's a punishment, you see," Caroline said with an appeasing smile.

"I suppose its good news in a way," conceded Vic.

"It is. And I have some *more* good news for you," gleamed Caroline.

"Oh, what's that?" asked Vic.

"I'm pregnant. I've known for a little while but didn't want to tell you until after the case. Now we have a double celebration." Caroline threw her arms around her fiancé, but Vic was far from delighted. However, he dared not show his disappointment and gave Caroline a gentle squeeze. No job, no flat, and now a child on the way. He didn't even have the option to find a paid job until his community work was complete.

The community service job assigned to Vic was to repair and paint a row of council-owned bungalows occupied mainly by the old and infirm. He did what was instructed to do and to a good standard, but the constant niggle in the back of his mind was the anger and resentment he felt at the situation that he found himself.

One morning when working on one of the properties,

Vic paused while repairing a picket fence to take a break. Leaning on a window ledge, with his back to the house, he lit up a hand-rolled cigarette when he heard a familiar voice.

"Oh, I thought it was you."

Vic turned around to see an old lady carrying a tray balancing a mug of tea and a plate of biscuits. At first, he didn't recognise her, but as she came closer, he realised that it was the woman he bought the ring from several weeks prior, which was the catalyst for all his misfortune.

"You're the nice young man who gave me some money for that tatty old ring I had," she continued.

"Oh, hello," a surprised Vic coughed, with the cigarette hanging from his lips.

"In fact, I gave the money you gave me to my neighbour. He's a lovely man, and he needed a few extra pounds to pay his electricity bill. The pension they give us doesn't go very far, but there are always those more unfortunate. Here, I'll leave this for you," the old lady placed the tray down on the workbench Vic was using and disappeared back into the house.

Vic's heart sank, and senses of guilt and regret immediately substituted feelings of disdain and anger at his situation. He stared at the tray, thinking that the old woman didn't even ask what he'd done wrong. Vic took a final lug of his cigarette and pushed himself off the window ledge and walked the few paces over to the tea and biscuits.

"Arghhhhhhhh!!!" he screamed as a searing pain from his foot reverberated around his body. The old lady came out if the house to see what the noise was.

"What's happened?" she asked before looking down at Vic's right foot. A four-inch nail had pierced his shoe and gone right through his foot.

"It's gone right the way bloody through," screamed Vic in agony.

"Oh, dear. Hold on. I'll call an ambulance," the woman said breathlessly before dialling 999 on her portable house phone. Vic fell to the ground and unceremoniously pulled the nail out of his shoe while making a cacophony of alarming loud pained noises. Fortunately, the ambulance was not long in coming and took Vic straight to the Accident and Emergency department of the local hospital. In the back of the ambulance, all Vic could think about between the waves of intense pain was that his heartless actions were catching up on him. He was finally coming to terms with his deception and the consequences of it.

Within 30 minutes, with shoe removed and pain killers administered and his foot propped up on a pillow, Vic lay motionless on a curtained-off bed, staring at a small stain on the ceiling. Then, with a dramatic swish of the curtain, in walked in a young female doctor. Without saying anything, she picked up the clipboard at the base of the bed and gave it a brief perusal. She smiled at Vic and raised her eyebrows.

"It's your lucky day," she said spritely, crossing her arms and staring down at her patient.

"Lucky? You call this lucky?" Vic replied, trying to prop himself up without putting any pressure on his injured foot.

"If you consider that the nail missed an extensor tendon by a matter of millimetres, I'd say you were lucky, yes," she countered. "Anyway, we'll have that cleaned up and bandaged in a short while. You'll be out of here soon."

"Oh, sorry, and thank you," Vic said meekly.

The doctor wrote some notes on her clipboard when Vic noticed a necklace she was wearing.

"That's an attractive necklace you have there," he said in his imitable sly way.

"Oh, this old thing?" said the doctor, lifting the pendant from her chest. "I only dug it out this morning. I've had it for ages, but it's not real; at least I don't think it is. An old boyfriend bought it for me. Knowing him, it'll be gold-plated and coloured glass. Besides, it's been in the back of a drawer for years, and it'll probably go back there tonight."

"I expect it is, but I'm a jeweller, and if I can have a closer look, I might be able to tell you if it's worth anything – just for your information, of course," said Vic. He immediately put aside the feelings of guilt and remorse he had just started to feel.

"Oh, thanks. Here you are," said the doctor as she took off the necklace and placed it in Vic's clammy hand. Vic's eyes lit up. He could tell straight away that the chain was 18-carat gold, and unless he was very much mistaken, the central flower design had been set with beautiful diamonds and rubies. He knew it was worth a fair bit of money – not as much as the old lady's ring, but still, a decent amount. Vic could barely withhold his grin, as all he could see were the pound signs flashing before his rapacious eyes again.

"So, what do you think, Mister Jeweller? Give me twenty quid, and it's yours," laughed the doctor as she finished writing her notes.

Vic reflected for a moment, looked at his foot, looked

at the jewellery and without further hesitation and with an ever-widening smile, glared straight into the eyes of the doctor.

"Well, doctor, you might not be a million miles away from your valuation. Perhaps this could be *your* lucky day.

The Box of Prophecies

During the early 1970s, childhood best friends, Craig Brewster and Becky Kirby, who was a few years older than him, would regularly take summer holidays together with their families in a holiday home in North Devon. The annual pilgrimage from Sidcup to the picturesque town of Bideford always took the same route, and they'd stop off at the same roadside cafes each year. It was a tradition that lasted until The Kirby's left town and went to live in Nottingham, to where Becky's father's job was relocated. The two families kept in touch for a few years, but occasional visits became just the odd Christmas card and eventually nothing. Sometime later, Craig discovered that The Kirby's migrated to Canada in 1981, and that was the last he'd heard of Becky and her family. However, Craig's memories would often drift back to the water-coloured halcyon days of his youth and the wonderful summer holidays spent with Becky in Devon.

Following one such meander down memory lane, Craig decided to take his family; wife Sally and children, Max and Charlie away for a few days' break to the West Country, where he hadn't been since he was a child. He wanted to show his children, where he spent so many happy childhood times. The plan was to take them there the previous year, but the area was in the process of being ravaged by terrible floods due to extraordinary high summer rainfall, and the government advice was not to travel to the area.

The Brewster's found a cottage a short distance from

the centre of town, but far enough away to enjoy the peace of the countryside. There was one place where he wanted to take his children in particular. In the nearby countryside was a clearing in a wooded area where Craig and Becky would invent games, usually pretending they were pirates stranded on a remote, uninhabited island. They were some of his fondest and clearest memories, and as such, he knew exactly where to find it.

Following a short walk across a field and through the woods, he excitedly led his children to a glade at the end of a naturally-made tree-canopied lane. It was a delightful day, and the gentle breeze allowed dappled, watery sunlight of a late summer's day through its branches and leaves on to the well-trodden ground. The memories were flooding back to him. It had changed little in the last 30 odd years.

"This is all so familiar. That's where we built a swing," Craig said, pointing at a 90 degree angled branch of an old oak tree."

"I can't imagine you swinging on a tree, Dad," said the nine-year-old Max.

"I'm surprised he didn't break it," the more cynical 14-year-old Charlie told him.

"Oy, don't be so cheeky, young lady. I'll have you know that I was once a skinny little boy in shorts," countered Craig, stopping in his tracks to address his daughter.

"You? Skinny? Yeah, if you say so, Dad," said Charlie, not believing a word of her father's story.

"I'd prove it to you if I had a photo," said Craig. "Do you know what? I might just be able to prove it. I planted a time capsule under one of these trees."

"What's a time capsule," asked an intrigued Max.

"It's usually a sealed box or something like that full of objects typical of the time. You would bury it in the hope that someone would dig it up years later to see what life was like in the past. You know, things like comics, stamps, coins, newspapers, toys, that sort of thing."

"Why can't you just look these things up on the internet?" asked Charlie.

"Well… you can, of course now, but the internet wasn't invented back then. Becky and I filled small tin boxes full of things that we thought people would find interesting in years to come. I'm sure I put a photo of me in mine," explained Craig eagerly.

"How exciting," Max said breathlessly.

"How lame," Charlie retorted, folding her arms and staring at the males with disdain. Ignoring his killjoy daughter, Craig continued explaining to Max.

"We thought it was such an exciting thing to do. We made a pirate's map of where we planted the boxes. 'X' marked the spot. It was our buried treasure."

"Do you still have the map so you can find your treasure?" asked Max naively. Charlie snorted at his comment and looked skyward.

"No Max, that's long gone, but the treasure is around here somewhere – at least it *was*. For all I know, it could have been found the very next day by some other children playing. But, let's look around here. I remember that Becky carved out a large letter 'B' with a knife on the tree where we buried the tins.

Max and Craig searched all the trees around the great oak for anything that looked like a letter 'B'. Charlie, sat down leaning against the oak tree, chewing gum and trying to look as disinterested as any teenage girl might. It didn't take long for Max to find something.

"Dad! Dad!" exclaimed the boy. Craig skipped over to see what he'd discovered. On the bark of a birch, he pointed out what looked very much like what they were looking for. It was faded and barely decipherable, but there was no doubt about it. It was a letter 'B'.

"Well done, son. Well done," he joyously panted. Max was delighted with his father's praise and looked in the direction of his sister, who tutted and gazed at her watch to illustrate her abject boredom with the whole scavenger hunt. "It's a pity we haven't got a metal detector, but go and find me some sturdy bits of wood, and we'll dig down. We didn't bury them too deep, so hopefully, we'll find our treasure." Max trotted off and picked up some pieces of broken branches and delivered them back to his Dad.

"They should be right below the carving," explained Craig and the two adventurers began prodded and scraping the ground frantically.

A few minutes later, Craig's stick hit something metallic. "This is it. It has to be!" exclaimed Craig. He tossed away his tool, fell to his knees and began clawing away at the loose earth like a burrowing badger. He pulled out a dirty, brown metal box and then another and placed them side by side.

"This is amazing. These are the boxes we buried; no doubt about it. Look, this one is mine; it's got a 'C' scratched on the lid. I just pray that the contents are still intact," he said, trying to catch a breath. Charlie, who suddenly became interested, sauntered over to the dig. With mud all over his trousers and shirt, Craig placed his dirty hands on hips at a job well done. Three pairs of eyes looked down on the two boxes. They were roughly half the size of a shoebox, but which considerably less depth and naturally, they were filthy.

"Open them, Dad," cried an impatient Max.

"Okay. Gather around," replied Craig. He carefully wiped away as much mud from his box before attempting to ease open the rusting lid. "Nearly there. Nearly there." It popped open, and to Craig's delight, the contents were dry.

"I don't believe it," said Craig, barely able to contain his delight. "Haha. Look!"

He wiped his dirty hands on an area of his trousers that wasn't caked in mud and carefully picked out his buried treasure. Inside the box was a folded up page of The Beano comic, a 5p coin, a David Bowie badge, an ice lolly stick (with a joke, too faded to decipher), a wrapper from a small bar of Dairy Milk chocolate and a small sealed envelope and as promised, a photograph of a boy in shorts.

"There you are. I told you. That's me," exclaimed a joyous Craig, carefully holding the edge of the blurry photograph.

"That's not you," said Max, squinting at the picture.

"It certainly is. I grant you, it's not a very good photo, but that's me alright." He dropped the evidence back in the tin.

"They're not exactly valuable items, are they?" sniffed Charlie.

"No, I suppose not," concurred her slightly disappointed father. I have to admit; I thought that I'd put in some things of much more interest. The David Bowie badge was probably Becky's anyway. She was a huge fan. However, if this is what I think it is, this will be fascinating." He put down the box and took out the envelope.

"What is it?" asked Max.

"I'm pretty sure this is a list of predictions. We imagined what would happen in the future and wrote them down. Yes, it's all coming back to me now," said an excited Craig. He carefully opened the envelope and removed the enclosed paper.

"You'd better read it out," said Charlie, who stood over her father, still trying to mask her interest.

Craig carefully opened the folded-up content and started to read out the list –

"Number one – *The Rolling Stones would win the 1974 Eurovision Song Contest.* Well, that was never going to happen.

Number two – *Humans will inhabit the Moon by 1990.* That's not as far-fetched as it sounds. A lot of people believed that would happen, back then.

Number three – *The Queen would marry Tony Blackburn.* Okay, that was silly.

Number four – *Crystal Palace would win the European Cup by the end of the decade.* I suppose The Queen marrying Tony Blackburn and going to live on The Moon was more likely than that happening.

Number five – *The existence of the Loch Ness Monster would be proven.*

Number six – *People will have cars that drove them around without them having to drive them by the year 2000.* Well, that's something that might be a reality soon."

"So nearly one out of six, Dad. Not bad," offered an unkind Charlie.

"Be fair, Charlie. I was a couple of years older than your brother is now, and we didn't have all the information at hand as you kids have today. Having said that, Crystal Palace weren't much cop then, and they still aren't. I should have known that they'd never conquer Europe," conceded Craig, laughing generously.

"Let's open the other one," said Max, excitedly.

As soon as Craig picked the box up, small drops of rain began to fall. He looked up and realised that the sunlight that struggled to break through the thick canopy was no longer present. The sky he could see was grey and threatening.

"Come on; we'll open it when we get back. It looks like it's going to pelt down in a few minutes. We'd better go." He carefully replaced the list in the envelope and placed it back in his box at closed the lid. Max picked up the second box from the ground, and they all began their journey back to the dry sanctuary of their cottage, picking up pace as the rain became more persistent.

The trio reached the holiday cottage just in time before a loud clap of thunder marked the start of a violent storm which shook the building.

"What happened to you? And Max too?" asked Craig's wife sally who stood cross-armed, wearing a pinny at the kitchen door. "You're both filthy." Charlie stood back, immediately disassociating herself from her father and brother.

Cradling the two dirty, unearthed tin boxes, Craig told her what they had been up to. Sally's face mirrored the indifference of Charlie at her husband's explanation as her eyes travelled back and forth between the mucky males.

"You boys had better get washed and changed; tea is almost ready. I've baked some scones to have with my home-made jam and cream," she told them before stepping back into the kitchen.

"Let me just clean the boxes up, and I'll go and sort myself out," replied Craig. He brushed past Sally with Max in tow and went over to the large sink. He grabbed a handful of kitchen towels, wet them under the tap and carefully started to clean all the mud off the metal tins.

"We'll open the other one after tea, son," he whispered to Max. Max nodded and ran upstairs to change. Craig gently placed the two cleaned tins on the floor by the back door and followed his son upstairs to clean himself up.

The rain had relented, and the sun was doing its utmost to force its rays through the clouds as soon as the family had finished their traditional Devonshire tea. Charlie left the table and went to sit in the living room with her iPod for company. Craig picked up the unopened tin and followed her out of the kitchen. He placed the time capsule on the coffee table in the living room and with Max sitting by his side, he carefully eased open the lid. To his relief, the contents were also in pretty good condition. He took out the items which were very similar to the ones he had placed in his tin.

"Now let's see what we have here." Craig took each

individual item out and laid them neatly on the table. "A Rod Stewart badge; a folded-up front page of Melody Maker with The Rolling Stones on it, a postcard of Paignton Pier at night with a large, bright full moon in the sky, a 10p piece – Becky clearly had more money than me, a 3 ½ p stamp, a Salt n' Shake crisp packet, a small Scooby-Doo pencil and gimmicky pencil sharper with Rod Stewart again, and a small envelope matching the one found in Craig's tin."

Both Craig and Max felt a little disappointed by the selection of items, as they both expected something a little more poignant from a 14-year-old as opposed to an 11-year-old boy.

"Let's have a look at Becky's predictions. I wonder if they are any more accurate than mine," smiled Craig as he carefully removed the list.

Again, he read them out loud –

"Number one – *Humans will not inhabit The Moon by 2000.* Haha, I must have told her about my prediction.

Number two – *Britain will have a woman Prime Minister by 1980.*

Number three – *Nottingham Forest will win the European Cup by 1980.* Blimey, those two came true. Forest actually won it twice by 1980.

Number four – *I will marry a plastic surgeon.* Interesting prediction.

Number five – *Prince Charles will marry and divorce and his ex-wife will be killed in an accident.*

Ashen-faced Craig lowered the paper and stared at his son. "That is beyond spooky. It's one thing suggesting that your Dad's football team will win a trophy, but *this* is in the realms of the supernatural."

"Are there any more?" asked Max, daring his Dad to read on. Craig went back to the list –

Number six – *In the early 21st century, New York will be targeted by terrorists, and a jet plane will crash into a building.*

Okay, now I'm scared. No one could have known that. And for a happy-go-lucky teenage girl, obsessed with Rod Stewart and tie-dying her jeans to suggest things like this is just odd. More than odd, it's genuinely frightening. Sally, come in and see this," Craig shouted towards the kitchen. Sally entered the living room, and Craig presented her with the list. After a moment, she sat down on the arm of the sofa and covered her face with her hand.

"Oh God, how on Earth would she know all this? And why?"

"I don't know, but I've got shivers down my spine just trying to digest it all," said Craig.

Max cuddled up to Craig and noticing something was wrong; Charlie came over to them to take a look at what was disturbing the rest of her family. She grabbed it off Craig to read.

"What a weirdo," she said.

"Stop it," snapped Sally as she snatched the piece of paper off her and handed it back to Craig.

"Sorry," apologised a chastised Charlie. She sat on the table opposite her Dad. "Perhaps, she's a psychic."

"She has to be, looking at what she wrote, but it's so morbid," replied Craig, still staring at the list. "These aren't just predictions, they're prophesies. I need to track her down."

"How are you going to do that?" asked Sally.

"I've bought my laptop, and we have internet access here, so, if she's anywhere on this planet, I'll find her," answered Craig. "But that will wait. We're here on a family holiday and what do families do in a cottage in the middle of nowhere when it's raining outside?"

"Watch television?" suggested Max.

"No," replied Craig.

"Sit on their own with their iPods?" suggested the ever-surly Charlie.

"Definitely not."

"Start my latest Danielle Steel book?" said Sally.

"Noooo," replied a disheartened Craig. The others just stared at the family patriarch with looks varying from eager anticipation to abject disinterest.

"They play board games!" Craig exclaimed to his underwhelmed audience.

"Board games? You mean *bored* games," Charlie elucidated.

"Come on. It'll be fun," insisted Craig as he walked over to a wicker basket beside the redundant, stone-surround fireplace. No one else said anything, such was their enthusiasm.

"We've got Monopoly?"

"No," came the collective response.

"Cluedo?" Craig continued.

"Not for me," replied Charlie unilaterally.

"How about Pictionary? That's fun." There were no further dissenting voices, so Craig took that as a yes, and bought the game over to the coffee table to set up.

Becky's predictions were put to the back of their minds, and the family spent over an hour of quality time together, enjoying the game; even Charlie did, her competitive steak coming to the fore. Once they'd been all 'gamed out', Sally heated through and served a pasta bake she'd prepared earlier. Everyone enjoyed the meal and following 'family time', was 'solitary time'. Sally sat down in an armchair to read her book; the children went back to their preferred pastimes – Charlie with her iPod and Max with his Gameboy. Craig connected up his laptop to the internet to do his promised research on the whereabouts of Becky Kirby.

His searches revealed nothing. "It's like she never existed. Becky, Rebecca, Becca, Bex; nothing," he said to himself, but loud enough for Sally to look up from her book.

"You know, she probably got married, Craig."

"Of course. Why didn't I think of that?" he asked rhetorically. "Mind you, that's not going to help me much, is it?" Sally just shook her head and resumed her reading.

"Come on, Max, it's past your bedtime now," Sally alerted her son as the sunlight outside was rapidly diminishing. Surprisingly, there were no protestations from Max. More curiously, Charlie stood up and informed her parents she was also going to bed too.

"You alright?" asked Craig of his daughter.

"I'm fine, but if we're not going to be allowed to watch television, what's the point in staying up?"

"I suppose you're right. Without the TV, is there any purpose to life?" Craig mocked. Sally received a kiss on the cheek from Charlie, while Craig was given a cursory nod, probably due to his flippant comment.

With the kids in bed, Sally drew the curtains and switched on a lamp beside her chair; the dull illumination barely making a difference to the dimness of the room. She took root back in her comfortable chair; her legs tucked comfortably underneath her, before happily returning to her Romance. Craig continued to his research, but without a surname, he knew it would probably be in vain. Sitting back on his chair, he exhaled and began prodding around Becky's tin. One item caught his eye as on it just looked out of place – it was the picture postcard of Paignton Pier by night. The condition was too good as the edges weren't particularly frayed or aged. Surely, there's no way it could have been in the tin for decades. Flipping the card over, he noticed there was some writing on the back. It was a message to him, written in tiny script from Becky.

A sudden flash of lightning lit the room up brilliantly and made Craig jump. It signalled another terrible downpour. Rain lashed the awnings and the garden furniture outside, making the downpour sound even more relentless and harsh, but none of this disturbed Sally's concentration. However, Craig's outburst did.

"Oh, my goodness."

"What? What's wrong?" shrieked a startled Sally.

"Just listen to this. There's a message written to me on the back of this postcard." Becky had written –

'To my old friend, Craig, I'm scared. I see things… bad things that come true. It's like they come to me in visions. I've always had this 'gift' as you'll see from my predictions. It's been over 20 years since we buried our treasure and I knew you'd be back one day to dig it up. I'm married to a plastic surgeon and live in British Columbia, Canada. I've returned to England and Devon for a visit, while my husband is away sailing with his buddies and I found our tins by the old oak tree.

I wanted to look you up, but I was frightened. I know you're married with a young child and I didn't want to see anything bad in your future. Craig, I'm drowning. I just wanted to leave this message for you in case. Farewell, my dear friend. Love, Becky. xx.'

"I'm going to have to see if there's a news story about a drowning in Canada," said Craig soberly.

"Are you sure you want to do that?" asked his wife gently.

"I have to. I can't just leave this here. Even if it's bad news, I have to find out," a determined Craig replied.

Sally remained seated in a state of shock.

"I've got a horrible feeling," confessed Craig. The hairs on the back of his neck stood up on end, and his hands became clammy as he began to type five words into the search engine on his laptop – *plastic surgeon wife Canada drowned*. A few seconds later, the results popped up on his screen. The first search seemed to confirm his fears. It read, *'Eminent surgeon and wife missing in a sailing accident'*. He nervously clicked on the headline and to his horror a photo of man and woman, who looked remarkably like his childhood friend appeared. He read the article beneath in solemn silence.

"Well, what does it say?" asked Sally softly as the rain outside began pelting down even fiercer than ever.

"I feel sick. Becky was right. The poor girl," replied Craig.

"Tell me, Craig, what happened?"

"She's… she's gone. She knew what would happen. Becky and her husband drowned after their sailing boat capsised. This is what it says – '*Coastguards recovered the bodies of Patrice Ferri and his English-born wife, Rebecca following sudden and severe gale-force winds caused their sailing boat to capsize off the shores of Vancouver… The couple had planned to emigrate to England with their newborn son, Craig*'. Craig?"

Sally got up and joined her husband, whose eyes were transfixed on the computer screen. He put her arms around him.

"You could never have known," she whispered sympathetically in his ear.

"She did," Craig replied. "Imagine living with the ability to see these horrible things and then foreseeing your demise. And her baby – Craig. She must have named him after me."

"That's heart-breaking, my love. She must have thought a lot of you. When did this happen?"

"Look," said Craig, pointing to the date of publication.

"The 28th August 2005," said Sally. "That's almost a year ago…"

"And two days after the accident. Today is the 26th of

August, "Craig interrupted. "She died exactly a year ago today and a year since we were supposed to come here originally for our holiday. It was like she knew the day of her death and wanted to tell me before it happened.

"Are you going to tell the kids?" asked Sally softly.

"No, I think it's best not to. It'll just scare them. I'll say I couldn't find any information about her and leave it at that," suggested Craig.

"Probably for the best," agreed Sally. "Come on, close your laptop, and we'll go up to bed. There's no point dwelling on it. I don't feel very much like reading, and I don't want to leave you alone."

"Thanks. You go up. I'll tidy up, and I'll be with you shortly," Craig replied.

Sally kissed him on the top of the head and made her way upstairs. Craig closed down his computer and unplugged it. The rain outside subsided, and a deafening silence filled the room. Still, in a state of shock, he put the paper and pencils back in the game box and took it over to the wicker basket. Before he placed it down, on top of the Monopoly box was a white feather. He picked it up and held in his hand, staring at it – it wasn't there before. His heartbeat which had been at quite a rate slowed down, and a feeling of peace and serenity filled his being. He held the feather to his chest, and a single tear dropped down his cheek. After a few moments of solace, Craig walked over to switch off the lamp. As he did, between a crack in the curtains, he chanced to see a large, bright full moon in the now clear, cloudless sky.

Craig placed the feather in Becky's tin on top of the postcard of Paignton Pier and closed the lid slowly. He knew, in his heart that Becky was finally at peace.

Deadline To Death

Writer's block is an author's worst enemy. With a canon of financially successful and critically acclaimed mystery novels behind him, novelist C.J. Billings (known to his friends and family as Chris), found himself in a situation whereas hard as he tried, the words just failed to materialise. Finishing his latest book, `Faces of an Angel' was proving the most challenging task of his writing career. The manuscript was 80% complete, and he knew where the story was heading, but he couldn't find the literary bridge to get him to his ultimate destination. He wasn't in a position to leave the work and come back to it when his creative juices started flowing again as his publisher was already turning the screw. Hansen was notorious in the industry for pressing and squeezing their authors for work. They paid handsomely and promptly, but would happily punish writers for breaking their strict terms, in particular, late submissions. 'If one does a deal with the devil, one should expect the discomfort of his thrusting pitchfork on one's posterior' was a phrase coined by the author. They needed a completed draft within a couple of weeks. This was by far the most complex and technically ambitious project he had ever undertaken, and CJ knew that even if his imagination could find a way to complete the story, there was still the editing to undertake.

"Just tell them you've hit a wall and you'll present your manuscript when you can," said Jane, CJ's well-intentioned, but naïve wife as the summer sun finally dipped below the horizon. CJ stood looking out of the window behind his writer's desk in his first floor London apartment.

"Sweetheart, publishers don't work that way – at least, Hansen doesn't. I don't have a lot of time left to complete this work and send it to them, and if I don't, I'll be in breach of my contract. It's Sunday night and another week has slipped by," CJ replied in clipped words trying to keep the antagonism for his employers at bay.

"But you're one of their most successful authors. Surely that should count for something, no?" she countered.

"It does, if I were one of their other minions, I'd be in overtime right now. Due to all the money I've made them over the years, they have been generous enough to grant me a slightly longer window to submit my work before penalising me. This book has become a terrible burden and not a labour of love," he replied, his face showing his frustration.

CJ sat down, shut down his laptop and buried his head in his hands as his wife looked on, not knowing what to say or do.

"I'm going to bed now," she said softly before leaving the room.

"I'll be in shortly," CJ replied, his hands muffling his response.

Just then, a Eureka moment. CJ stood up, stretched and clapped his hands in delight.

"If that's where she ends up, then that's where I will go, he said to himself triumphantly and strode into the bedroom where Jane was taking off her make-up at her dressing table.

"I'm going away," he announced, leaning against the

wardrobe.

"Where?" Jane asked, wiping away her mascara with cotton wool.

"Bude in Cornwall."

"And why are you going to Cornwall?" asked Jane, pausing at her task.

"Well, that's where Jessica ends up, so I figure that if I go down there, it'll inspire me to finish this bloody book and I'll be able to breathe again. We used to go on family holidays there when I was young. It's been years since I've been."

"How long do you intend to go for, Chris?"

"I don't know. Not long. A week or so. Just as long as it takes me to do what I have to do."

"Well, okay. I can't have you moping around this place all day, I suppose. It'll do you good," replied Jane generously before returning to her exercise. CJ bounded over and kissed his wife on the top of the head. He felt like a door had been opened in front of him and through that door were the answers he'd been looking for.

The following day, and after a pleasant four-hour drive from London, with the summer still sticking to the seasonal rules, CJ got to his destination. He checked into a bed and breakfast and immediately took a stroll down to the seafront. He stopped at the edge of the beach. It was early evening, and the sands were sparsely populated. Looking out to sea he took a generous intake of sea air. He stood motionless for a couple of minutes gazing at the beautiful view expecting a flash of inspiration; just waiting, but nothing was forthcoming. Jessica, his protagonist, was still hiding out from the police in a cottage, just as she had been for several weeks.

Realising that he was probably asking too much of his imagination so soon after his arrival, he sauntered back to his accommodation. A hundred yards or so from the guesthouse, he was surprised to hear a woman's voice behind him.

"Excuse me, are you CJ. Billings?"

CJ halted and turned around. A short, rotund woman in her early seventies greeted him. Her face was beaming.

"Yes. Yes, I am," he replied.

"Oh, I have all your books. I think you're wonderful," gushed the woman, taking several paces towards her hero.

"That's very nice of you to say…"

"Margaret," she replied. Her wide smile gave her ruddy cheeks a glow from the setting sun.

"That's very nice of you to say, Margaret," said CJ holding out his right hand which Margaret clasped between both of hers.

"Are you here alone or with your family?" she asked.

"I'm on my own. I've just popped down to Bude to finish off my latest book," he explained.

"Ooh, how exciting," replied Margaret as she released CJ's hand, her smile broadening further if that was even possible.

"I hope you don't think I'm cheeky, but I live just down the road, and I wondered if you might pop in to sign all your books that I have kept?"

CJ looked at the woman's face and without hesitation,

agreed to her request. Margaret clasped her hands and led the way to her cottage, which was only a stone's throw from where CJ was staying.

"Here we are. Do come in," beckoned Margaret upon opening the door to her house. "Mind your head." CJ stooped down slightly and entered the comfortable looking, well-furnished home.

Margaret toddled off to the kitchen, leaving CJ standing in the middle of her living room, perusing the multitude wooden and porcelain knick-knacks that adorned every available surface.

"Oh, where are my manners? Please do take a seat, CJ," she said upon re-entering the room, with arms laden with several paperback and hardback books. CJ sat down at one end of the floral design sofa, and Margaret did the same at the other end, dropping her load of books between them. Margaret reached over to a small table by the arm of the sofa and picked up a ballpoint pen which was nestled between several bottles of pills and handed it to CJ, who began to sign the novels.

"I'll put the kettle on in a moment. You'll have tea with me, won't you? Perhaps you haven't eaten yet? I've got a nice home-made chicken and mushroom pie in the oven. I can heat it up for you if you like?" CJ felt unable to refuse, and as he hadn't eaten for several hours, it didn't seem like a bad idea.

"That would be lovely, Margaret. As long as I'm not putting you out at all?"

"Oh, no, not at all. It's not every day I can welcome a celebrity in my cottage." CJ smiled, and Margaret stood up and once again disappeared back into the kitchen. CJ continued to sign the books. There were eight in all – five hardbacks and three paperbacks. He had got through seven books having written a standard, *To Margaret. With very best wishes, CJ Billings.'* when Margaret re-entered the room and re-took her seat, unable to take her eyes off the famous author.

"It won't be too long. I do hope you like it. It's an old family recipe."

"I'm sure I will, Margaret. You have a lovely home," CJ said, looking around the room. His eyes then caught sight of an easel in the corner with a half-finished painting positioned on it. "Oh, you're an artist, I see."

"Thank you. Yes, I am. I'm not a professional, but I like to dabble a bit. It's one of my pastimes, I suppose."

"Do you mind if I have a closer look?" asked CJ, pointing at the work.

"Be my guest," replied his hostess.

CJ stood up and walked over to the painting. He switched a desk light on that was positioned beside it. It was a harbour scene. The sky in it was stormy and the sea choppy with huge white waves crashing against the harbour walls. Although unfinished, it was so alive.

"I love it. I really love it," announced CJ in a hushed voice. Margaret joined him by his side.

"Really? Do you really?" she asked, almost embarrassed.

"I do. It's magnificent. So cruel, but so alive." He half-expected Margaret to jump up and down in wild excitement, but she simply offered an affirmative hum and stood back. CJ continued to stare at the vista for a while, mesmerised by the realness of the scene. The use of dark blues and greys in her delicate brushstrokes brought the picture to life. Then it came to him – the inspiration he'd been searching for weeks. He points at the artwork. "That's where Jessica ends up. That's the finale," he said with determination. He turned to face Margaret, but she was no longer standing beside him. Sounds from the kitchen of utensils dropping in the sink confirmed her whereabouts and CJ reclaimed his seat on the sofa.

Several minutes later, and with the gorgeous aroma of a home-cooked food filling the air, Margaret appeared from the kitchen with a tray. She set it down on a small foldaway table and brought it over to CJ. His mouth watered as he gazed upon the plate laden with the pie, mashed potato and peas all generously smothered with a thick gravy.

"I do hope you like it," said Margaret happily.

"I'm sure I will. It looks delicious." CJ began tucking into his supper as Margaret watched him joyfully from the other end of the sofa.

"I haven't got any beer, but would you like a glass of cider?" Margaret asked, remembering that she had forgotten to fetch a drink. CJ's mouth was full; all he could offer was a vigorous nod of his head.

When Margaret returned with a large glass of cider and with CJ's mouth empty, he complimented her on her excellent supper.

"You cook as well as you paint," he said.

"Thank you very much," she replied. "Tell me how near are you to finishing your latest book?"

"Not too far. In fact, I was going to say to you that your painting has inspired me. I was having so much difficulty in finding the right way to bring a conclusion to my story, but there's something in that painting over there that has shown me my direction. To be able to create such a dramatic image, I guess there must have been some upheaval in your life?" explained CJ, finishing off his food.

"Let's just say things haven't always been as idyllic as they appear now," Margaret said without the chirpiness her voice previously embodied. She stood up and removed the tray from the small table and took it into the kitchen.

CJ thought for a moment, not wishing to intrude further and continued, "I probably shouldn't be giving anything away, but you wouldn't believe the trouble I've faced attempting to bring my story to a conclusion. It's tough to find an escape for a character when being pursued by police for a crime that she may or may not have committed." A mighty crash of crockery and glassware came from the kitchen as soon as CJ finished what he was saying.

"Are you alright?" shouted CJ as he rushed over to the open kitchen door.

"Yes, I'm alright. I'm so clumsy," responded Margaret, who was already on her hands and knees picking up the pieces of broken plate and glass.

"Here, let me help you," said CJ as he knelt beside the old woman.

"No, honestly, it's alright. See, I've nearly picked it all up now," replied Margaret forcefully as she stacked the shards atop one another in her left hand. "Please, go inside and sit down. I'll be back in a minute." CJ did what he was told and sat quietly until Margaret re-entered the living room. She resumed her seat and in a much less lively manner than previously, continued to enquire about CJ's story.

"You say that she may have or not committed a

crime?"

"Yes, but I don't want to give too much away," says CJ.

"So what is she doing in Bude?" enquired a stone-faced Margaret.

"She's on the run and has ended up in Cornwall. There's nowhere she can go unless it's into the sea."

"May I ask what this woman has done?"

"I'll tell you as long as you don't tell anyone," CJ said with a wink.

"I won't tell a soul. You can count on me," replied Margaret.

"She is accused of a serious crime; I can't say what as it's key to the plot. I won't say if she did it or not, but without going into too much detail, the police have been on her tail and eventually track her down to a Cornish fishing village and, well, you'll have to see what happens when you read the book." There was a short silence before Margaret replied. She looked ashen-faced.

"That sounds fascinating," she says, forcing a smile. The red-cheeked ruddiness had disappeared. A pale, almost ghostly appearance had replaced it. "I'm glad your visit has given you almost instantaneous results, CJ," she continued.

"Please, call me Chris."

"Okay, Chris," said Margaret, a smile slowly returning to her face.

"I've taken up too much of your valuable time, and I should get back to my digs to continue my writing. Thank you so much for your hospitality and your delicious food," said CJ standing up and preparing to exit the house.

"Oh, it was my pleasure, CJ… er Chris," replied Margaret, beaming once again. "I wonder, if you have time, you might come round again tomorrow, perhaps for tea?"

"Yes, I'd like that. I'd like that a lot. Shall we say 4 pm?" he replied. Margaret nodded enthusiastically. They shook hands warmly, and CJ left the house. As he made the short journey back to his accommodation in the dusk, he looked over his shoulder, and there stood Margaret, by her front door, waving at him. He waved back before entering the B&B. He ran upstairs, sat on his bed and untied his shoes. It had been a long day, and CJ decided to leave his laptop in its case until the next day.

Following a good night's sleep and a hearty breakfast, CJ decided to take a walk to the Old Harbour to have some quiet time to work out the ultimate plotline of 'Faces of an Angel' in his head. The view he had was similar to the one in Margaret's art, but with bright blue skies. The general hubbub of passing holiday-makers and the low tide gave him a feeling which was in stark contrast to the raging waters and desolate isolation of the painting. After a while, and with his mind in a better place than it had been for some time, CJ walked the short distance back to his guesthouse where he set about writing the conclusion of his book. So involved in his storytelling was he that it was almost 3.45 pm when he realised that he had a tea date to make. He closed the laptop and placed it under a pillow.

A few minutes later, after picking up a bunch of colourful flowers from the small florists across the street, CJ knocked on the azure-coloured front door of Margaret's cottage. She opened it immediately and welcomed him in.

"I'm so glad you came," she gleamed. "And flowers too? They're lovely. Thank you."

"You're most welcome," replied CJ as he handed over the bouquet. He was ushered into the house enthusiastically. A wonderfully heady aroma of fresh baking filled the air. He sat down in the same place as he did the previous night, while Margaret took the flowers into the kitchen. She appeared a minute later with them arranged in a large vase which she just about managed to find room for on a shelf in the corner of the room.

"I do hope you've got a bit of an appetite on you as I've made a cake or two." Margaret laughed to herself and again stepped back into the kitchen. Re-appearing with a tray featuring no less than three cakes, she placed it down on the foldaway table. "You've got a choice of Coffee and Walnut, Cherry or Lemon Drizzle."

"Wow, you don't do things by half, do you?" CJ asked, impressed by the display in front of him.

"My late husband always said, `Do things properly, or not at all'. I guess as a successful author; you probably use that same guideline, Chris?"

"You're right, Margaret, but I would have been more than happy with a shop-bought Madeira," CJ replied.

"I don't do shop-bought, my lad," Margaret giggled.

A few minutes later, the tea was poured, and the cake was being consumed.

"Tell me; I'm interested to know how you come about your characters. How do you think them up?" said Margaret before taking a bite of coffee and walnut cake. This was a question that CJ had been asked about by every journalist and fan he'd ever spoken to, but he didn't let that on to Margaret and answered her query as if it was the first time he'd ever mentioned it.

"Initially, I think most characters are based to some degree on people I've known or at least made acquaintance. After that, I think even subconsciously; you take little quirks and nuances from everybody and even characters from previous books. In the book I'm writing now, who knows, I might take some personality affects from you and your life, Margaret," CJ mused. She smiled sympathetically before taking the teapot away.

"I'll make a fresh brew," she announced before walking off to the kitchen again. CJ realised that it was the second time that he'd made mention of Margaret's personality, which created a change in atmosphere and caused her to disappear. He couldn't work it out and questioned if he might ask her if he'd said something wrong.

"I hope I haven't offended you," CJ said to his invisible host.

"Offended me? Not at all. Why do you say that, dear?" asked Margaret, still out of view.

"It's just when I've mentioned your life, you've gone a little silent." There was no answer until she re-appeared with a fresh pot of tea. She placed it down carefully.

"I don't want to go into it too much, but as I said yesterday, my life hasn't always been as pleasant and happy as it is now. I'm originally from South London, and in my younger years found myself in an impossible situation and without the support of family or friends, I had to get away. I moved down to Cornwall following an unpleasant position I found myself in. I just wanted to get away and start again. I never got married or had children, and I have always regretted that. However, it just wasn't to be, I guess. We all have our little secrets, don't we?"

"We do indeed," replied an intrigued CJ. I have to say; your situation mirrors my lead character to a degree. Do you know what I'd like to do? I want to dedicate my new book to you."

"That is indeed an honour, but I'm not sure if I'm worthy of it," said Margaret with a lamenting lilt to her voice.

"Of course you are," CJ replied, taking Margaret's hands in his. She smiled but looked slightly uncomfortable. "Is everything alright?"

"You get lots of aches and pains at my age. I take those to keep me alive," she laughed, pointing over her shoulder at the bottles of pills still in situ on the small table at the end of the sofa. "I'm sorry I'm beginning to feel very tired. I need to have a nap. It's been a long day."

"Of course. You've gone to so much trouble for me, I'm not surprised it's taken it out of you," conceded CJ. "I'm going to spend two or three days finishing off my novel and editing it, but I'd like to come by and see you again before I return to London. Is that okay with you?"

"Yes. That would be nice," said Margaret, slightly breathlessly.

"Let me help you clear everything away before I go," said CJ.

"No," replied Margaret stridently. "Leave it to me. I'll do it later. You get back to your book. I want you to finish it as soon as possible as I can't wait to read it."

"I'll see you in a few days then, Margaret."

"You will," she replied, staying put in her seat.

CJ left the cottage feeling a little guilty for leaving Margaret in her condition, but his mind was so excited with the thought of finally completing his work, the feeling soon dissipated.

As promised, CJ spent the following three days hard at work on his laptop in his bedroom and by lunchtime on Friday, he had finally completed and edited the first draft of `Faces of an Angel'. He found an ending to give the woman her comeuppance.

'Standing on the harbour in the freezing November night with the wind howling and rain firing down from the heavens like live ammunition, Jessica looked down to the waves crashing against the stone wall. Behind her, she heard the distant shrill of a police whistle. Looking around through the unrelenting downpour, Jessica could make out flashlights. It was the two police officers that had been pursuing her around the country. They'd finally found their prize, and now there was nowhere left for her to run. She turned back and looked down at the dangerous waters below. One enormous wave almost envelopes her, but her mind has been made up. The whistles and shouts of the police officers were getting closer. She would hang for what she did. The only course of action was to jump.

"Jessica!! Jessica!! Don't move," shouted one of the policemen rapidly approaching her, his voice almost drowned out by the brutal weather.

It was too late, she had made her mind up, and with a prayer and a final gulp of air, she closed her eyes and fell into the violent brine. The intense swirls took her under immediately.

The police officers ran to the harbour wall, looking over the edge, trying to seek out Jessica in the water, but it was fruitless. It was an impossible task. Soaked to the skin with raindrops cascading from their noses and chins, they looked at each other in silence, before turning away and walking sombrely back to the town. To them, justice had been done, albeit not in the way the crown had expected.'

On completion of the manuscript, he once again went back to the harbour that helped inspire him. The tide was on its way in and although the day was pleasant and light danced over the gentle waves, he could just about imagine the vastly different conditions in Margaret's painting of the same scene once again. After saying a silent farewell to the harbour, CJ made his way back to the town and his elderly friend.

CJ brushed himself down, cleared his throat and knocked on the door. There was no instant response like there was the last time he visited. He knocked again, and to his surprise, a younger woman of about 30 opened the door.

"Oh hello, I've come to see Margaret," announced CJ.

"I'm afraid you're too late," said the young woman forlornly. The look on her face and the timbre of her voice suggested that Margaret had not just `gone to the shops'. "What happened?"

"You must be CJ Billings. Margaret told me about you. You'd better come in," said the woman.

CJ entered the cottage, and the woman closed the door behind him.

"By the way, my name is Emily. I live next door. Margaret passed away yesterday. I only spoke to her on Wednesday when I popped in to see how she was. You were all she could talk about. She's been quite ill for some time, but her face lit up when she mentioned meeting her literary hero. I'm just here to get her things in order."

CJ looked around the cottage. All appeared to be the same as when he last visited, apart from one thing – the unfinished painting of the harbour was slashed in two. It was still in place, so it didn't seem like it had been an accident or ripped in rage, but as a deliberate and calculated act.

"There was something that Margaret wanted to give you." Emily handed CJ a hardback book; his book. The one he hadn't yet signed. He took it from Emily, and an awkward silence prevailed.

"Where is she now?" CJ asked after a while.

"She has been taken back to London, to her family," Emily said.

"I thought she didn't have any family?" asked CJ.

"Oh yes, she had family alright. They didn't want much to do with her, but she certainly had a family." Another uncomfortable silence followed before CJ piped up.

"I suppose I'd better be off then."

"I guess so," agreed Emily.

"Thanks for the book… my book," said CJ as he opened the front door. Emily nodded and smiled sweetly. CJ left the premises and closed the door slowly behind him. He walked solemnly back to the B&B and prepared to make his way back home.

It was late when CJ arrived back home, and his wife was already asleep. He made sure he crept around his home quietly, careful not to wake her. He walked into his study and placed his laptop and book down on the desk and sat down, staring at the novel. From the feeling of happiness a few hours earlier, CJ felt numb. His emotions would change again and intensely as he picked up the book. 'Confession of a Killer' was his first published novel, and from its pages fell a folded up piece of paper. He put down the book and picked up the paper. He opened it up. It was a letter from Margaret. Hairs on the back of his neck stood up as he began reading the note –

Dear CJ,

You'll be reading this after my death. I wasn't frank with you about my past, and I wanted to make this confession to you. However, I would like to request you keep the contents of this letter to yourself. You may well be shocked by what you read, but please try and be objective. What I did was a terrible thing, and I've had to live my life with the guilt for the last sixty years.

Firstly, our meeting was not the first time we've met. I was surprised to see you in Bude, but I knew you wouldn't recognise me. You and your family would take holidays in the village when you were a very young boy. Your parents would take your older brother and sister on boat trips, but you didn't like the sensation of the moving boat, so I used to sit for you in the same cottage you spent time with me recently. It was so lovely to see my little Christopher again after all these years. I'd been following your career carefully and with great pride. However, this is not my confession.

Before I moved to Bude, it was the early 1960s, and I lived in South London as I told you. I was a live-in nanny for a well-to-do family. They were quite ghastly in their language and mistreated me; making me work my days off and implemented curfews. However, that doesn't excuse what I did. Their child, a boy never stopped crying, and one day, I was trying to feed him in the nursery when he started choking. I just watched him. I didn't pick him up. All I could think about was how upset his parents would be if he died, and that thought delighted me. It would make up for all the angst and emotional pain they placed on me. I just stared at this child coughing and gasping for air in his high chair. It was like something had taken me over. Suddenly, I snapped out of it, disgusted at my non-activity. I picked the child up, put him over my shoulder and thumped his back, trying to dislodge whatever was trapped in his windpipe, but it was too late.

The coughing and crying stopped and then the boy's body went limp. I placed him back in his cot and just stood, unable to move, watching him. His mother finally came to the room only to see me standing over the child's lifeless body. She looked at him, then at me and ran downstairs to call the police – not an ambulance, but the police. I was arrested, but released on bail which my family put up. Although I didn't inflict any harm to the boy, I did nothing to help, and I knew their lawyers would ensure I'd be found guilty of murder and hanged for it. I had to escape.

I moved around the country for a few months with the money I had saved until the police search died down. Perhaps they didn't have enough evidence on me after all; I don't know. I then found my way down to Cornwall and fortunately found a job as a housemaid in a big house a couple of miles away. I changed my name to Margaret Burns and made sure I didn't speak to anyone about my past. After a time, my employers; a kind couple, allowed me to live rent-free in one of their cottages, which they bequeathed to me after their deaths. I didn't marry or have children as I didn't think it would be right. You were the closest thing I had to a child. I loved you and looked after you as if you were my own.

When we met again, and you told me about your story, it chilled me to the bone. It could have been about me. It bought back terrible memories, and it was something I didn't want to think about. The incomplete painting that you were so impressed with was started six decades ago. It has remained incomplete as a reminder to me of what I did; I kept it there in my living room as a penance. I used to visit the harbour even in the harsh winter and thought on many occasions *about throwing myself off. I often wish I had.*

So, that is my story. You could do some research and find out my true identity, but I would ask you to leave things as they are.

Christopher, I hope you can find in your heart to forgive me.

Margaret. X

CJ felt anaesthetised. He folded up the confession and slipped it back within the leaves of the book. He placed the novel in the top drawer of his desk and shut it solidly. After a couple of moments, and amidst a disbelieving, sickening silence, he opened the lid of his laptop and clicked on the file – *'Faces of an Angel (1st draft)'* and highlighted the entire work.

The similarities between Jessica in the book and Margaret were uncanny, and the question he asked himself was – How could he live with himself knowing the inspiration for the completion of his story was a child killer? There was also the fact that he promised to dedicate the book to her. However, if he didn't deliver the manuscript to his publisher sharpish, he'd be in breach of his contract, and his career could be over. It was a lose/lose situation. With his finger hovering over the delete button, the outcome of his conundrum would, without doubt, be life-defining and unwinnable.

Other Books by Elliot Stanton

About the Author

This is Elliot Stanton's fourth book and the first he's written featuring short stories. His previous novels are humorous in nature, and all have various aspects of true-life events, but this time he decided he wanted to try something different. In the spring of 2019, he decided to write a series of Tales of the Unexpected–type stories and 12 months later he'd written enough tales to create *The Crimson Scarf and Other Short Stories*.

Elliot is married with two teenage children and lives on the outskirts of North London. His interests include history, watching sport, music and travel. His favourite location is Las Vegas, where he has visited many times. In fact, Vegas is the location of his second novel, *For A Few Dollars Less*.

He is a member of Mensa, and a keen retainer of trivia so enjoys partaking in pub quizzes with a regular group of his friends.

Writing is his main passion and intends to write more novels and books of short stories in the future.

Available worldwide from
Amazon and all good bookstores

———————

More from the author at:

www.elliotstanton.com

———————

www.mtp.agency

www.facebook.com/mtp.agency

@mtp_agency

www.ingramcontent.com/pod-product-compliance
Lightning Source LLC
Chambersburg PA
CBHW031958050726
47590CB00006B/1958